road to reboot

a novel

by

Jenz Johnson

First published in trade paperback 2008.
Updated edition 2010

Library of Congress Cataloging-in-Publication Data
available upon request.

ISBN 978-0-9779586-0-3

www.reboot2.com

Printed in the United States of America
Birdrock Press
La Jolla, California

For my parents

road to reboot

contents

"The future is not some place we are going to, but one we are creating. The paths are not to be found, but made, and the activity of making them, changes both the maker and the destination."

—*John Schaar, professor emeritus of political philosophy, University of California at Santa Cruz*

"If you want truly to understand something, try to change it."
—*Kurt Lewin*

The LAN party is in full swing.

In the middle of the darkened living room, a pair of black speakers blast *Bat Out Of Hell*, rattling bottles on the table. Over the fireplace sits a 60-inch flat-screen TV with a row of five PC towers lined up in front, green and blue lights flashing from their cases. Someone has brought an *Area-51* and it sits in the center with a hub blinking rapidly on top. A cable from each PC snakes through the shadows along the floor, winding under the coffee table, around stacks of shoes, to a controller in the hands of one of the five gamers crammed on the couch.

"Die, rodents!" a freckled face shouts over the din. A fist flies up in triumph. The group leans forward, faces splattered with light, madly manipulating their controllers up and down, pushing each other out of the way with their elbows.

"No!" one of them yells.

"Sweet lord!" another hisses.

A girl in an oversized sweatshirt wraps her arms around one of the gamers, and behind them, another player sits on the back of the couch with his feet between the cushions, occasionally kicking one leg up can-can style when he scores. Their faces are frozen for a second by a bright orange flash.

You look at the plasma screen and see a character leaping from a large turret, blasting the retreating opponents. "Aarg, maties" booms from the couch.

"Good god!" a gamer yells. He stands up. "Crapazoid!"

"Damn, where did *that* come from?" another says, looking dazed. He is wearing a fedora and sweatpants, but no shirt. His pale stomach is streaked with bean dip. The statistics roll up the sides of the screen. Below them characters shoulder their weapons, jerk along a path, then topple off the side of some ramps. There is a frenzy of motion as the opposing team scatters.

"God shall smite thee from the heavens," intones a tall student on your left. His head is a mass of blond curls which fall over his forehead and stack up on the top of his sunglasses. He passes out stapled booklets. "Here, read it and weep, my brothers," he says. The booklets are neatly bound and contain profiles of the characters in the night's tournament.

"OK, we're gonna start the real rounds any time now," he says. "Just as soon as we get some badly needed cabling."

He looks up and notices you.

"Hey, Matt," you say.

He stares and shakes his head. "Where the hell have you been?"

"Picking up the gear," you say, raising your bag.

"I mean before that."

"Around," you offer.

"Around what?" he asks.

"I took a scenic route," you say.

He scoffs.

"Metaphorically speaking," you explain.

"A scenic route?"

"I wanted to try to ..."

"And the a zillion text messages I sent?"

"That was you?"

"Jeez."

"I thought it was spam."

He ignores you and eyes your grocery bag. He tugs at the bag and peers in. "Anyway, you better get these downstairs." He juts his chin in the direction of the stairwell.

You take a deep breath and head downstairs. The sounds of yelling and tables being dragged across the concrete floor grows louder. You step into the basement, which is pitch black except for lava lamps scattered along a row of boxes. You squint and look around. A projection screen shows footage of Iron Butterfly with psychedelic green and purple lights. You navigate around the bubbling patterns on the floor.

"Finally," a tall, freckled gamer says looking up from his machine. "Burgie's in a real twist." He stretches an arm out and motions to the corner. There, you see the double-chin profile of Burgie leaning over the back of his machine. His silhouette bobs up and down, a penlight in his mouth. Yellow lights flash in unison from a rack of switches.

You pick your way through the maze of equipment, open boxes and cases of Coke. Near the back wall, you squeeze by the three rusty washing machines and a couple of dryers. A pile of clothes sit on the floor, soaking in a dark pool of water. A couple of large canisters of pretzels and Reese's Cups are stacked on top of the dryers. You hesitate and consider popping a lid.

Burgie stands up, adjusting his pants and setting his penlight down next to a neat row of switches. A couple of spare hubs are slung over his arm on their power cords like dead fish.

"Hey," Burgie shouts. "Guys!" He glares around the room.

The clamber in the basement continues full throttle, the din respectfully ignoring him. He throws up his hands, then ducks close to the network gear and disappears from sight. You head in his direction. When he re-emerges, he straightens to a full four inches taller than you, with curly hair and a full wiry beard. He scratches a large pale stomach that protrudes from his T-shirt, and then takes a long swig from a liter of Dr Pepper.

You hold up the grocery bag. "I got the stuff," you say.

"Jeez, not Harry's!" he mumbles when he sees the bag. His smeared glasses reflect the screens around him so you can't see his eyes to tell if he's really upset.

"Hey," you say. "It's better than nothing."

"Always the cheapskate," he mumbles.

"Well, it was the best I could do on short notice."

"Short notice?" he mutters. "You've known about this for a couple of weeks. You didn't reply to Matt."

"Thought it was spam. Anyway, a lot's been happening."

"Yeah, well tell me about it." He rummages through the bag.

"Well, for one thing…" you begin.

"This isn't even CAT6," Burgie snaps. "You brought CAT4. I can't believe it."

"What?" You look into the bag. "They're RJ45 connectors. See." You hold up the end of a cable. "Aren't they?"

"Jeez," he says. "This stuff works off an entirely different protocol."

"I could have sworn…" You take a deep breath and shake your head. The entire day has been going the same way. Small snags that you can't seem to escape. In fact, your entire life seems to be sinking. Not that you could do anything about it.

Burgie continues to dig into the wires, pulling out tangles of heavy black coils. He shakes his head. "Remember. It's not what's on the end that counts…"

"…it's the stuff in between," you mumble back. He drilled this line into you the last time you were connecting Monster cables at his apartment.

"Christ, yes," he says, and his arms flop at his sides. "And don't ever buy shit from Harry's again. Ever." He picks through the grocery bag, moving aside the opened bag of Cheetos and a half-eaten can of bean dip, and holds another cable close to his glasses, turning it sideways to read the label. "We're going to have to subnet these puppies on a completely separate switch." He glares at you. "Where've you been, anyway?"

You start to answer but you think better of it. "Driving around," you say at last, coaxing a few Cheetos into your hand.

Burgie turns back to the pile of cables. "I should be thankful they can handle 100 megabips. OK. Let's get these bad boys pulled upstairs, and I'll figure out the configuration. Man, these aren't even color-coded." This just adds insult to injury.

"Listen," you say, "maybe I'll just sit out the first few rounds. I mean, I'm not really in the mood."

"That processor of yours is looping something fierce." He studies you. "Don't wimp out. It'll take your mind off of things," he says.

You wait as Burgie pulls a cable through a tangle of cords.

"Listen," he says, "you're making a big deal out of nothing. This so-called morass of yours?"

"More like my whole world collapsing…" You want to describe how you can't shake this sinking feeling in the middle of your chest, how so little nowadays gives you any relief.

"Minor league," he says. "Remember Señor Jim?"

"Just by name."

"He was in worse shape than you."

"He was?"

"He was in over his head," Burgie says. "Then overnight he turned things around. Made tons of money." Burgie starts winding the liberated cord around his arm, one end across his palm and the other under his elbow in giant loops. "The before and after of this guy defies gravity." Burgie separates the coils and lays them flat on the table.

You stop chewing.

"One minute he was slaving away at his job like a code hog, just like you, putting in the late nights, you know, grinding out the deliverables. Then the next thing, he is flat on his back. Dan said it was the big C. Or a complete disconnect. Hard to know for sure. In a blink, he disappears off of the face of the earth. But then, the next thing, he's decked out, hair cut, spiffy coat and shoes polished, if you can believe it. Get this: His old company hires him back as a subcontractor. He sets up his own business, charges consultant rates—triple his old salary."

"He did?"

"Yeah, he makes out like a bandit. Lives cheap and invests in Yahoo. This is back-when. Gets out early with the jackpot," Burgie says. "I don't know how he does it. All of a sudden—and this is the strange part—he's just totally different. I mean, he looks good, super friendly. Even sends me source code for a problem I was having. Out of the blue. *Gratis.* Now that blew me away. Of course, these days, he rarely surfaces, at least not in the flesh. A real privacy freak. But tonight…"

Burgie lowers his glasses for effect. You nod for him to complete the thought.

"Tonight, he will probably make an appearance."

"Really?" You perk up.

Burgie pushes his glasses back. "So, don't wimp out on me."

"Yeah," you say. "Can't be as bad as I think it is." You hope.

"So," Burgie says, suddenly in a tired voice. "Don't do this to me again." He reminds you of the cables which he raises within inches of your face.

"Yeah," you say. "A misstep."

"God, Harry's. Of all places."

"Since Monday, I've been just, well, driving."

Burgie nods, but he only partially hears you. His mind is now fully engaged in the hardware. "Listen. Let's get things connected."

"Yeah, OK."

You wipe your hands on your jeans and look around the basement. It is pitch black, except for gray silhouettes that move ghost-like around the room. Faces chatter in the flicker of orange screens.

"Hey, I can't connect at all," a teen blurts out from your right. Burgie waves him off.

"And these screens really suck," he says.

"Hey, next time, bring your own."

"But I can't see anyone," he says pointing back.

"Listen," he says with mock patience. "We aren't connected yet. Try a ping."

"I tried it, but nothing."

"Yeah, like I said, we aren't connected."

"But these screens. The resolution is so nineties!"

The kid keeps going, past Burgie's tolerance level.

"Yeah, yeah," he says finally. "Back to your desk. Listen, we'll restart in about five. Most of you teenies down here have a curfew, then we get serious…"

"Hey," the teen protests, sounding hurt.

"No offense," Burgie says and smiles. "We'll link upstairs and piggyback the machines."

"So, what're the teams?" another freckled kid says, pushing in from your left. He can't be more than fifteen and waves his controller in the air.

"Hey, give me some air, will you?" Burgie yells.

"But…" the kid says.

"It's not going to happen until I can get these puppies connected, all right?"

"Yeah, OK."

"Sit down," another says behind you. You look around. The small gaggle pushes each other back and forth, huddled around a small monitor. The screen is divided into pint-sized quadrants, each containing a view. "Why do we always get the shit screens?" another asks.

"Because we are crap!"

"Yeah, second-class definitely. Just wait." He guffaws like a mad scientist. "Revenge will be ours."

"And you…" Burgie says, without looking in your direction exactly. "Time to shake a leg." Burgie finishes labeling the ends of the cable with a felt pen and hands you the end.

"Yeah," you say. You grab the cable and head upstairs, the coils trailing behind you.

The living room now has another group of four set up in a corner, and two more gamers pushing in front of the bookshelf in back. Their machines are lit, and they're jacking in.

"Hey, wait a sec," one says, getting situated on the chair. He grabs a bag of Doritos and puts a Big Gulp within reach. You spot the lights of the kitchen and veer towards them, tripping one gamer who has walked in hauling a TV. He barely recovers.

"Watch it!" he says.

The kitchen is a mess, with everything piled on two tables in the middle. On the first table are cans of dips and opened bags of chips. The other table is stacked with drinks, bulk candies, large blocks of chocolate, orange boxes of day-old brownies, black-and-whites, Krispy Kremes, industrial sizes of Oreos, Chips Ahoy, Fiddlesticks, Ginger Snaps, Newman's, Mother's Frosted and a large Happy New Year cake looking a little weathered.

You set the cable down and survey the goodies. The dips are in a bad need of a facelift. You rummage through the refrigerator, gathering boxes of Chinese leftovers, a half-eaten meatloaf, old French fries, two leftover burgers, half a burrito and soy sauce. You empty the ingredients into a row of plastic tubs, grab a potato masher and begin a frenzied mix.

"This should do the trick," you say to yourself.

With a burst of mustard and soy sauce in each, the dips are finished. Sheep Dip, Roughage Whip, Hamburger and French Fry Dip, Burrito Mash, Onion-Jalapeño and Leftover Chinese Dip. You jot down the names on Post-its, then pile some pork rinds on a paper plate with a ladle of each dip around the edge. You rearrange the bowls so they line up.

"Hey," someone yells from the living room. "Cable Guy!"

You take a chip then sample the Onion-Jalapeño and Leftover Chinese Dip. It's good with a good kick to it. There is a big percolator of coffee with open jars of instant set close by. You pour the brew into a large Styrofoam cup, then supercharge it with a mound of instant and let the powder settle.

"Cable Guy!"

"Yeah, OK," you say. You take a long couple of gulps and begin to feel better. The night may not be as bad as you think. At least, you can get your mind off of things for a while. You head into the living room, the cable snaking behind. Locating a switch against one wall, you squat down and carefully plug in the jack. The lights blink rapidly with the 100 Mbps indicator switching to green. Suddenly, the row of lights blinks rapidly in synch.

There is applause from the basement.

"We're set," someone yells down to Burgie.

You place the plate of dips on your coffee cup and head downstairs again.

"Let's do a round of pings, guys," Burgie shouts over the ruckus. "Upstairs is a different subnet, all right?"

"This sucks," another says.

A long coil has been pulled off the pile of cables and laid out along the side of the stairwell. Quickly, someone races around the room connecting up the remaining boxes. Burgie punches the keys, sniffing the packets as they flash on his screen. He scratches his beard and takes another long drink from his liter before looking up.

"Who's up there? On top, I mean," you ask.

"The Holodeck? Those are the luxury booths." He smiles and goes back to his keying. No doubt there is better ventilation upstairs. It already smells like a locker room downstairs, and the real sweating has not begun. "Where's your controller?"

"I forgot it," you reply.

"Man, you are in bad shape," he says and nods in the direction of a stack of old controllers. "Over there." He looks around. "You can set up next to Jonze," he says, "the newbie." You see an older man in khakis and a plaid shirt, maybe in his forties, standing awkwardly next to a TV, waiting for someone to approach him.

You wander over.

"Hey," you say.

"Hey," Jonze says beaming. "Should be fun."

"I hope so," you say, lifting your plate, squeezing in front of the screens.

"My first time here," he explains. "So, if I get in the way..."

"No worries. We are all newbies at some level."

He laughs. "Yeah."

There is a machine on the floor, and you plug in. Jonze balances your food for you as you lower into a bean bag.

"What's this?" he asks pointing to the glob on the plate.

"Onion-Jalapeño and Leftover Chinese Dip."

"Wow."

"Yeah there's more in the kitchen."

He sits down at a nearby table.

"But be careful," you warn. "The Onion- Jalapeño has a kick."

You are joined by a couple of teens who take positions on the floor. You set your plate carefully on a stack of *PC Gamer* back issues. A couple of sneakers are kicked off and thump on the floor.

"He's God," says one of them referring to one of the teens.

"Nice to meet you," you say. "Thought I might run into you one of these days."

God is a tall, shy youth with short cropped hair. He smiles quickly. "Yeah?" he asks. He giggles.

"My first time," says the older man.

"That's OK," God says. "You can be on my team."

"Wow." Jonze beams. "Thanks."

"OK, chums," Matt shouts from upstairs. "Time to rock and roll. Burgie, you set?"

"Yep," shouts Burgie as he takes his position. The screens come alive with movement.

"What are the teams?"

"It's on the screen, dummy."

"Hey, this sucks," a pudgy gamer says from a corner chair. "We're gonna get creamed."

"Not if you do something other than shoot up the place, Dan."

"Yeah, use some strategy for a change."

"We're still going to get creamed," Dan says.

"OK, let's get moving," says God. "The longer we mill around, the better targets we are. Come on." His character quickly jumps up on the screen, pivots around, then heads off down the hall.

You look down at your hands on the screen and find a large bazooka-like weapon. Your boots feel a bit awkward. You shoulder the weapon and prance behind a small group of fellow Blue Team members. Bullets bounce off the wall, and you quickly race up the ramp, then down a set of stairs, slowing up at the corner.

"Go to that side," God says to you. "I'm going up top."

"Roger," you say. "Jonze, follow me."

"Listen, I'll pin them down. You guys head for their flag. Stay close together."

Jonze uses his real name on screen, and he nods his helmet before bumping into a wall. Bullets strafe the walls, and you let out a couple of bursts of rockets. The hallway lights up. You back up, cross to the other side, then edge forward, looking through your scope. Bullets fly, and you squat down, aiming at two Red Team members as they emerge from behind a vehicle. You let loose and the scene explodes.

"Two kills! Yeah."

"Let the blood flow," yells a gamer in a shrill voice.

You are joined by other members of the Blue Team, and you funnel into a large courtyard in the center of the building. Along the top, there is a walkway and a tall tower overhead.

The Red Team streams from a door on the other side. Suddenly a hovercraft flies in from the top and unloads a stream of rockets in your direction. Jonze is flipped over, and you run for cover. More Blue Team shows up along an adjacent wall. You hide behind a pillar as another craft floats in. Suddenly the first craft explodes. Pieces are strewn around the courtyard. You take aim on the second craft, then let loose a rocket that catches a wing. The craft spins out of control and explodes in the center of the courtyard.

"Bull's-eye!" God yells proudly. "OK, time to close in. Get moving."

You race to take position behind a torn piece of the fuselage. Red Team members venture forward, but they are picked off one by one.

"Crapazoid," you hear from upstairs.

"Cool," says Jonze, and he is back at your side.

"Cover me," you say, motioning with your free hand. But Jonze is frozen.

"Just a sec," he says. He picks up a Coke and takes a couple of gulps.

"Let's go."

"Just needed to refuel."

"OK, hurry."

Jonze comes to life on the screen and swivels around to lay in a barrage of bullets. You move forward to see a Red Team member firing from behind a large slab. You lower your rockets, and let loose two in succession. Part of the slab is blown away, but there are still bursts of fire. You rush behind an overturned hovercraft. You take aim again at the slab, and see it explode.

"Good one," says God.

Red Team begins to retreat. Jonze joins you, and you rush forward. Past the main door, you find an abandoned hovercraft and get in. Jonze follows. Punching the controller, you turn the hovercraft around, the jets flaring up in bright blue, then you power down the valley to Red Team's fortress.

"Hold up," says God. "I've got to re-position."

You pull behind a wall as enemy fire opens up from the roof. You wait as Red Team reinforces. Large guns are positioned along the top. Suddenly, you see the enemy fall from the roof.

"Christ!" someone yells.

"What the?"

"OK, now!" says God.

"Jonze, you drive."

"OK," he says. "Boy this is great. I think we're going to win."

"Let's not count our chips just yet," you say.

The hovercraft jerks forward, hitting a large dip hard. You manage to line up the front entrance in your sights and let a stream of rockets loose. The explosions clear the way as more Blue Team members scramble up the sides, running quickly in front of the craft. A member of your team is picked off.

"I'm down," a gamer squeals from across the basement.

There is a large explosion in front of you, and you jump out. Racing for cover, you enter the fortress.

"Come on," you say. But Jonze is down.

You scramble toward the ramp. Red Team takes up position over the doorway to their flag. You fire off a rocket. Suddenly, a Blue Team member is running down the ramp with the stolen flag.

"Got it," you hear from upstairs, and you switch weapons to a rapid fire, cranking out a steady stream of bullets as cover. A Blue Team member grabs the red flag and zigzags down the ramp. You lay down cover as he races toward the fortress door. Suddenly Jonze shows up in a troop transport.

"Over here," Jonze says.

You jump in and the transport takes off.

"Go, go, go!" God yells.

The transport disappears in the distance.

"No-o-o-o!" yells the team from upstairs. "This sucks!"

The game is over and your team has won. Stats roll up the screen. Blue Team has out-killed Red Team, with God racking up an impressive 68 kills. Everyone else's performance pales by comparison.

"Yeah!" a gamer yells, jumping to his feet. "Revenge is ours!"

"Good round." God smiles.

"Yeah," you say beaming.

"It just sucks," a hefty gamer says, his voice suddenly booming next to you. He has followed Matt downstairs.

"Listen, Dan," Matt says. "The teams were fair."

"Like hell," Dan replies. "How much fun do you think it is getting blown up all the time? I couldn't even move without getting picked off."

"Listen, Dan. Don't go running out trying to shoot up everything. You know, you could wait for some cover. Maybe back up or don't go back to the same spot where you were picked off last time. Ever think of that?"

"How much fun is cowering? I'm supposed to stand behind a rock all the time?"

"Well," Matt says. "You can have fun winning."

"He just has one weapon he likes," Burgie explains. "Let's grab something before the next round."

"It just pisses me off," Dan continues. "Who was doing that anyway?"

"God," says Matt with a smile. "Can't say I didn't warn you. He shall smite thee from the heavens."

"Jesus," Dan says.

"Better," Matt quips.

"Then I want God on my side."

"Don't we all," says a voice from behind.

You turn to find a tall stranger in a black T-shirt and baseball cap looking on. The gamers make room for him as he nods at Burgie.

The group is suddenly quiet.

"It's him," Burgie whispers to you.

Y ou rattle off a quick message to Burgie from the back of the darkened conference room.

There is no response. The blinking cursor waits on the screen. You look up and find Gordon, the office manager, standing in front, his face lit from the projector below like a Halloween lantern. You have this sinking feeling that this is not going to be good. It is Monday before the LAN party

"OK, people," Gordon says. "Let's settle down. This isn't going to take long, so please bear with me."

He clicks the next slide.

At the center of the room is a large polished table. Most of the staff sits around with cups of coffee, their notebooks open. Chairs are lined up along the sides, with extra rows squeezed into the back. You lean forward, backpack wedged against the seatback. You can't see anyone you know. Burgie and Jack are already in their usual spots. You press the backlight and rummage through your email, then take a gulp of the cold foam and set the lukewarm cappuccino on the floor. The room quiets and the screen fills up with another Powerpoint slide, bullet points neatly aligned and clipart of people doing sports.

Gordon's glasses blink like fisheyes. The room slips into a murmur.

You look again. There is a doughnut on your finger. It was a quick scavenge in the break room, left over from the previous week. Although you can barely see it in the dim light, you can smell the sweet chocolate of the frosting. You take a quick bite.

"This is not looking good," the woman next to you says in the dark.

Her comments don't add to your feeling of well-being. You look up at a screen filled with boxes and diagrams.

"What's happening?" you ask.

"Hard to say, but Gordon is a little too cheerful this morning," she says.

"He's always cheerful at meetings."

"Well, not this cheerful."

"Anyway, it's almost lunchtime," you say. "When's the meeting supposed to end?"

"Anytime now," she says. "He's been beating around the bush, but I think his final slide is just around the corner."

"I can barely keep my eyes open," you say. Gordon's droning voice and the slides have you fidgeting in your seat.

You turn your attention back to the doughnut and realize maybe it was left out in the lunchroom for a reason. It crunches on one side and feels spongy on the other, with pockets of gooeyness. You look closer and notice that there is an unusual swelling along the bottom side, maybe from yeast, but more than likely from unhealthy causes. You examine it, lifting it in front of the light from the projector. You hold it at eye level. The frosting looks slightly wrinkled. It resembles a bad toupee.

You sniff at it, but it smells OK.

"OK, people," Gordon says finally. "That's what it's going to look like."

Your mouth begins to sour.

The room is silent as people strain for a closer look. For a long time, you only hear the breathing of the woman next to you and an occasional cough from across the room. On the screen is a slide with a large organizational chart, each section aligned in neat horizontal rows, with employees designated by their first initial and last name. Gordon's name is in boldface at the top, but you don't see your section anywhere.

"Jeez," you say, swallowing hard. The taste is turning into a moldy burn, with just a hint of slime.

You look again, but cannot find your section anywhere. Your stomach feels queasy. You catch your breath; your heart is beating hard.

Suddenly, the lights are back on, and Gordon strides up the side of the room, manila folder in hand. No one moves as he silently pads to the door. You start chewing slowly, cheeks full, eyes straining to see the slide. But the screen has changed, and it now shows the company logo and *Thank you.*

The room is dead silent.

"I guess this was coming," the woman says. "You hear rumors and you think, well, maybe this won't affect me." She smiles at you, but with the remnants of the donut sticking to your cheeks, you are having a hard time responding. Her face saddens and she gets up.

"Jeez," you say again, your tongue sticking to your teeth.

People begin to get up.

"It's official," she says. She stands and turns toward the door, the row slowly shuffling out. "Stiff upper lip."

You shake your head then gather your things, adjusting your backpack. You are suddenly tired, your legs feeling wobbly and back unusually sore. You take a deep breath then move quietly to the door.

You feel suffocated, and stop to catch your breath in the hallway. It is only a short distance, but you feel that you need to sit down again. You find yourself leaning against a wall, breathing slowly, thinking about your long trek back to your cubicle.

You're famished. The break room is a few doors down and you step inside.

You catch your breath and feel safe, ensconced in the smells of Krispy Kremes and coffee. You approach the counter, eyes skipping over the powdered coffee creamer, ignoring stained plastic spoons, the multicolored packets of sweetener—both real and synthetic—and Styrofoam cups. You spot an empty donut box and wince. It is like an accident near the side of the road, and you are afraid to look. You find the coffee has warmed down to a thick gel, but fill a Styrofoam cup with the thick substance.

You quickly step to the fridge and spring it open for a cursory look. Your stomach automatically rumbles when the door opens. (You realize your stomach has acquired the instincts of a refrigerator light, cultivated from years of scavenging.) New bags, each with someone's name scribbled along its side, sit along the top and middle shelves. The ones in back appear to be squashed by the new crop. Below, you find a jumble of other bags the janitor has moved. These are the leftovers from the weekend. You also find a half-drunk Dr. Pepper, Mountain Dew and Pepsi, a left-over burrito, and a tub of potato salad, half-frozen lasagna, a baggie of coleslaw—the makings of a quick breakfast post-meeting. You find a carton of milk and pour it in, concocting an ad-hoc cappuccino, and make a mental note to return.

After a quick slurp, you feel revived. A couple shuffles past the door to the break room and you decide to venture back to your cubicle. You walk out in the hallway, past the network closet.

As you pass her in the corridor, Dolores hooks an arm. You are startled and twist to regain your balance, lifting the remains of your cappuccino out of harm's way. You steady yourself, but Dolores reels you in. You find yourself squeezed between her and Rex, their eager faces on either side.

"Good timing," she says, her eyelashes fluttering.

"Yes, very serendipitous," Rex adds, leaning forward to make eye contact. "Don't you think?"

You are close enough to smell her sweet breath, a combination of coffee and Tic Tacs. She looks like an oversized Raggedy Ann with big freckled cheeks and big stuffed arms with dimples at her elbows and wrists. Her hair is pulled back into two large braids, tied with ribbons, and revealing large, buoyant earlobes. She waits a beat or two.

"I had this horrendous donut," you begin.

"So," Dolores says, ignoring you, her lips parting into a knowing smile. "This module of yours. This *XLib…*"

"Yes, puzzling," Rex murmurs, his eyes sunk deep under bushy eyebrows.

You try to get your bearings. You'd forgotten about *XLib*, but now the mere mention of your module has you back-pedaling. It has been a real thorn. Maybe that is where your sinking feeling all started. The epicenter. Your stomach begins to rumble.

"I don't understand," you say, steadying your mock cappuccino. You take a hasty slurp from your cup and come up with a full nose of foam. She pulls back quickly to avoid blowback. You try to clean the foam off by dipping your face down to your free hand, but your hand is still pinned to Rex's side. The buttons of his cowboy shirt rub against your wrist as you manage to half-dry your nose on a sleeve.

"Gordon says D-day is this Friday. Am I right?"

"Actually June 6, I believe," Rex pipes in, pleased at himself. Dolores gives him a quick look.

You try to remember the exact deadlines that Gordon set, but your mind is a jumble. Overhead you glimpse a flicker from one of the lights. Kaufman has warned you about these flickers, about the seizures that even the smallest of flashes can trigger. You've made a mental note and keep a wary eye for any changes. "I mean…"

"You don't get it, do you?" she snaps and moves forward, unafraid of the foam that remains on your nose. Awkwardly you straighten up and try to sidestep, but now she is even closer, her smile replaced by a scowl, her lilac perfume mixing with the hot peppermint of her breath.

Lenny and Margaret from QA stop to listen.

"We have to get started," she says. "Otherwise, it will look like *we* are delaying things," she says, indicating Rex as well. Your mouth is dry; a pasty film sticks to your tongue.

"That Documentation is complacent..." Rex adds.

You look over at Rex, who is still smiling but has a worried wrinkle creeping across his forehead and threatening to take over this entire face. His mustache begins to droop.

You study Dolores.

"Listen, I see your point," you say. But you don't understand what the fuss from Documentation is all about. After all, *XLib* is just a silly set of utilities, not exactly core product. *Odds and ends* is how Gordon described it when he dumped it into your lap. Yet Dolores has been nagging you *ad naseum* to start the documentation. You tried to explain that there wasn't much to document. You had some inspired beginnings, but these all fizzled. Somehow, the various routines failed to work together. You restarted—then restarted again—but little survived the initial unit testing.

"You've got to do more than just *see*," she says, her earlobes bouncing. Her eyes bulge out emphatically. "Is this some sort of *game* with you? Some sort of cat and mouse game?"

"No ..."

"Who do you think you are?" Her face is bright red.

Your stomach tightens and your voice breaks. "Me?" Your mouth feels numb. You desperately want to be somewhere else, to be *someone* else right now.

"You wander in here late every morning. As if you didn't have a care in the world. You don't do any real work, as far as I can tell. This place is some sort of coffee shop to you, isn't it? Where you can sip your cappuccinos and schmooze with your buddies? You don't have anything pressing. No deadlines. No responsibilities. No work. You are somehow privileged, exempt from any rules..."

You flush. You want to defend yourself, but you don't know where to begin. So far she's been pretty accurate.

"Or are you just lazy?"

"Dolores, calm down."

"Or maybe you're just clueless."

"Listen," you say, but she continues to barrel through.

She edges toward you, and you trip backwards, your pack knocking into someone. A small crowd has gathered. All eyes are on you.

"What's with you?" Her face is lit up, and she glares at you. "No one else can do anything, because you're the only one who knows anything about *XLib* and here you are, sitting on your thumbs. And all you can say is 'I understand?'"

Her nose is close to yours and each word flings droplets of saliva in your eyes.

"You're ..."—she tries to think of the word—"pathetic." She is practically screaming.

The hallway is suddenly quiet and she looks around. A group of programmers have stopped and are whispering to one another; heads rise over cubicles to catch the action. You see Burgie and Jack turn the corner. As they approach, they are surprised to see you at the center of the gathering.

The coffee shakes in your hand. You want to take a quick sip to energize yourself, but the cup is too far away. The bottoms of your feet begin to itch, and the hallway gyrates around you.

Burgie, who is now behind you, nudges your backpack then clears his throat. Dolores glances at him. You can feel the heat of his large frame on your back like Saturn easing into orbit. He produces the remnant of a Snickers bar and proceeds to feed it into his mouth with tree-shredder precision. To your left, Jack swallows. He is short, with a pug nose and thinning sandy hair that he spikes up like Bubble Boy.

Dolores takes a deep breath, and she pulls her sweater around her large frame as Burgie chews loudly. "You'll do this?" she says.

"I can't," you say.

"What do you mean *you can't*?" she asks.

"I mean, there won't be any time. Not now. Not for you, not for documentation."

Her face is suddenly bright red. "You are absolutely the worst..."

"We're gone," you say. "Don't you get it?"

"Gone?" she snaps. "How can you be *gone*?"

"We're toast," Burgie explains between bites. "That's the news of the hour, fresh off the presses."

"Toast?" she asks. You realize that Dolores and Rex were not at the morning meeting.

"Yeah, the noun referring to bread that has been browned due to exposure to heat," he says. "The connotation is generally positive, except in our case."

She looks back and forth between you and Burgie. Her mouth is open to say something, but nothing comes out. Instead, she blinks and swallows hard.

"Fried," you say still tasting the last of the doughnut. "We've been sacked, Dolores. Laid off. Rationalized. Given the ax. " Your stomach re-knots itself with each increasingly severe synonym.

"Jeez," she says.

"So find someone else," you say, straightening up and glaring at her. "There's nothing to document. Not anymore."

She steps back, startled, and looks around. It all sinks in to you now.

"There's been another layoff?" she stammers.

"Bingo!" says Burgie.

She quickly places her fingers to her lips as if she is going to heave right on the spot. Her eyes tear up, and she blinks uncontrollably, her bulging eyes stealing a frightened look to Rex.

"You mean...?" Rex begins.

"Yep," Burgie says.

"But we absolutely must get the product out the door," she says. "Or we're sunk."

Burgie stuffs the Snickers wrapper back in his pocket with a muffled burp.

"We have sunk," he says. "Come on." He starts walking silently toward the elevator in long loping steps, arms straight at his sides, Jack in tow. People look at Dolores as her big eyes blink rapidly and begin to tear up.

"It's nobody's fault, OK," you say to Dolores and hurry down the corridor behind them, your backpack bouncing from side to side. The elevator is close by. The three of you stare at the floor indicator.

"So much for beating the lunch rush," Burgie says, squeezing into a packed elevator.

You catch one last glimpse of Dolores as she stands with Rex in the hallway. She looks at you from the distance, still stunned, her body breathing in spasms, arms lifeless at her side. Then the door closes and the elevator begins its slow painful descent.

The heat hits your face like a furnace as you step into the noonday sun. The parking is packed. Cars edge slowly out, gravel popping under the tires, ricocheting off windshields and onto the concrete. Drivers hang out their windows, sweating, trying to catch even the faintest of breezes. As a dust devil brushes by, you squint and lick the sand from your teeth. Your eyes slowly adjust.

"We act as though comfort and luxury were the chief requirements of life..." Burgie intones as he walks slowly around the pylons in front of the building. Over the chain-link fence, the desert looks like a barren junkyard.

"It's not?" Jack says.

"...when all that we need to make us happy is something to be enthusiastic about."

"Who said that?" Jack asks. "The Dalai Lama?"

"Albert Einstein."

"Whew," Jack says in disbelief. "He really was a genius."

"Makes you wonder why we stuck it out so long at this place," Burgie says. "Doesn't it?"

"Yeah," Jack replies brightly.

The cars creep forward. People stare at you through dusty windshields. A crowd shuffles along the sidewalk, disappearing into the underpass on its way to the parking annex.

It's a miserable afternoon. To the north, the city bakes in the heat, a shimmering pool of asphalt.

"This way," Burgie says, his forehead already drenched with sweat. His large frame swivels abruptly. Instead of heading out to the parking annex, he veers around the building to the rear. To the west, a power plant spews a slender braid of steam into the desert sky. You walk single-file in the shadow of the building, then out the back gate. The air smells of bleach.

Burgie has parked his green Prius near the dumpster. The side mirrors and bumpers are a flat gray, and a black strip protrudes from the rear, with an assortment of Burgie's recent add-ins. The windows are tinted, and the locks have been replaced with digital keypads. Brazenly, the car sits in a no-parking zone.

"Sure beats walking over to the annex," Jack says.

"Hey, it cuts off a full 25 minutes each way," Burgie boasts. "This space opened up when the company went through its last cost-cutting. Remember that second dumpster?"

He surveys his space as if it is his ranch.

"When it vanished," he continues. "I moved right in."

"You squatted a garbage spot?" Jack says.

"Why not?" he says proudly. "Except for the occasional overflow on Fridays, it's perfect. Security got hit in the last layoff, remember? They don't care."

He smiles and punches in his code on the door. The locks spring open. You move around to the passenger door, which is wedged near the concrete retaining wall.

"New batteries," he says. "I saved a bundle."

"Really?"

"Yeah, old laptop batteries. I wired them together with a little software. Hot swappable, too."

"Neat."

A lone figure shuffles along the side of the building and past the loading dock, cigarette in hand.

"Hey," you say to Myra as she approaches. She has short-cropped hair and wears a casual men's jacket over jeans and sandals. Her face is a mesh of fine lines like soft leather, with deeper lines around her nose and mouth.

"You guys off to lunch?" she asks, her hand shielding her eyes. She takes a small puff from the cigarette in her other hand and looks at you calmly as you answer through the smoke.

"To Shakey's," you reply.

"Sharey's," Burgie corrects. "It's Sharey's now."

"Yep, pizza buffet," Jack says.

"$4.95," Burgie says, fishing around in his beard.

"I thought it was $6.95," says Jack.

"With coupons," Burgie says, "$4.95"

"OK," she says. "Sounds good. Do they have any vegan?"

"Doubt it," Burgie says. "Sorry."

"OK," she says, disappointed. "Guess I'll just tag along anyway. You mind?"

"The more the merrier," says Jack.

She gives a small smile and takes one last go-for-broke drag on her cigarette, before flicking it on the concrete slab and crushing it with a sandal.

"You guys get screwed too?" she asks, as she squeezes into the back seat behind Burgie.

The car is quiet.

"I'll take that as a *yes*," she says, and she stares out the window.

Burgie switches the car on and settles back with a creak. He taps a small monitor on the dashboard and checks the video of the fence and a few discarded boxes behind the car. He swivels a joystick to rotate the camera, carefully scrutinizing the back alley as he moves out of his space.

"Just a sec," he says, once he has cleared. From the trunk, he unrolls a small kid's swimming pool and drags it to his space. "That will keep the squatters away," he says as he throws a couple of jerry-rigged switches and the car scoots along the side of the main building.

"Screw them," Myra snaps as she gazes up at the top floor and gives "them" the finger.

The car pulls onto the frontage road, then quickly into the darkness of the freeway underpass. Back in the sunlight, Burgie edges out onto the freeway with a bump. Sharey's is two exits away. With every bump in the road, you bounce up and down, nicking the roof.

Burgie hooks the steering wheel with a coat hanger and stretches back like an oversized kitten, wiggling his hips against the shag seat cover, cracking his neck, and raising his arms. A strong hot breeze hits you. The bouncing continues, and you have the nagging Tacoma-Narrows-Bridge feeling.

"Auto-pilot?" you ask, referring to the coat hanger, and he nods with a muted smile. He uses one finger positioned at the bottom of the hanger to keep the car on track.

"Upgraded the shocks," Burgie says proudly. "From eBay."

"Pretty nice," you say.

"Actually," he explains, "the shocks were for a Ford pickup, but the specs seemed to match up. Might need some tweaking."

"A little bouncy," you say.

"Yeah," he replies grinning. "But you get used to it."

Your head bobs in agreement.

"Dennis missed the bullet," Jack says from the back seat.

"I think Lucas and Big Bob also," Myra adds.

"Peter's got a sweet deal," Jack says.

"If you don't mind brain atrophy," Burgie says. "He's been doing maintenance for years."

"He likes it," Myra pipes in. "They'll never get rid of Old Slick. That clunker will be here when Intel processors roll into your iPhone. He'll have a job for life."

"The Slick has been there, what, fifteen years?" you ask.

"Twenty, maybe twenty-five years. That thing sits in the back offices of every customer and just polls the floor. And no one knows how to code it. It's patched and spaghettied out the ying-yang," Myra adds.

"I'd like to see Dolores document that dinosaur," Burgie says, turning in your direction.

"Alex survived," Jack adds. "Again."

"The janitor?" you ask.

"Yep. Low-tech will always prevail, wasn't that Busby's Correlate?" Jack asks.

"*Any sufficiently advanced technology is indistinguishable from magic,*" Burgie intones. "Arthur C. Clarke."

"Really?" Myra asks.

"Don't get him started," you say.

"Alex has been there forever," Myra says. "He pre-dates management."

"What management?" Jack says, and everyone chuckles.

"*The first myth of management,*" Burgie recites, "*is that it exists.*"

"Murphy's Law?" Jack asks.

"As applied to management," Burgie adds. Then, "*Technology is dominated by those who manage what they do not understand.*"

"I wish I knew what I was going to do now," Jack says as an aside. His honesty is definitely out of place. The car is suddenly silent. You glance back and see Jack and Myra looking up, heads nodding.

As he pulls off the freeway, Burgie unhooks the wheel and begins making turns into a series of side streets. At the restaurant, the parking lot is packed. There is only room for a handful of cars, since it shares its lot with a fitness center and a nail salon. A small space is hidden between two SUVs, and Burgie swings to the opposite side of the aisle for his approach.

"That looks pretty tight," you say. "Maybe we should look for parking on the street."

"Shouldn't be too bad," Burgie says, eyeing the parking space carefully. "You guys better get out here."

"I'll give you directions," you say, as Myra and Jack unload.

"OK, you be the marshaler," he says.

"The what?"

"That's what it's called. Hope you've read up on the Air Standardization Coordinating Committee air standards 44 and 42A. I like to use the standards wherever possible."

"Listen," you say. "You want to do this by yourself?"

"First off, to move me in, your arms are bent like you're being arrested…"

"Can we just get on with this? We don't have much time."

"…then wave your hands side to side. Like this."

His hands scrape the roof over his head.

"To move left, point your right arm down and keep the left going. To move right, point the left down…"

"OK, OK. I got it."

"Wait. For me to stop, cross your hands above your head."

"OK," you say. "It's getting hot out here."

You take your position in the space and move your hands over your head in a side-to-side motion. Burgie smiles and moves toward you.

"That's it. I always wanted to taxi a plane," Burgie says out his side window.

You point your right hand down for him to move right.

"Wrong arm!" he says.

"Hey what's going on?" Jack shouts from under the shade of the restaurant awning.

"I'm marshaling," you say.

Jack puts a hand to his ear for you to repeat, but you are not sure that this is a standard hand signal you should acknowledge.

You correct your arms and Burgie moves his Prius in. Then with both arms lowered, you move them up and down to indicate *slow* and he creeps along until the car is close to the barrier. Then you cross your wrists overhead for Burgie to stop. He kills the motor and gives you a double thumbs-up. He opens his door, but it does not clear more than a few inches. He twists around, rolling the window down.

"Not as much room as I thought," he says with his head out the side. His forehead is drenched and there are large wet spots across his chest and under his arms.

"Emergency evacuation?" you ask.

"Yep," he says, then rolls up the window. Turning around, he leans both front seats back and leans the back seats forward. He dips from view, his heels kicking like an oversized scuba diver. A minute later, the hatchback pops open and he rolls out the back, a Dr Pepper in tow, knees tucked under his immense stomach. He steadies himself on the rear bumper before swiveling around.

"Had to disconnect my video," he explains holding up his small minicam, "just to be on the safe side." His pants are twisted, and he quickly adjusts himself. His T-shirt is completely soaked.

"Just out of curiosity, how do you signal emergency evacuation?"

He slips the camera back in its holder and reconnects it.

"Probably like this," Burgie says, standing up straight, pointing low to one side, rotating his hands in large circles. "It means 'fire in the engine,' but that would probably get me out pretty fast."

"I'm impressed," you say. "Now all you need to do is learn how to take off and land, and you're all set."

He smiles proudly, pushing his black curls off his forehead. After a long swig of Dr Pepper, he stows the bottle under his shirt. The bottle looks more like a growth than a roll of fat. But you figure no one would really question the protrusion, fearing what the answer might be.

Myra and Jack are waiting in the entry. Smells of fresh-baked pizza fill the air as you edge through the door. Burgie takes a deep breath, and lets it out slowly, licking his lips and rolling his eyes.

"Heaven," Burgie whispers.

The place is packed, mostly with techie types, and you see a couple of tables of employees drinking from 32-ounce Coke cups. There is a row of picnic tables and benches that have been added to the smattering of bar tables and round tables.

The buffet overtakes the bar, with seven or eight pizzas perched under heat lamps, and a steam table of pasta, garlic bread, fried rice, potato skins, nachos and even some Chinese dishes. At the far end is a soda fountain. Small Styrofoam salad bowls are stacked next to a pile of forks.

"Four?" the Chinese hostess asks raising four fingers. "Ten minutes," she says. "Very quick."

She jots down a Chinese character on her paper. You back up next to the stack of throwaway papers and gumball machines. On the wall is a picture of President Clinton with the owner. The caption reads "Best Eggrolls In Arizona! Bill."

"It's $4.95, right?" Jack asks.

"With coupons," she says. "$2.69 for drink. Free refill."

Burgie produces the coupons and gives you the knowing eye.

After twenty minutes, you are seated with the salad bowls piled high with thin slices of pepperoni, cheese and sausage pizza. There was an assortment of Chinese dishes at the bar. You piled wontons, broccoli beef and bamboo shoots on a couple of your slices. Another has chopped noodles and shrimp. They are all steamy hot and smell great. Burgie lines up paper cups from the office and fills them from his bottle. He looks around, then stashes the bottle in his lap. Myra has stacked the vegetables from the salad bar on her plate (mostly tofu and baco bits). Jack is folding a slice into his mouth.

"This buffet is pretty schizophrenic, don't you think?" Myra says.

"Yeah, not bad," Jack says.

"Gr-aute," Burgie mumbles, then swallows. "Great."

"So what're you going to do?" you ask Myra after a while. "Those guys already have the want ads." You look over at the table of co-workers. Ed is dividing up the paper by ripping each page down the middle. "Are there classifieds on Monday?"

"Guess I'll update my resume on Monster," Jack says. "Only about eight months old."

"An eternity," Myra says. "That's a full generation for a processor. You need to pump it up."

"Yeah?" he says. "The hard part is just not knowing what I'm going to do next."

"Fear of the unknown," Burgie chimes in. "Apeirophobia."

"Really?"

"Quite common," Burgie says between bites.

"That's the fear of infinity," Myra says. "I know my Latin."

"Same thing," Burgie says, "...if you think about it."

"I've got anuptaphobia," she says.

"More like androphobia," he says.

"I'll ignore that." She gives him the evil eye.

"The hard part is my folks," you say. "They'll think it was my fault, of course."

Everyone nods.

"Which it wasn't," you emphasize.

Your mother will comfort you for a few minutes, but then the questions will begin. How could this happen? Did everyone in your section get laid off? Didn't you see it coming when you didn't get the promotion you wanted? And blah, blah.

It would be different if you were on your way up. Or if you were in the limelight—a rock star, an actor, or a writer. These occupations have the mystique, along with the ups and downs. In fact, the ups and downs *are* the mystique. Once you became famous, everything would fall into your lap—women, money, cars, and gadgets galore.

You imagine yourself as the Wilt Chamberlain of the coding world, bedding scores of hacker groupies that hang around the back entrance after your code goes gold. They wait outside after the go-live party and try to grab a printout or a book, as you tuck into your impossibly fast Ferrari 612 Scaglietti with its 6-liter V12 parked in your reserved spot. You wave with a smile, push your glasses up and fire up that baby to a side window of fans yearning to be sitting in your passenger seat.

You look over at Myra who is daintily re-hydrating the baco bits.

If you were the Brad Pitt of the technology world, you'd swagger up to the podium, hair askew (but in a good way), shirt unbuttoned to your navel (hell, unbuttoned all the way!), signing an autograph or two from adoring fans, having phone numbers pushed into your pockets by prying fingers, nonchalantly picking through your state diagrams with a toothpick in your front teeth.

"Yes," you would say, "I remember sitting in that very cubicle, getting my notice when that new sort algorithm struck me, one that would shave another 16 microseconds per 1000 off of the critical indexing. That very spot!" And you would laugh at the mess you had been in. You wouldn't mind a layoff or two, or working for a manager formerly assigned to Abu Ghraib prison. Things would make sense. All of the suffering was just paying dues for a better life.

"You finished?" Burgie asks incredulously. "Just one run?"

You look down and see a plate of partially-eaten slices.

Burgie gets up and returns with a mountain of soft-serve. "The dessert bar is near the bathrooms," he says.

Myra plops down with fruit cocktail and an almond cookie. "What we should do," she says firmly, "is form our own company." She looks around the table. "Look at the talent that's right here." She breaks off a nibble of her cookie and surveys the table.

"That would be great," Jack says. "I hate doing resumes."

She takes out a pen and uncrumples her napkin.

"Between us, we would have some great ideas. Who needs the likes of Gordon? If he can run our company into the ground, just imagine what we could do?"

Jenz Johnson

"Run it into the ground?" Burgie asks.

"No, I mean we don't need his so-called management. We have enough brain power just at this table to launch a dozen companies. We just need one good idea to run with. It can't be that hard." Her pen is poised over the napkin. "Come on. Let's brainstorm this," she says. "Think of Compaq. This is the way they got started."

"You mean HP," Burgie says, lifting a spoonful. "They're HP now."

"We can do this," she says, ignoring Burgie. "Throw out an idea. Even a crazy one."

"Cray started this way," you say.

"The CDC 1401," Jack says.

"1604," Burgie corrects. "The 1401 was a glorified IBM card sorter."

"OK," she says. "Come on. We can do this."

"Yes, but doing what?"

"Consult?" you say. "We could hire ourselves out."

"Well, yes," Myra says.

"I know," Jack says. "You know how when you refill your water bottles, it keeps overflowing and you get yourself soaked?"

Everyone looks up at Jack.

"In front of the Food Warehouse," he explains. "We could rig an automatic shut-off for those things. Just like at the gas pumps. We'd make a bundle."

Burgie makes a buzzer sound and returns to his eating.

"Or," he says quickly. "You know how the freezers fog up when you're looking for ice cream. At first they're pretty hazy, so you open the door, but then they really fog up and you can't see anything. And you have to open them even wider, which just compounds the problem more. We could come up with some sort of fan that blows the glass. Like the kind they have when you walk into a store."

"Jack," Myra says, looking disgusted. "Your ideas are shit."

Jack winces and looks down at his leftovers.

"What about an on-line business of some sort?" you suggest.

"Well, like what?" Myra shoots back.

"I dunno," you say. "Like books or tools?"

"Been done," she says, rolling her eyes.

"Or, places to rent?"

"Yeah, done."

"Or porn," Burgie adds without looking up.

"Please!" Myra says. "Let's not whore ourselves out just yet. We're not that desperate."

"We're not?" Jack asks.

"It would be very lucrative," Burgie notes.

Myra shakes her head and re-crumples up her napkin.

"Maybe we should be heading back," you say when nothing else is forthcoming. "It's almost 2."

"Jeez, we deserve to be laid off," she says. "We're a bunch of real losers."

Burgie swallows the last of his dessert and pushes away his empty plate. "That's the last time we invite you along."

"Yeah," Jack says, his chin sinking.

"Sorry, guys," she says. "I just feel like shit today."

"OK," Burgie says. "No harm done. Losers today are winners tomorrow."

"Yeah," Jack says brightening.

"You're right," she says and pulls out her purse.

You chip in your share and Myra adds a couple of dollars for the tip.

"It's a buffet," Burgie says. "You don't tip when it's a buffet."

Myra shrugs and leaves the money, looking around.

"Be right back," she says and heads toward the restroom.

Burgie slides the bottle under his shirt and eyes the remains of the meal. He pulls your plate closer and locates the uneaten pieces at the bottom.

"You mind?" he asks.

"Be my guest," you say. "Couldn't finish them."

"Too much MSG?" he asks, munching through the noodle and shrimp slice.

"I'm just feeling pretty low all of a sudden."

"Hey, this is pretty good. Did you make this creation?"

You nod.

He takes another large bite to fill the other cheek. He picks up the broccoli beef and pepperoni slice.

"I feel kind of stuck," you say. "It felt like a dead-end job when I was hired. And now, it really is a dead end. I don't even like what I'm doing. The coding is all drudgery. It's just been one big mistake after another."

"Yeah," Burgie says. "Feels pretty crummy, all right."

"The story of my life," you stuck. "Stuck with nowhere to go."

He takes a long slurp from his cup.

"There's hope, though," Burgie says as he scavenges around the other plates. He stacks the left-over slices then rolls them together into a tight burrito. His mouth opens, and he loads the package in. "You've got some options," he says finally, his glasses bouncing with each bite.

"Well, I don't see any. I'm pretty much fried."

Burgie swallows.

"I mean at this juncture," he says. He takes a quick swig.

"Like what?" you ask.

He pushes your plate back. It's now completely clean.

"You could always reboot."

Y ou bet," Gordon says to his phone, as you are ushered by Agnes into his office. He points to a chair as you enter. You carefully lower yourself and the leather squeals like a pig. Gordon looks up with a frown.

"Sorry," you say quietly. You try moving to the other cheek. You feel like you are back in the principal's office.

Burgie's words play in your head. Maybe you could get out of the mess you are in. Maybe there is a way you can swap out some of the obsolete chunks of yourself for something completely new, just like upgrading to a new version. You could replace your internal operating system for a newer model. How difficult could that be? Maybe patch in a more upbeat personality, for example, or a brighter, hipper self. That would be nice.

You've tried to change yourself before. You remember buying a diet book once when you couldn't fit into your usual pair of jeans. Or when you started watching more sports on TV, trying your best to fit in during football season. But it didn't take. There you were the next morning, hair plastered to your forehead, the same groggy face blinking back in the mirror.

It's not so easy to change. It's not just the memory lapses, or the missteps, or the way your will power vanishes when you need it the most, or that you lose your concentration or just get sidetracked. No, these things you might eventually overcome. It's that you yourself have deep, lingering doubts. You see the sheer futility of it all. How changing even the smallest thing is a major uphill struggle. Even setting smaller miniscule goals, like getting to work on time, meets with overwhelming resistance.

Today, for example, you couldn't find your keys for the longest time. You searched under every pile of clothes, even looked in the refrigerator, the sink, the freezer—all without success. When you did find them (behind the Right Guard in the bathroom), there was a large smear of SpaghettiOs in the middle of your shirt. Probably from the reclined dinner in front of the tube the night before. You lost time digging out last week's T-shirt, a bit wrinkled, making a mad dash out the door. When your car finally sputtered to life, the gas gauge was low, your A/C refused to start and, well, everything else just tumbled out of control after that.

The world, itself, resists change. This much you have found out. How can you make big changes when you cannot overcome even the smallest of obstacles? How can the whole evolution thing be expected to happen when you feel like Bill Murray in *Groundhog Day*, with every day the same bad replay of the one before?

"You bet," Gordon says, the sleeves of his off-blue shirt rolled at the wrists, tapping a legal pad with his black Mont Blanc pen. His cologne smells like cherries. "That son of a gun is plain lucky is all. I've never seen anyone chip away in a sand trap like he does and end up two strokes on anyone. Yeah... I know... Dumb luck..." He laughs.

Your eyes wander back to his credenza, which has a series of trophies, a couple with badminton birdies on the top, another with a racket and one with a cowboy hat.

"You can count on it," Gordon says leaning forward. "Don't you worry. Just minor bumps." He nods a number of times, then ends with an "OK, you too."

He sets the phone in its cradle, and then rearranges some papers on his desk.

"OK," he says looking up.

You sit up in your chair, your legs scrambling.

He smiles.

"You doing OK, Jenz?"

"Yeah, I guess," you say, your hands sticking to the arm rests.

"Well, you will do just fine out there. It's a difficult time. We all feel the pinch." He smiles warmly. "And it's not easy letting people go, let me tell you. The hardest part of my job is trying to communicate a larger vision to folks, when most of us—myself included—would much rather be taking care of our personal lives. Don't you think?"

"Yes, sir."

"You play golf?"

"No, sir."

"Any sport?"

"I like tubing," you say.

"I mean a competitive sport? A team sport?"

"Well, tubing can be very competitive."

His smile suddenly fades.

"Well, the point is this. We're a team. A family. And hard as it is to time our thoughts off of ourselves, we have to do things many times to benefit the team. We each have a role to play, and others count on us."

"But, sir, I'm being laid off. I'm not going to be part of the family for very much longer, am I?"

"Yes. That's true. But my point is this. Your team still counts on you. What you do over the next few weeks will make a big difference to those people around you. You can't just forget about them now. It's hard I know to think in those terms, but the fact is when you leave they still have to make a living. You wouldn't want them to lose their jobs just because you lost yours, would you?"

"No, sir."

"Whether or not you think it is fair that you were laid off, you can't take out your vengeance on them. They didn't do anything wrong, did they?"

"No," you say. "I don't have any bad feelings toward them."

"See, that's good. That's the way to look at things."

"Thank you, sir."

"So, I hope you won't mind me saying that coming in late and coming back from lunch late: these things are just signs that you may feel hostility and resentment towards your team. Maybe you blame me."

"No, not really," you say. "Not exactly."

"It's OK if you do. I can understand how you feel. I've been caught in a few layoffs myself. It's not easy being on the other end of it, let me tell you. And I have been fired more than once in my career."

"You have?"

"You may not see it now, but being fired is one of the most positive things that can happen to you. Your being laid off: It will be a chain-reaction to many good things to come. Mark my words."

"Yes, sir."

"So, I have to ask you this. And pardon my frankness here, Jenz. Do you think you can finish *XLib* before you go?"

You fidget in your seat.

"I guess so," you say. "I mean I will try."

"I know it is a lot to ask, but it will mean a lot to us here. And to your fellow teammates. Frankly they're a bit concerned."

"I know, sir."

"Even though you are relatively new here—what was it, nine months?..."

"Six, sir."

"Yes, six. You've made a lot of good friends. They are counting on you. Their jobs depends on how well you do."

"It's just that *XLib*, sir," you say, "well, it's getting a bit overstuffed. I mean…"

"Overstuffed?"

"As in an Overstuffed Burrito," you explain.

"I'm afraid I don't understand. Is that a technical term?"

"Well, not exactly. I mean a lot of new functions and features get added to it, and it is becoming a bit too bulky. I'm not sure it will be that reliable even if I am able to finish it."

"Yes, that can explain your frustration. It's a lot of work to put on your shoulders. Yes, I agree."

"So, it's going to be hard to really finish it, I think, in the time I have left."

"Two weeks. Yes, I see what you're saying. It's not a lot of time."

"Yes, sir."

"But it's important. It's important that you finish it."

"OK, I'll try."

"It's important not only to us, the large family of ours. But you will see, that it is important to you as well. You may think that one little software module may not make a big difference in your life, but your own sense of self is at stake here. Your confidence in what you do."

"Yes sir.

"Listen, Jenz, let me share something with you. It's unfortunate but it happens: managers at other companies talk with one another. They're not supposed to, but they do. We all play golf together or meet up at the same functions and conferences. And of course, over a couple of drinks, you find out a lot of very interesting things. You hear plenty of doozies out there. And you hear which of the applicants looking for work are the ringers. Which ones are the heroes. Even before you see their applications on your desk, you know which ones to stay away from."

You swallow.

"You want to be one of the heroes, don't you?"

"I don't think I'm hero material," you say. "Actually speaking."

Jenz Johnson

"I think that you are, Jenz. I think you have what it takes. That's why I hired you in the first place. The point is, when you put everything you've got into something, into making *XLib* work, whatever it takes, you will be rewarded. If not in this job, in the next."

"Sounds like the concept of heaven, sir."

He laughs. "Yes, maybe you're right. But, you see, your reputation will precede you. And you will feel ten feet tall. Let me tell you, there's no better feeling."

"Yes sir."

"You'll see."

"Yes sir."

Agnes has a satisfied look on her face as you close Gordon's door. She is sitting in a small cubicle outside his office, her beige glasses dangling on a gold braid around her neck, her hair piled on her head. At a side table, another secretary is typing nonstop at a computer. She looks up briefly.

"I hope you had a good talk," she says without looking at you.

"Well..." you say. "It was...informative."

Agnes frowns and stands up, pushing her swivel chair under her desk and approaching you with a folder in her hand. She slides her glasses on her nose, then sets the folder carefully on the counter. Her eyebrows are replaced with two thin lines that seem stuck on her forehead like decals.

"Now as far as your car permit, you will need to turn it in on the same day as you exit with your name plate, ID card, key and handbook." She glances over her glasses at you. "Not at 5 p.m., but on my desk by noon. Your computer access will be terminated at that time, promptly. You will not receive your check until 4:45 p.m. during your exit interview with HR."

"OK."

"HR will go over this with you, but I thought I would inform you, as a courtesy, to give you fair warning that we have rules that must be followed. Rules. When you break the rules, you suffer the consequences."

"I still have another couple of weeks," you say.

"Of course."

"These are our records that Gordon asked me to keep," she says. "They are not part of your personnel records. That is, unless your exit is less than satisfactory. I'm sure that Gordon explained this to you. I keep tabs and I'm sure you don't want any of this…" and she waves the folder "… to find its way to HR."

The young secretary looks up at you, then quickly returns to her keying. Her fingers race across the keyboard, her eyes fixed on a notepad propped up in front of her.

"Of course, we always hate to see good people go," Agnes says and smiles smugly as her eyebrows move up and down. She places the glasses on her nose and looks through your records.

"Katie here will get you the forms. Have them filled out for HR next week."

She lets her glasses fall to her blouse, gives you one last glance then turns to the young woman at the other desk.

"Katie, can you get him started?"

Katie looks up, fingers continue to fly across her keyboard.

"Let's put things away for the day, shall we?" Agnes does not look up but moves stiffly to her desk.

"OK," she says rising to her feet. "That's not a problem."

Katie is shorter than you thought she would be. The row of manuals and notebooks that line the front of her desk completely hide her.

"This way," Katie says. She wears a cashmere sweater over jeans and walks awkwardly around the side of the counter. "They're in a back cabinet. You probably can get them yourself if you prefer." Before you can reply, she pivots around and you follow her.

Katie shuffles along in sandals, with a slight limp. It's as if her right foot has one pace and left foot another. With a small motion, she pulls her sweater around her and smiles. The hallways are empty, a few stragglers in the cubicles sorting through papers.

"You do Gordon's memos?" you ask as you catch up.

"Yes, I do most of the grunt work," she says.

You glance down and notice that she doesn't really bend her right ankle. Although she doesn't exactly favor the ankle, it gives on its own and her shoulder dips involuntarily. "I was sort of tricked into this job. But that's OK."

"Tricked?"

"Well, hired for documentation, really. But you know, in retrospect, I think I'm pretty lucky. Agnes wanted to get out of the typing mode herself and dreaded having to learn to use a word processor. And well, I was keying a mile a minute with Dolores. As you probably noticed, nothing escapes Agnes' gaze." She laughs.

"The next thing I know, I was given a raise and desk near a window. So, I didn't complain."

"I don't think Agnes likes me very much."

"No, not too much," she says. "But don't take it personally. She doesn't like very many people around here. Just Gordon." She smiles. "That's just her style."

"I guess so," you say. "But I don't like the fact that she's keeping a dossier on me."

Katie laughs again. "Yes, I think she missed her true calling. An informant."

You smile at the image of Agnes in a shady bar passing along clandestine information.

When you reach the cabinet, Katie opens it quickly and stoops down. There are stacks of forms, neatly organized with their numbers and titles labeled on the shelves.

"You will need the T103, T104 and U24. There were some COBRA forms, but we are out of them. Were you getting any benefits yet?"

"Some," you say. "I'm still on probation I guess."

"Well don't feel bad. Gordon really watches his expenses, and parceling out the benefits, especially the health benefits, is one way he saves money. It's his idea, really. But I think it's happening a lot out there. Especially these days. That's one thing I like about working here. The health benies, once you're eligible, aren't half bad."

"But you've been here awhile," you say.

"Seems like a lifetime," she concedes. "Technically, I'm still part-time, but I put in enough hours that I qualify for health benefits. Gordon is good that way. When he sees that you are putting in the time, he's pretty forthcoming."

She collects a stack of forms, placing one on top of another.

"OK. Well, look these over. Bring them back to me. If you have any questions, just let me know. Agnes really has kept out of this part. As far as she is concerned, anyone who is laid off doesn't deserve much."

She grabs the forms and pushes them to you.

"Luckily, the state has some regulations. To cushion your transition."

You look down at the stack and feel queasy. You're as good as gone now. The forms make it all official. Soon you will be out knocking on doors.

"Listen," she says. "Don't feel too bad. Is this your first time?"

"Yeah," you say. "I'm trying to get used to the idea of not working. I mean in a couple of weeks. It's a little disconcerting."

She gives you a light pat on the shoulder.

"You'll do all right," she says. She gathers the forms.

"I don't know about that," you say.

She smiles.

"Trust me," she says. "It's never as bad as you think it is. It may seem like the end of the world right now, but after a good night's sleep, you'll feel a lot better."

"I don't really think it's going to help."

"You'll do fine. Come on, this way. Let's get you a resume kit. You'll feel a bit better once you get rolling on your resume. The idea is to think positive. We are all afraid of something, but if you focus on your talents, you'll see things go a lot more smoothly."

"OK," you say. "It would be nice to have some. Talents, that is."

She closes the cabinet, and then turns to head back down the hallway. You straighten the forms and start walking also, colliding with her, the forms crumpling up against her back.

"Oops," she says, catching her balance.

You try to gather the forms, but they flutter to the ground.

"That's my fault," she says.

"No. That was definitely me," you say. You drop to a knee and brush the forms toward you.

"Not a problem," she says. "We didn't break anything, did we?"

"I guess not."

"So, no harm done," she says. "Come on."

Some of the lights are now off, and the hallway darkens, looking more like a warehouse than an office. She moves slowly in front. Her shoulder blades show through her sweater, gliding up and down.

"We're out of the K209's," Katie says to Agnes as she passes, "so I'm getting him set up."

Agnes ignores her, and you follow Katie to the elevator. Katie's jean skirt falls below her knees, and you notice how her black hair is tied in back with a light blue tie with a small tattoo showing between her shoulder blades. She presses the button, and the elevator lurches down.

"So," you say.

She looks over with a smile.

"You've been here a while."

She smiles.

"I mean, you like it? I mean working here?"

"Yes."

"Typing."

"Sounds pretty boring, I suppose. But for me, that's all I need. Some job that I can forget about when I go home. It pays well and leaves me alone. So, from this perspective, it is ideal."

"But working for Agnes…" you say.

"She's not half bad. I could have a lot worse. But you know, if you don't mind having a control freak for a boss, then she is all right. Besides, I'm typing most of the time, so Agnes leaves me alone. She knows that if she asks me to do something, the memos don't go out."

"But your career…?"

"No, my real career is Africa." She stops and looks at you. "That's where I'm really needed. Not physically I mean. But to organize funding. It's a problem the world is just beginning to understand. It's my passion. And working here, I have the time and resources to pursue it."

"Africa. You mean the continent?"

"You've heard of it?" She laughs and resumes walking. "Yes." She sees your confusion and smiles. "It's in bad shape. The problems in Africa. Botswana, Zimbabwe, Malawi, Mozambique. They're really bad. The children suffer a lot. You see their faces, so young and innocent, and it just breaks your heart. Most of them don't know what is happening. They're the real victims. And little real help gets through. And the big money gets siphoned off."

She stops.

"So, I help to organize things. There's a lot of people here that just need a push to send a small amount. I just make sure it finds its way to the ones that need it. At a micro level. Person to person."

She smiles.

"So, my job is not a big part of my life. And you? What do you do besides computers?" she asks.

"Not much I guess." You shrug. "I like games," you say.

The elevator rattles as it descends.

"And do you read?" she asks.

"Yes," you say. "Learned when I was in first grade."

She laughs. "Touché. I mean do you read books?"

"Mostly computer stuff. You know magazines and blogs."

"Blogs are cool."

"Yeah, I suppose." You shrug. "I like movies," you say, although it sounds like blather.

"Well, maybe they are easier to digest," she says. "Did you see *Fight Club?*"

"I like Brad Pitt in that movie," you say. "I like the character."

"He's pretty sweet," she purrs.

"I mean, I think he's a terrific actor."

"Well, that, too." She laughs.

"He says his lines so well," you say fumbling.

She nods.

"Did you see *Snatch?*" you ask.

"I'm sorry, what?" She looks at you.

"The movie, *Snatch?* He was good in that one."

Just then, the elevator arrives at the first floor and she heads out without really answering you.

"OK, this way," she says.

You follow her. There is a maze of cubicles, but she finds her way to a cabinet next to a copy machine.

"I think this will help you," she says. Stacked neatly in the cabinet are a series of forms, each with their label.

She looks through the stacks and finds the one that she is looking for. She lifts a small stack and lays it over her arm, handing you a single form.

"HR will probably have a small meeting in the morning, but you can probably skip it."

"Agnes says that I won't get my check until around 5 p.m."

She laughs. "She wishes. She tells everyone that, but frankly the company is on the hook to pay you on your last day. But you can have it sent to your home, and just skip out early."

"Well, I don't know."

"Whatever you want to do." She looks around. "You know, most of the people are out looking already. Ed's not back. He's a veteran. He just left with most of his group, and called in that he was having an off-site."

"Really?"

"Yeah," she laughs. "Agnes had a conniption fit. She has a thing about rules if you haven't noticed. But Gordon isn't going to do much. Besides, Ed's doing it by the book, you know, calling in."

"Oh."

"He's gone. Maybe his whole group is going *en masse* somewhere else."

"But the references?"

"You mean from Gordon? Is that what he told you?"

"Well, not exactly."

"I don't think so. HR is supposed to be the only ones that talk to perspective employers." She shrugs. "The past doesn't bite you that often," she says. She considers her statement. "Of course, when it does, it bites down pretty hard."

You look around. The place is vacant.

She rummages around in the cabinet.

"HR has these resume kits. There's always plenty on hand. Agnes doesn't hand them out until the last day, but HR doesn't care."

She hands you a small packet.

"Gordon is just trying to keep his head above water," she says. "Come on, let's head back."

She closes the cabinet and turns. She walks quickly down the hall. Once inside the elevator, you press the floor button and wait.

"Anyway, you'll do OK," she says. "I can tell."

"Really?" you say.

"Yeah," she says. "You're just a little green. That's OK. People like you because you're honest and really care. Most people here don't really care that much."

"I thought...," you begin to say.

"To them, it's just a game. Sam's the best at it. He knows. He sloughs off work better than anyone, and still gets more staff."

"Really?" you say.

"Oh yeah. He's Gordon's favorite. It's a game really."

"It is?" you say.

"I wouldn't worry too much about things," she says. "They usually have a way of ending up all right."

The door opens, and she is walking before you can respond.

Halfway down the hallway, she stops and extends a hand. "Hey, it was nice getting to know you. Good luck." You take her hand. It is delicate and warm. She smiles, then gathers her forms, placing them over an arm. "If you have any questions, here's my extension." She jots her full name and extension on a post-it. "This way you don't have to speak with Agnes, or someone in your section. Just press 7 and dial the extension."

"OK."

You nod and watch her as she wanders back to her desk.

For a moment, your life rewinds.

You are back in your bedroom at your parents' house. Linus Torvalds, the Finnish wunderkind and creator of Linux appears at your shoulder. He leans closer to inspect your work, and you smell his Nordic cologne. Next to you: a can of Pringles, a two-liter bottle of Coke, still cold, and a stack of splayed manuals, each open to the right reference page. Your feet are up on the chair, the keyboard on your lap. You have been debugging since late afternoon, hunting down the bugs, the snafus in your code.

Linus nods. "You are almost there," he says with a smile. "Remember: Given enough eyeballs, all bugs are shallow."

"I only have two," you say, frustrated.

He laughs at this.

"OK, OK," he says, a hand resting on your shoulder. "That's OK. Just keep going."

You are hacking up a storm, your fingers springing across the keyboard, eyes jumping along the lines of code as they scroll up. Your latest project is writing a spider. Not the kind that hides in your closet or throws its web up in the oleanders outside. No, this spider is virtual, a robot of sorts that crawls across the Internet, retrieving information just like Google. Your first spider appears on your screen. You watch it come to life, take a small step, then vaporize. It is not bad for your first attempt.

If the truth be known, you are not programming the spider per se, but a class of spiders, a blueprint with each movement described in methods and behaviors, small chunks of code you write carefully. You call it Spider, a superclass, from which you plan to instantiate a litter of actual virtual spiders, each with their own name, each marching across the web.

But first, you have to get one spider to work.

You begin forming a list of things on the page that you want your spider to investigate further. You throw away the images, metatags, the layout of the page—none of that is important. The links are the most interesting, since they point to other web pages that may contain even more information. Of course, there is the raw content which you want to scan for interesting tidbits. Your spider needs to think about what he consumes.

But how do you tell the spider what information is useful and what needs to be thrown away? Google doesn't have this problem: It consumes everything and brings it back to its terabyte server farm. But your spider needs to be discerning.

You push back from the screen.

You examine the consume method for your spider, scrolling up the screen so you see the entire module. This method contains the logic on how the spider digests its food. But each spider will have its own diet. Some spiders will go out in search of the latest movies. Others will find new music or the latest releases of software. So the consume method will be different for each one. Or maybe, this is a whole new method, a *digest* method, which instructs the spider how to store information it finds.

You quickly break your consume method in two: a consume and digest. Yes, this is how to do it. The spider needs to know what it is supposed to digest, so you pass a list of subjects that it must recognize with each bite. Quickly, your fingers type up the new digest method, attach it to the Spider class. You instantiate a test spider and get it crawling across a single web page. It comes to life on the screen, then immediately vaporizes in an ugly crash, horrific errors spewing at the bottom of your screen. You throw up your hands in disgust.

"Keep going," Linus encourages.

So, you lean forward and spot an odd indent in the method. This caused the logic to abort early, and you know what it needs, just a single squiggle bracket } to patch it up. You rebuild the spider, and set it lose again. It begins to move. You dump its digestive track on the screen like the good internist that you are. You look at its virtual retina to see where it is going, names flying across the screen.

"See," he says. "Keep your focus. It is key to everything. Don't think about anything else."

You rub your eyes and pull close to your screen. Your fingers automatically begin tapping at the keys, paging down through the lines of code, reformatting sections to make them more organized. You imagine the flow of logic, each step your creation will take. You feel that you have it now and assemble the components back together and rebuild your spider.

The spider comes alive, moving, consuming, digesting. The screen lights up and you follow the flashes of diagnostics at the bottom. You see the spider take its tentative steps, out beyond your room, landing on a distant site. Technically the spider doesn't go anywhere. Each destination is grabbed and its web pages loaded into your computer's memory. You merely fetch the name of the page—its URL—and presto, it is pulled into memory where the spider can roll it around and dissect its contents. The web site knows nothing of the inner workings of your creation: It may even think that it is human. You smile at this, but suddenly the spider hits a wall. Errors fly up the sides of your screen in red. The spider curls and dies. You shake your head and adjust your glasses. Your fingers sneak away from the keyboard into waiting can of chips. You crunch and stare. You re-start the spider, get it moving again. Somehow it is looping at the same location, retracing its steps back to the same sites, then dying when it can't escape its loops.

How do you get the spider to venture out to different paths? Its movements must have more intelligence. It must have some way to broaden its range, otherwise it revisits the same pages again and again, and gags.

"Randomize," you whisper to yourself with a smile. "That would do the trick."

You page through your Spider class again, digging into the crawl method, seeing how the spider chooses the next link to go to. You quickly scrawl a few lines of code, grabbing a random number from the Random object.

"Dinner!" your mother shouts through the door.

You lose your place, and have to start at the top of the method and read down again. It is frustrating. You find the spot and continue coding. In a few minutes, your code is finished. You love working at this level of indirection. The computer program—not the spider itself, but the plans that the spider will follow once it is created. It is one level up from the actual virtual world, like a commander overseeing a battle.

You feel giddy and excited at the prospects, and instantiate a new spider. It begins to crawl, starting at its usual first page, then venturing to a new page, then another. The bright lines of characters light up your smudged glasses and you are beaming. Your code is working. Even the spider seems alive with excitement.

"There," you murmur. You quickly decide to make that spider go faster, getting rid of statements that drag on its movements. Each step he seems to be thinking. This isn't right. He plods along without any real spring in his step.

"No, don't clean it up. Stop. What have I told you!"

You retract your hands from the keyboard. It was too tempting.

"Remember," Linus cautions, pushing his glasses up on his nose, his eyes glaring. "Never optimize until you are done. Never. You know this."

He is perturbed now. He leans back as you plow ahead. You quietly back out your changes, the lines reappearing on the screen. You read through the Spider class again, making sure that there are no misspellings or strange indents. These could be disastrous.

"Dinner!" your mother shouts again, this time with a bang on the door. You push away from the desk and open the door a crack.

She is holding a spatula in hand, glaring over her glasses, her gray sweatshirt pushed up at the sleeves, hair pulled back and frizzy. The smell of food comes drifting in. It smells like another meatloaf you will have to suffer through. She is glaring.

"Dinner!" she says again. "I'd like to see you occasionally."

"Just another second."

"You know, you've been in your room for two days." She looks worried.

"I know. I'll just be a little while longer."

"You haven't exercised." She begins her list. "You are not eating well. You don't see your friends at all."

"I chat with them on-line."

"And you need fresh air. Remember when you used to play tennis?"

You have a vague memory of the game.

"That was a nice game," she says.

"I'm right in the middle of something. If I don't finish now, I will probably give up."

"Do you know that one in ten young people get Diabetes? It's from not taking care of yourself. One in ten."

"I'm feeling OK."

"You're not."

You look at her.

"OK," she says. "How about some dinner?"

"Maybe later."

She shakes her head and smiles. "You know there're more important things in life than computers." She waits, but sees that you want to get back.

"OK," you say finally.

She smiles and retreats down the hall.

Jenz Johnson

But she is wrong. There is nothing more important than computers. School is a bore, and you try your best to keep out of everyone's way. You've long since given up on sports or dating. But you can survive each day, knowing that there is something fun waiting for you to explore on your machine, a chance to explore and push your limits in a whole new world. You want to explain this, but she doesn't want to hear this. Programming is what you understand, what makes you tick.

Linus understands. Coding is all he ever wanted to do. Now, there is no denying he is great, even popular. He smiles, as if he knows your struggles. You throw the pencil back at the desk and walk into the hallway.

You remember as a youngster sitting in front of a computer, pecking out the assignment statements, trying out do-while commands, exploring the arithmetic of bit manipulation. You could always retreat to your computer and explore new things. Your parents encouraged you; they saw the possibilities then. Now your mother has become increasingly worried. You cannot find enough time in front of the computer. The worst part is being continually interrupted.

Still, deep down, you feel you can code with the best of them. Maybe not Linus, but Bricklin & Frankstron, Knuth, Kapor, the Woz, the big names. They are your heroes. You've read their interviews. But mostly you wait for them to guide you to the next big breakthrough.

"Hey," your father says looking up from his plate, still chewing. His legs are crossed and propped up on the coffee table in front of the TV, a glass of wine resting on a coffee table. "The prodigal son emerges."

"Hey, Dad," You smile. "I think I got my class going."

"Your Spider?"

"That's the one." You find a plate waiting for you on the counter. It has two thick slices of meatloaf, a mound of mashed potatoes, string beans and a roll.

"I was almost finished," you say. You wander over to a spot on the couch and your father mutes the TV. "You can watch it if you want."

"Same old…" he says. "So, tell about this class."

"Not much to tell. It crashed and sputtered around."

"Yeah?"

"Yeah," you say.

"You two," your mother says. "Can't you remind him about the garbage?"

"Yes, don't forget to take out the garbage." He says this dead-pan.

"OK," you say.

"Remember the chores you have to do."

"I forgot."

"And some exercise is not going to kill you," she says.

He puts his paper up, and your mother pulls up a chair next to you.

"This is how you are going to spend your time?"

You move the mashed potatoes on top of the meatloaf; tap it down so it covers the sides in a neat potato box. The string beans are pushed away to the sides as a sort of a moat.

"You're not going out?" she says. "You're going to look like this all semester? No job? No friends?"

"Dear," your father says. "Let him eat."

"Look how he eats," she says and looks away. She is still holding a spatula. "Your hair is all over your forehead."

You move your hair off your forehead, then chew through the meal, practicing some speed eating you picked up from the IFOCE website.

"What, no herring?" Linus says from an empty chair. He has floated out. You smirk. "No cabbage rolls or grilled reindeer?"

"What's so funny?" your mother asks. "It's funny to look like this?"

"Nah," you say, and push the plate away, the meatloaf house only half demolished. "I'm full. Can I go?"

"Go?" she asks. She starts to say something, but stops.

"Can I be excused?" you repeat.

You plant the glass on top of the meatloaf house, balancing it as you get up from the couch and move to the sink.

"Maybe some dishes later?" she asks.

"I'm kinda busy."

"It would help your mom" your father says.

You scrape the remains, do a quick rinse and stack them on the side.

"Maybe," you say.

"A pot or two," she says, but you are already on your way to your room, Linus in tow, ignoring the barrage of other work being heaped on, as you carefully close the door and fix the chain.

When you are back at your desk, computer glowing, your code begins to unfold. You are readying your first army of spiders to crawl over the web. You survey your methods again.

Your stomach gurgles. From your backpack, you dig deep and produce a bottle of Cheez Whiz, half of a can of chopped green chilies, and a single serving soy sauce. Quickly you assemble a snack in the remains of your coffee cup. Linus smiles in anticipation. You stir the concoction with a heating coil used normally to reheat your coffee. The mixture sizzles, and the air fills with the aroma of a Mexican café. You plunge a Pringle into the finished dip and bring up melted and chunky ooze that you load into your mouth. The flavors overwhelm you, and you settle back into your programming.

"You deserve this," Linus says with a yawn. You nod knowingly with a crunch, and you both look back at your code. Within minutes, you are in full swing. Linus retires to your bed. Halfway through your dip, you decide to devote yourself to the minutiae of life. This is your life's work, you decide. You know you are good at something, and this is it. You can sit above the fray and uncover important precepts hidden behind the code. Digging deep, understanding the trail of clues.

The house quiets down. There is a clanging of dishes; the TV is turned off; and, finally, you can burrow deeper, embellishing your work, preparing for the launch of one of your latest creations.

"Most great people have attained their greatest success just one step beyond their greatest failure."
—*Napoleon Hill*

The second floor is completely empty. Each stall is a shamble of papers, file drawers open and books on the floor. At your desk, you stare at a stack of printouts and the half-filled cup of coffee from the morning. You drain the last of it and shut down your screen.

Alex the janitor has started his rounds early, and he rolls up with his trash bin, squirt bottles dangling from his belt, smelling of ammonia and cleanser.

"Hey, kid," he says, smiling, with a full beard and Rastafarian hair. He is in his mid-forties with broad shoulders and a slight potbelly. He was one of the first of the company to actually welcome you, and is always smiling, crow's feet crinkling at his eyes. Although it's not always clear what he's smiling about. He gives the impression that there's something very comical about daily situations, as if he sees the sitcom possibilities that elude the principal players. You don't know what part you are playing, maybe the clueless role.

He holds up the memo from his bin. "I read about your demise, kid."

"Yep," you say, shrugging.

"Sorry to hear you're leaving so soon." He reads it over again. "Well, shit happens. Don't let it get you down, OK?"

He wears a thrift-shop cardigan over a tie-died shirt and moves quickly around your cubicle in his drawstring pants.

"I'm not, I guess."

"Good deal," he says. "And listen, I've got a six pack in the van if you need to unwind or something. Kind of like exit counseling, but faster. Sort of helps take the sting out of the day, you know what I mean?"

"I'm OK," you say, "thanks, though."

"Yep, seen this all before. To these guys"—he juts out his chin indicating the management—"it's business as usual. They probably don't even talk much about the people being axed. It's more like a lottery to them, you know, like pulling names out of a hat."

He points at the sentences in the memo, rubbing his beard and appreciating the language.

"See, it seems to be in an order of when you were hired. You notice that, kid? The last one hired is actually at the top of the list. Look, the names are listed almost by hire date, not by project or alphabetically. Hmm, that says something right there."

"Yeah," you say. "It still feels the same, whether you're at the top or bottom."

"That's probably how they made their decision, too. Most likely they had a number that they had to let go, and they just went down their list by the amount of time with the company, adding up the salaries. When they hit their number, they stopped. They didn't bother to list the names alphabetically. So, they were probably in a rush, too."

"A LIFO stack," you say.

"LIFO?"

"Last-in-first-out. It's a type of collection. A stack. Stored in memory. For example, when you fill your grocery bag, that's a LIFO stack. The last groceries in the bag are the first ones you take out when you get home."

"Never thought about it."

"Well, it's important when you are coding. Although you also see FIFO's. First-in-first-out. They're queues, as opposed to stacks."

"I see," he says, leaning against the trash bin.

"Like a teller line at the bank. The first one in line gets served first. Very convenient. You see more FIFOs in real life. There are more LIFOs in the computer world."

"Well." He laughs, "you sure know your stuff, kid."

"Yeah. You're the *only* one that feels that way," you say.

"Listen, you can still come to my dojo on Wednesdays if you want. It might help you see things more clearly. I'll cut you a special layoff price. A deep discount, kid."

He smiles with a big grin.

"Thanks," you say.

"I know what you're thinking," he says. "This marshal arts stuff is a little strange…"

"Yeah," you say. "I guess."

"…that you don't need it," he continues.

"I guess. I just don't see myself getting into martial arts at this late stage. I don't think my bones can take it."

"Well, it's *aikido*, not *judo* or *karate*. We're not into breaking bones. Not unless we have to," he says, laughing when you look up,

Jenz Johnson

slightly worried. "Aikido is a really beautiful way to move. They say it's the graceful way to run away. In a fight, you see all the openings and can move through it without causing harm to anyone. It's a real spiritual thing, and it helps to develop your inner self. Anyway, it's fun for me. And Gordon doesn't seem to mind that I clear out the aerobics area in our so-called Fitness Center on Fridays. As long as no one drinks in class or out in the parking lot, we should be OK."

He smiles at this.

"There are things that you see and things that you cannot see. A good aikido master can see these special points on your body as if they were lit up."

With two fingers he points at a couple of different places.

"It's really a gas," he smiles. "Besides, this"—he motions to his duster—"just helps me pay rent. And of course, for me, it's good business development."

He gazes at you with a satisfied look on his face.

"Come on, let me show you. Stand up."

"It's OK," you say. "Really."

"Come on. It's a little surprising. You'll like it."

"I really have to finish up," you object, but before you can turn back to the screen, Alex has pulled you up on your feet. He smiles and holds your shoulders in front. He steps back.

"Now, stand straight. There you go. Your energy or *chi* flows up and down your *chakras*." He smiles, pointing to exact points along the front of your T-shirt.

"See, your fingers control your wrist, and your wrist controls your hand. And when you line up the wrist and elbow, like this," he says as he takes your hand and gives it a slight twist. "This happens."

You are on your knees.

"Ouch," you say. "I didn't see that one coming."

Your head is pounding and dizzy, and your entire arm has a dull, throbbing pain.

"Funny how the body just snaps in a whole new direction, isn't it?"

You nod.

"The tail wags the dog. Except in this case, it's the pinky."

He is still holding your hand, but gently releases it.

"Didn't hurt, did it?"

"Nah, it was OK." Your arm has a tightening ache.

"Surprising, huh?"

You nod again, finding your feet, and shuffling over to your desk. The chair feels good against your back, which has suddenly started to twitch.

"You finished here?" he asks.

"I guess you could say that."

He laughs loudly. "*Touché*. I didn't mean it that way."

"Yeah, I know. A little gallows humor."

You place the Coke cans into the recycling box and close some manuals and set them back onto the bookshelf above the desk.

"I'll get the recycles tomorrow."

"OK."

He grabs the trashcan and empties it.

"You managed to survive this one."

"Yep," Alex says. "I don't hold down such a big paycheck. Plus they get someone they can trust. I taught Gordon's kids before his divorce."

"Taught them?"

"Yep, at my dojo. Of course, at that time, I was staying at the Y and earning my rent through a summer program. Then went over to Himmel Park, taught there on Saturdays, sort of free of charge. I met Gordon's wife there, and she was a beauty to behold all right. She would have been so nice to spend time with."

"Gordon's divorced?"

"Yep, over three years now. Of course, the kids were a mess. Correction: are a mess. The young one was fat and could barely move and probably spent his evenings in front of the TV scoffing down chips."

You wonder what kind of chips.

"Gordon's career is number one. His family, well, a distant second. The older one wasn't much better," he continues. "Constantly running at the mouth, arguing, disrupting class, acting like a real smart-aleck. I remember that part. I calmed them down, and his wife was pleased."

You try to visualize Gordon married and end up empty.

"Anyway, she left him. I don't know the details, but the kids were all shook up. And Gordon was a mess for a while. Still is. She was always playing second fiddle, and she just got bored."

He moves to the other side of the office and looks over the divider.

"Yep. Anyway, I needed work and, well, here I am."

He dusts the tops of the cabinets, and sprays the windows over the bookcase.

"You seem off-balance, kid."

"I guess it shows," you say.   "I don't know exactly what I'm going to do next. I've been thinking about that."

"Well, that's normal."

"I mean for work…"

"Do you know how to run a coffee bar?"

"Nah," you say.

"Can you make a good espresso?"

"Not really, just drink them. Mostly cappuccinos."

"Well, I could always use help down at the dojo. That's my daytime job. Actually, it's my life."

"Thanks," you say. "I was kind of counting on programming work. That's all I really know."

"Well, I'm sure you know other things, even stuff that you can earn some cash with. Hey, just look at me. Not that I'm your best example, but I always seem to have enough cash to live on. It's a question of what you want to sweat. I mean, some people sweat their jobs, others sweat their girlfriends, or cars, or lord knows what. You know? It all works out."

"I guess."

"So, I think you should just settle out. Gordon's mostly hot air." He looks at you.

"Listen, you could use a beer. You'll feel better. Take your mind off of it."

"I don't know."

You look at the screen, and hardly have the energy to turn it off. You wonder what the computer is actually thinking when it is not on. There must be something happening. Or what kind of logic is present in the circuits as it is powering down? It's not the same rigorous logic that it has at full power. But what exactly does it think is true or false?

"OK, got to go. Wander over to my van when you're done."

"Maybe…," you say.

"An invincible determination can accomplish almost anything and in this lies the great distinction between great men and little men."
—*Thomas Fuller*

Welcome to my little world," Alex says as he slides open the door of his van, flipping on the lights to illuminate an interior of bright orange and violet posters, Janis Joplin at the mike, Jim Morrison looking up in a fisheye. The van smells of incense and old smoke. Along one wall is a row of large pillows stacked on a narrow couch, with a small armchair and mini-fridge next to it.

"Make yourself comfortable."

He moves a small coffee table, clearing a stack of *Be Strong* magazines.

"Go ahead, sit," he says and pulls off his cardigan, sitting comfortably in his tie-dyed shirt and drawstring pants. He stretches back and wipes his forehead off with a handkerchief, as you sink into the pillows. The van smells of sweat and incense.

"What a day! Hey, you into Hendrix?"

"Not really," you say. "Paul Allen is big time, though. His museum in Seattle was going to be entirely Hendrix at one point."

"I found downloads of some of his best live stuff. Most of this is bootlegged. Can't buy this anywhere. Helps to put the world back into perspective."

He sits in the armchair closest to the driver's seat and bends over to open a small refrigerator.

"How about a cold beer? Or some iced ginseng?"

"A beer is fine," you say.

He sets it on the table, moving a magazine into place as an impromptu coaster and flipping on a small fan overhead.

The beer foams over the spout, and you sit back down. From the wall, a picture of a young defiant Bob Dylan looks down, his hair curled up in an afro. Next to him, Jimi Hendrix. On the other side, there are pictures of Japanese samurai.

"Woodcuts," he says following your eyes. "Or actually reproductions of *Chushingura*. My favorites."

You lean forward to take a closer look. The samurai are suspended in action, swords held over head, spears poised behind a shoulder. Rows of Japanese characters line the white space.

"Get comfortable," he says, shedding his sandals and throwing his feet on the table. He carefully stuffs a small pipe, taking a quick sniff and clicking his lighter until a thin puff of smoke escapes. He takes a long drag.

"*Chushingura* means the Forty-Seven Ronin. It's a story based on an actual event that happened in 1701 in the court of the Shogun in Edo."

"I always liked samurai, well, in the movies at least," you say. "Especially Toshiro Mifune. I thought he was great."

"Me too." He smiles. "At that time," he continues, "these samurai were fiercely loyal to their *daimyo*, a Lord Naganori Asano. He was tricked into drawing his sword when a sleazebag by the name of Kira provoked him in court. Unfortunately, drawing a sword in court was punishable by death, and Asano was forced to commit ritual suicide."

Alex looks at the pictures, pointing to a scene where a samurai is facing a court, short sword in hand.

"His retainers vowed to avenge his death, even though it was prohibited. With their lord dead, they became *ronin*, masterless samurai. Today, these would be your average consultant, although this comparison doesn't do their roles justice. Each one of these forty-seven ronin took a different identity, melting into the landscape to avoid detection, to keep under the radar."

You are suddenly aware of the music, a stumbling, blazing lick, at once seemingly out of control, but finding its beats and counterpoints.

"Wow!" You smile.

"Yeah," he says. "This one is Ōishi who became a disheveled, fat drunk. When he was a true samurai, he was pretty fierce, an expert with a spear. So, during the days he would drink and beg. But at night he honed his skills, practicing in the dark so that no one would see. He could wield his spear in close quarters. That's why he holds it behind his back."

He points to a picture of a large samurai, flying in the air, with a spear raised over his head.

"The ronin eschewed any responsibilities, and their families lived in the poorest quarters. They were forced to take on the lowliest of jobs. None of this mattered to them, however. Their focus was on something far more important. Their lives were dedicated to righting a wrong."

He leans his head back and stretches out his arm.

"Then on December 14, 1702—a full year after the death of their leader—they arrived at Kira's residence. And under the cover of darkness and in the middle of a blinding snowstorm, they entered his home. They immediately cut down his bodyguards with quick strokes.

"Kira whimpered in front of them for his life. But the only honorable course they gave him was to commit *seppuku* himself. Which he refused. They killed him quickly. As they walked to the grave of their Lord Asano, people from the town were all out on the streets. News spread fast, and they gave these warriors the accord of heroes. Which they were. When they reached the grave of Asano, they all committed *seppuku*. What they did was wrong by the samurai code, taking revenge without permission, and they accepted the punishment. Their story is told to this day."

You are speechless.

"That's the samurai spirit," he says in admiration.

He nods, trying to say something. You take a small sip of beer.

"How do you like my place?" he asks.

"I like it," you say. The samurai pictures seem to pulse on the walls.

"My home actually," he says proudly. "Here and my dojo. But I prefer here. I can drive up to the foothills and park most nights along the streets. The end of Euclid is my favorite spot. Euclid and Sunrise. It's like living up there without the high rent."

He smiles.

"Of course, I'm pretty discreet. Don't want to disturb the neighbors."

He takes a long drink.

"I keep moving around. Keeps them guessing," he says seriously. "Listen to this part," he says, turning up the volume. "Allman Brothers. This band was at its height when they did this concert at the Fillmore East. Dickey Betts and Duane Allman, trading licks. Gregg hammering on the organ. Two drum kits." It's a driving blues sound, and it quickly fills up the van. "Chicago blues at its best. Did you know that Duane was the lead guitar on *Layla*? Everyone thinks it was Clapton. Duane dropped by while they were recording the song, hung out for a while, laid down the track. He called it the 'crying bird' sound. Man, how it soars. It was his tribute to Charlie Parker."

The music continues.

"You don't mind, do you?" he says and notches back the light in the van. "The windows are blacked out. Security came around here the other night, so I need to keep a low profile."

He clicks on a row of black lights, and the inside of the van walls come alive. There are waves, hula girls, pineapples and palm trees.

"Maui Modern," he explains. "My theme." He smiles and leans back.

"*Layla?*" you say.

"Yep, you've heard it, I'm sure. A great tune. You only hear the extended version all the time, the 7-minute version with the piano and Duane's guitar. There was an earlier version that bombed on the charts. It was around the time Clapton fell for George Harrison's wife, back in those days. Talk about a real jerk, Clapton ended up marrying her, then leaving her. The guy's screwed up big time.

"But the song refers back to *Layla and Majnun.* It's a Sufi tale. It's about a teenager driven to near insanity by the love of a woman he cannot have. Clapton was reading this and, supposedly, he felt that this was him. Go figure. In the story, the boy abandons everything for her. But the heart of the story is the parents. Clapton dismisses this part entirely. It's their only son, their jewel, for whom they had great hopes. And he pisses it away for this one woman. They never see him again, yet all he can think of is this woman. Clapton's lyrics are crap."

"I could never understand them," you say, looking around at the posters.

"Yeah. You weren't missing much. Anyway, it was Duane on guitar. That's what made it great. Now, Clapton plays it everywhere he goes, but it was Duane's solo. Of course, when Duane flipped his cycle, well…"

He takes another sip.

"… that was it. End of an era. Dickey Betts never could do much more than keep the band hobbling along, playing his country tunes, and drinking beer. That's my cue."

He leans over to the refrigerator and pulls out another beer.

You're drifting off as he talks.

"Hey," he says and the van comes back into focus. "Don't go south on me, now."

He takes a long hard drink from his bottle and smoothes his beard.

"Come on."

"Sorry," you say. "I guess a lot is going on."

"A lot is always going on." He laughs. "If it weren't, you'd be bored to tears. Trust me."

"Well, maybe a little more good stuff and a little less bad stuff."

"Hey, there's always more crap than chrome. You somehow have to cherry-pick the good stuff. Separate out the seeds and stems."

"It's hard to keep focus when my job is pretty much done and Gordon is going to kill my career."

"You still thinking about him?"

"Yeah. I think I blew it today."

"He fumes well. He writes some great notes that he stuffs in my closet. But you give him more power than he has."

"Well, the power to give me the ax," you say.

"Yeah, he can do that. But this part about killing a career..."

"Won't give me any reference, that's for sure. Probably drive a nail in my next job, if I ever find one."

"Are you sure he said that? Well, that part is overplayed."

"Well, he wants me to finish my code. In two weeks. If I don't deliver, well, I'm not sure what he'd do. He wants me to work wonders. It's a mess anyway. I couldn't do what everyone wants me to do even if I had three months." You shake your head.

"Well, that computer stuff is beyond me," Alex says. "It's probably why I lasted so long at the place." He smiles. "Ever notice that the ones that know the least stay the longest? Look at Agnes. And Gordon. They don't know shit about computers. Did you ever notice that Gordon rarely uses his."

"PowerPoint presentations."

"Whatever. But his keyboard is always covered, and not a speck of dust between the keys. I don't think he ever takes it off."

You look around at his walls again.

"Mind if I give you a suggestion."

"Go ahead," you say. "I could use whatever you got."

"Start fighting!"

You are not concentrating, and the words seem to have no meaning at first.

"Like a samurai," he says, nodding to the pictures on the wall. "I mean, you are on a collision course right now, and there's no turning back. You are trying to second-guess the consequences. That's all wrong. There's a samurai saying, 'Test your armor, but only test the front.' If you keep on thinking what will happen if you fail, then you are focusing on the wrong shit. It's the fight that you need to concentrate on."

You nod at this.

"As I look at it," he says with a smirk, "most of the little memos going back and forth put you right at the center of it. The center of a cyclone."

"Not me," you say.

"Man of the hour." He nods knowingly. "You are going to have a fight on your hands. I hope you realize this. When a boss's career is in the air, you are going to have to be prepared. Time to start training."

Your stomach grinds at the thought of Gordon jumping on you again.

"What do you mean Gordon's career?" you ask.

"He's not exactly the most popular manager in the eyes of our parent corporation. Although I don't see a lot of the memos coming in, I do see his genuflecting on the ones going out. It doesn't sound like he is making good on his promises, always wants a little more time. That doesn't go down well. And, frankly, your little piece of the pie is a key wedge."

"But it's only a bunch of silly utilities. Sam keeps adding more on..."

"Well," he smiles. "They may be silly, but they are definitely part of the main course. Which reminds me..." He looks around the van. "Are you getting hungry?"

"Nah."

"You sure?"

But you are now worried. The thought of being called into Gordon's office is enough to get your stomach aching. Just the thought of his pen tapping on the desk makes you nervous. You rub your hands and begin thinking of a way to avoid another meeting.

"It's just that I'm not a fighter. Not really."

Alex laughs, seeing you squirm at the thought.

"We all are. It just takes some focus and training. You should see some of my students. They come in like lambs and leave with a bundle of new knowledge. Like lions," he says, pounding his chest in jest. "Of course, most people think that the janitor is out of the loop. But, man, you can tell a whole lot about a civilization from its garbage. You'd be surprised to open up the memos, discarded printouts, budgets, projections that go into the trash. It's better than any murder mystery."

"You go through the trash?"

"Oh yeah," he says with a smile. "I like to keep up with current events."

He laughs and takes a long drink from his beer.

"Shit," he says. "I collect the stuff like it was going out of fashion." He tilts up his bottle with a big grin and drains the rest with four or five gulps.

"The real question is what do you want to do? That's the question."

He studies you, and you avoid his eyes, looking instead around the van.

"I've never known what to do," you say. "That's my problem."

Alex laughs at this. "That's rubbish of course."

"No," you say surprised. "I've always just seemed to wander around from one thing to the next."

"Well, that's what we all do." he says. "That's the definition of being mortal."

It's not the kind of mortal you had in mind.

"I mean you know, don't you?" he says.

"Well, not really."

"Well actually," he smiles, "your body does. It just doesn't filter up here." And he taps his dreadlocks at the temple. "This thinks it's in control. When in actuality, it's usually the last to know."

"Let me put it this way," he says, draining his beer. "What are you waiting for?"

You hadn't really thought of yourself as waiting for anything.

"I mean, here you are, wanting to do something. Trying to do something. And, presto, you're not doing anything. Right?"

"Well, I'm not sure what to do?"

"OK," he smiles. "So, you're waiting for...?"

You shrug.

"A signal?" he asks with a glint in his eye. "A sign? A thunderclap, for example?"

"No," you say. "Not exactly. I guess some idea of *what* I should do."

"Some clarity?" he asks.

"Yes, I guess you could say that. Some understanding."

"Kind of eliminating any risks of doing the wrong thing."

"I suppose. But I feel like I'm in a bind. It's not real clear that there is anything that I can do to extricate myself from, well, you know, being kicked out on my ear, never finding a job in this town. Or, I could try to sink more hours into something I know won't work anyway…"

"Like whoring yourself?" he asks.

"Yeah, that."

"I see," he says. "So you are in this kind of bind."

"Yeah, I can't see any way out."

He laughs loudly at that, a big smile turning his face into bundles of wrinkles and crow's feet.

"Oh, you will find a way out, all right," he says. "The question is whether you land on your feet or your ear."

He begins to laugh, his shoulders bouncing up and down.

"Exactly," you say, unable to control your laughing either.

"You will go flying out that door, one way or another," he roars.

"It's just the velocity," you say. "The trajectory."

"Hah!" he laughs. "Yes, the trajectory."

You are laughing, seeing yourself tumbling out of the second-floor window, tumbling end over end into the night sky like a falling comet, Gordon standing near the window with his foot extended out into the night air.

"It's a question of which planet you land on," he chuckles.

"Which galaxy," you shout. "With Gordon's boot, it could be at the edges of the known universe!"

You both double over at this, the van filling with peals of laughter, shaking, the music serving to underscore the pure lunacy of it all.

"But," he says, slowly recovering himself. "That's, of course, your answer."

"What? Uptas Minor?"

"No, to your question, kid."

"Yeah?"

"Yeah." He smiles. "It don't matter."

He is smiling, taking a long easy drag, smoke trailing up past his eyes.

"You're history. You are gonna be kicked so far out of this place, it doesn't matter what you do."

"In fact," he continues. "Your path is unfolding as we speak. Here," he says, giving you a poke in your chest with two fingers. It's a gentle poke, but strangely you lose your balance and tumble to the floor of the van.

He bursts out laughing again.

"That's you, all right," he roars. "Destined to find the floor."

He is doubled over again, laughing, tears now streaming down his face. But you are suddenly taken with a wave of remorse as you struggle to find some handhold along the side of the van. You are scrambling on the carpet between the couch and table.

"Ha!" he says, pointing again at your efforts. "There, you see!"

Your feet are tangled up and you cannot move. You fumble, feeling along the corners and wall for any aids.

"Here, kid." He extends his hand. You look up and grab it tentatively, his large hands gently giving you a tug. You try to smile, but you are on the verge of losing your temper. "Hang on, wait."

He helps you to your seat again.

"Hey," he says with a big smile. "Maybe we've had too much for tonight."

"That's not it," you say, turning angry.

"No, I know it's not."

You are breathing hard, feeling stupid and unable to do anything right. And to add insult to injury, Alex is looking at you with complete pity, as if he sees a fool unable to find his way.

"It's like this, kid," he says. "You've got everything it takes."

You are not listening to his spiel now.

"But you are missing one thing," he says gently. He looks at you until you raise your eyes from the floor of the van. He turns and lowers the volume on the speaker.

"You are missing the first step. You have to take it, and not turn back."

You are breathing hard, your face flushed.

"What was that? A little spill? Right?" he says. "And look at you. You are completely unnerved. Why?"

"Listen, I don't appreciate being knocked around, OK?"

He holds up his hands. "My apology if it seemed that way." He is looking hurt and a little surprised.

"I don't like being pushed around," you say.

He is nodding at this.

"OK, fair enough," he says. "Maybe you're right about that. So, I apologize."

You brush off a knee, your head pounding and the whole evening souring.

"Accepted?" he says extending a hand.

"OK," you say. You shake his hand and find his grip to be very soft and warm. He smiles.

"Take a good deep breath," he says, his eyes looking closely at you.

"Can I get you something to drink? Some water? A Coke?"

"I'm OK," you say.

"Then, can I say something?" he asks.

"Yeah, OK. I'm sorry, also, for jumping on your case," you say. You begin to feel better. "It's not you that I'm angry at. It's me. I'm tired of always stumbling, of falling, of being pushed around. I've been pushed around my entire life. People call me nerdy and goofy. I was always an easy target. And it's not that I exactly feel great about myself. I would settle for good. But everything I do turns to, well, crap."

You realize that the layoff is the cap to a long string of missteps over the years. You never really felt like you fit into the company in the first place, you realize now. Now, sitting in the van, trying to recover from an awful day, you are fumbling to stay seated.

"OK," you say, trying to avoid his eyes again.

"You have to take that first step."

He looks at you.

"You don't want to take any steps. And I don't blame you. Nothing seems to be that clear right now. But sometimes you cannot wait for things to clear up. You have to step off."

He looks around his van.

"Actually, it's not as hard as it sounds. Take me," he smiles. "I can't say that I will always live in my van, that I have all the answers, but it's about taking action. You must always react the best you can. You must see your situation as clearly as possible, then react."

"OK," you say.

"If you want to, I can help."

"Well," you say. "As long as I won't spill on your floor again."

He smiles. "Yeah, well sometimes I don't know my own strength."

He pauses a moment.

"Here's what I've learned," he says. "For what it's worth. Lessons from a janitor." He smiles. "First, never turn back. That is, set your sights, have them firmly in mind. Then never let them go. Never."

His face grows serious when he says this.

"Now, this is not to say that you can't make mistakes and correct yourself. But, be firm."

"But what if you don't even know your sights. I mean, what you want to do?"

"Then, turn your back on everything that is wrong."

His eyes soften as he says this.

"You'll throw some babies out with the bathwater. But you have no choice."

He looks around his van, at the pictures of samurai that line the walls.

"I gave up a life long ago, one that I didn't like, one that did no one any good. I didn't want to be part of a conspiracy. I never went back to it. I'm not saying it wasn't comfortable. I'm just saying that kind of life wasn't for me."

He strokes his beard.

"OK," you say.

"It's a big step."

He smiles as you try to absorb the gist of his advice.

"Next, learn from everyone you come in contact with. From the guy behind the counter, from your enemies, your best friends. Each one has something to say, something that you can learn. You'll find that you begin to attract the people you need to make your next steps."

He smiles at what he has just said.

"Even janitors." He laughs aloud. "Finally," he says. "Summon that new person you want to become. See him. Become him. We all do this at some point in our lives. We see small little similarities of that person in the movies, or walking down the street, or in our dreams. When you see him, nurture that person, until, you'll see, one day you'll become him."

He strokes his beard, and you are staring at the same picture as he is.

"You can't go wrong with samurai," he says. "They have always been my heroes, you know."

The pictures on the wall appear to be growing smaller, blurring.

"Yep," he says.

Suddenly your head grows very heavy, as if you have absorbed about as much as you can hold. The small van throbs with the music, and you gaze at the ceiling, with its small posters, faces, and scalloped edges. You see the samurai in the pictures move ever so slightly in your periphery, as if they are stepping out of their frames. Your eyes grow tired and the sounds of the van begin to recede.

"Hey," Alex says. "Lean back. Take it easy."

In another moment, you are asleep.

"The greatest warrior is the one who conquers himself."
—*Samurai proverb*

I n the dream, there's a small foot bridge, and it winds through dry grass and manzanita bushes, then up a short distance to a red bluff. Over the ridge, the ocean fills the horizon and you shield your eyes from the sun. You are floating over the path, trying to reach the ground, but distracted by the smells of the sea that drift up. You hear the waves against rocks in the distance.

From over the ridge, a figure approaches with deliberate strides, his sandals clicking in steady rhythm. You watch him as he comes closer. Then he is very close, and suddenly, his eyes lock in, looking directly at you. He is in large baggy pants, his kimono open in front. And there are two swords, stuck in his belt as he walks unhurried to you: Toshiro Mifune as he was in his younger days, playing the samurai Miyamoto Musashi in *The Samurai Trilogy*, his beard scraggily, top knot neatly tied back. He stands next to you, gazing out across the landscape, blue kimono fluttering in the breeze, the white prints of bamboo jumping across the front and sleeves. He rests his hands across his swords, squints his eyes, but does not turn.

"Quickly," he grunts, turning and looking at you, his eyes steel gray. You glance over to see your car parked at the top, beyond reach.

You know it's a dream but do not hesitate. Instead, your feet are moving, hands out of your pockets now, swinging at your sides, glasses clean, and the smell in the air is wet and scented. Over the rocky trail, you pick your way, close behind the samurai, watching his shoulders dip with each step, his legs beating the fabric. You try to keep up, keeping an eye on his back. The trail winds around the side of the mountain, and down to a short plateau with a solitary pine tree. You turn and look around, the sun shining in your eyes. You are closer to the ocean, and its sound is hypnotic, luring you to its blue waters.

"Keep your eyes ahead," he shouts. He pokes you in the back, and you find yourself in front somehow, walking briskly, the sound of his wood sandals now in back. His breath hits your neck, and you hear the knocking of the swords against themselves.

"Walk straight. Look straight."

You follow the path, and it rises up and down, the ocean pulling closer to you, then hidden as you walk behind a small hill. When the path winds around, you stand looking out over a choppy ocean, Mifune peering across to a small island, where four flags whip in the air. He puts a hand on your shoulder, and you step into a small wooden row boat on the sand. With a shove, the boat lurches as the ocean hits the bow, turning you around to face the open waters. You pull back on the oars, and Mifune sits in front, staring.

He is in simple burlap kimono, now with a wide straw hat that shields his head from the morning sun. There is a large black and white emblem on his back, with a Japanese character.

"But where are your swords?" you ask. None are visible when he turns to look at you.

"You are looking for the wrong things," he says. "My swords are of little value. You know this, right?"

You don't, but nod that you do.

He taps his head. "Here," he says. "And here," he says pointing to his eyes. "When you approach everything as training, you will not be discouraged."

You check your watch and find it in Japanese and unreadable.

"Ganryu Island," he says, turning to face forward.

You remember Ganryu Island, off the shore of Japan. There in feudal Japan, Miyamoto Musashi was tricked into coming out of retirement to fight.

Your boat dips as Mifune tears a few strips of white cotton from his inner kimono, ties a small white band around his head, then ties back his sleeves. The ocean sprayings, rocking the boat, throwing you down to the wet floor of the boat. Quietly he lifts you up and sets you back on the bench.

"Shh," he says with two fingers to his lips.

His hands are rough and callused.

You nod and continue to row, until the ocean currents push the back of the boat and shove it closer. Your stomach is feeling queasy. Clouds are forming, and the island comes into view. There is a line of men in tall hats waiting in a row along the shore.

He picks an oar and holds it up to the sky, tilting it and rotating it, until he finds a line he likes. He presses a knife blade into the paddle side, then leaning into it, splits the wood and moves the blade through the crack until half the paddle falls to the floor. He does the same on the other side, then shaves off the end, so it is blunt. With long strokes he shaves down the rest of the oar until it is a straight shaft. Picking it up, he holds it and moves it quickly from side to side. With the back of the knife, he smoothes out the roughness.

He turns to show you his work, with a glint in his eye.

"Strategy is everything," he says. He studies the shoreline as he approaches, shading his eyes, then sitting calmly. When the boat hits sand, you get out and pull it up on shore as Mifune jumps and runs low toward the smirking Kojiro, a brash samurai who challenged Mifune to a duel of swords. Mifune had become a simple farmer by then.

The judges suddenly sit up and begin to speak. But Mifune does not stop. He races toward Kojiro, who had been seated, and who, seeing the farmer racing toward him with a wooden staff, hesitates. He stands slowly, then in a quick motion unsheathes his long sword and throws the sheath away.

"You will no longer need a sheath for your sword," Mifune says, holding his wood sword in both hands and rushing quickly in. Kojiro moves to the side and Mifune stops, edging forward as Kojiro recovers, then pushes toward Mifune, the blade raised high over his head, casting a long shadow down to the sand.

"You are late," Kojiro scoffs.

"I slept in," says Mifune, glancing over to you as you hold the bow of the boat in the dipping tides. "Isn't that right?"

You nod in agreement.

"He is my second," Mifune says. "Slightly rough around the edges," he says. "But my battles are his battles."

"It is your last day," Kojiro says. "Who cares what riffraff you bring! Bring your mother if you think she will help."

Kojiro moves to his right, and Mifune turns, the head band fluttering, feet sinking into the sand.

"It is just a dream," you want to tell him.

"You see," Mifune says, turning so you can hear him, "he is already at a disadvantage. Look how he walks."

"I'm walking just fine," Kojiro says. "I'm younger. I'm quicker."

"None of which matters," Mifune says.

"What matters to an old man anyway," Kojiro says, tilting his sword at a fresh angle, his feet edging forward. "A warm bed? A hot meal?"

Mifune laughs, grimly. "You will never know."

"Each position he takes," Mifune explains to you, keeping an eye on Kojiro's sword, "has a counter position. Either it is defensive, or it is offensive. His strike becomes your block. From which you move to counterstrike. Am I right, Kojiro?"

"Yes, this is just the basics. Who cares?"

"But you will see that I don't need a block position."

And Mifune points his wood sword at the nose of Kojiro, then raises it high over his head.

"With no block, old man," Kojiro says, "you are a sitting duck."

"He is quicker in his own mind," Mifune smiles. "We are all quicker and smarter in our own minds. So, of course, you need to adjust. Am I right?"

"Not so," Kojiro says. "No adjustment needed."

"But he has a sword," you say. "You are going to be killed."

With his free hand, Mifune scratches inside his kimono. His eyebrows pull close.

"Ha! Fleas!," Kojiro blurts out. "And a *bokken*. You are a true farmer now. You even smell like horse manure!"

Mifune is pleased by this comment.

"But you must keep your focus. " he says facing you, his eyes glaring straight into you. "Don't look to the right or left. Do you understand this?"

Kojiro's face is now lit up by the sun, his eyes widening, a slow smile forming, as he shifts his feet. There is a murmur of the judges as they confer in the distance, their hats dipping, small cups of tea at their lips.

"The world is filled with such fights. They are meaningless. Only the one that you are in should be kept in your thoughts," he says. "And you must always practice. This one will be practice also."

"Is this a lesson?" Kojiro laughs. "I should be doing the teaching. Your moves are yesterday's tactics. It is a new age, old timer."

"Yes, it will be a lesson for you too." Mifune smiles.

Suddenly, Kojiro moves in, the flash of his blade streaks through the air. The judges turn. Mifune is up in the air, staff over his head as the long blade of Kojiro quickly slices toward Mifune's head. You are pulled closer, next to Mifune as he rotates, crosses under the blade, his staff careening towards Kojiro's head. Kojiro's blade pierces the samurai's headband, but Mifune is already ducking, his staff finding a spot below Kojiro's hairline. There is a solid thud as it opens the skull in a swift motion. Kojiro is startled, his eyes wide open in surprise.

He opens his mouth as if to say something before collapsing in the ocean water.

Mifune lands, his feet digging into the sand, breathing hard. There is a thin stream of blood flowing from Kojiro's temple. He looks at you, letting his wooden sword drop to the ground.

"Do you understand?" he asks. The sea gulls overhead looking on. "Do you understand what you have just seen?"

You nod.

"Then you know the way from here," he says, his eyes squinting at you.

You blink as he rushes back to the boat, past the judges, pushes the boat out into the ocean and is gone.

Y ou bolt up. The van dead silent except for Alex snoring. On the table are the last of the bottles and a box of granola. You find your backpack and shoes and move to the door. Alex is deep in sleep. You want to tell him about the dream, but you decide not to. You look instead at the samurai that line the walls, the *ronin*. You pull on your shoes. You give the warriors a silent *goodbye* before pulling open the door and stepping outside into the cool, night air. You take a deep breath. The air feels clean and revitalizing.

The main building is lit up, and you walk across the vacant parking lot toward your car. Two guards are sitting on the concrete planters, smoking and flicking away the ashes. You move quietly across the pavement, occasionally gazing up. Although the night sky is a deep black, you see small ribbons of violet intermixed. Some clouds are building up, and you can smell rain on the gusts of winds

You head out of the parking lot, onto the dark sidewalk that leads to the underpass. From a corner of your eye you see a figure to your right, but when you turn, it's gone. Still you hear the ruffling of fabric, like the samurai in your dream. In fact, you have the strong sense that you are being followed, or that you are dragging a piece of cloth stuck to your shoes. You stop and shake it off, then listen to the traffic whooshing from the freeway. Again there is movement to your right and without turning your head this time, you see someone nodding, or rather bowing slightly in a Japanese way. Rubbing your eyes, you let the thought go.

You see a couple huddled at the side of the freeway, their backs against the street lights. From the distance, it's no one you recognize, although they appear to want to cross, waiting as the trucks and cars overhead stream by. You veer off to see what is happening. When you reach the spot, it's a Mexican couple. They look up fearful, the mother with a small girl on her back, and the father with a makeshift pack.

The man smiles a nervous smile.

"*Es bueno*," he says. "*Justo algún extranjero divertido.*"

The woman smiles and looks around.

"You're crossing here?" you ask.

But they don't understand. Their faces are hidden in the shadow of the lights, though they appear dark and wrinkled, the small child is sleeping with a shawl draped over his head.

"This is dangerous, even now," you say. "You have to run fast."

They nod, but obviously don't understand. In rush hour, it would be impossible, but now there is a chance when the traffic breaks. At their sides are large woven satchels, and the man divides his attention between you and the freeway.

"OK, I'll help," you say pointing to the bags.

"*No, no,*" the man says. "*No, es pesado.*"

"You have to cross very fast. How do you say fast in Spanish? *Andele?* Is that it? *Andele.*"

They both look fearful but pick up the bags and are ready to scamper across the road. Quickly you stop them.

"Wrong word," you say. "Let's see, not *mañana*. Oh yes, it is *pronto*. We must *pronto.*'

They smile nervously, looking at each other then back to you.

"OK. We have to wait then, I will count, OK? You know one, two, three. Like that?"

"*Si, si. OK, entendemos. Uno dos tres.*"

"Yes."

"*Si,*" the man says holding his wife's wrist.

But the traffic is very busy. There are cars going in both directions. And some large trucks. There are no breaks in the traffic. Just as one side of the freeway lets up, the other side gets busy. Her child appears to be heavy and sound asleep, and already she is having a hard time balancing herself. It will make crossing very difficult.

"OK," you say. "I have a better idea. Let's go another way. This way."

"*No comprende.*"

"Muy better. No big cars. No big autos," you say. "Safer."

They nod and talk with one another in Spanish.

"It's OK," you say. "This way. Underneath. Under."

And you sign this with one hand being a human figure with your fingers walking like the yellow pages under your other hand.

"This way," you say.

They hesitate, but the man finally picks up his satchel and they follow you. They move quicker than you imagined. You take the woman's bag.

"*Gracias,*" she says with a smile.

Jenz Johnson

"*Andele*," the man says, smiling. You realize what the word means now.

"OK, *gracias*," you say.

And you share a smile.

"Where are you from? Mexico?" you ask as you walk down a dirt trail to the underpass.

"Guatemala," he says.

You nod at this.

"OK."

You walk single file down the frontage road. There are distant sounds of thunder and a couple of streaks of lightening. The woman turns a bit frightened in the direction of the storm.

"It's OK," you say. But you notice the storm has gathered some wind and is heading toward you. "This will work out."

There is a sudden pop of thunder and the woman jumps. Her husband puts a hand on her shoulder. The whole sky behind them lights up, and you see their eyes very clearly now, fearful, wide-open and nervous. A couple of drops fall. Then the shower abruptly begins to pour. Thunder claps overhead and you are soaked. The husband takes his poncho and drapes it over the woman and her daughter.

"This way," you say and you reach the underpass without too much trouble. "Big storm, huh?"

The thunder catches up and rumbles overhead. When you turn you see another figure standing at the freeway, but it is only the silhouette of the samurai, and you catch a nod from him. The rain falls in steady curtains on either side. But the underpass is dry.

"OK?" you ask. "It's good that we got off the freeway."

They nod.

"We better wait this out," you say. "Very wet." And you wring out your T-shirt. She smiles and sets her satchel down. Her daughter sleeps through the sounds. The husband moves the bags up the hill a ways as a small gutter forms with rainwater along the side.

They sit on their bags and wait. They seem to be very experienced at waiting. You find a large rock to sit on and take your pack off. Your phone is clipped to your belt and has escaped any rain. With a dry portion of your shirt, you wipe off the screen.

"Here," you say, as you rummage in your pack. You bring out some half-eaten bags of chips, a bag of M&M's and a small plastic bottle of Coke. "This might help."

"*Gracias*," she says, but refuses.

The man brings out a small bag and sets it on a satchel between the two of you. He unfolds a paper and inside are tortillas. He takes out a knife and cuts a small wedge of something green and gelatin.

"*Por favor,*" he says.

"Thank you," you say. "But really I'm OK."

"*Por favor,*" he says. So, you tear a small piece of tortilla and take the small chunk of gelatin. It is very good.

"Very delicious," you say. The woman smiles and looks to her husband. "I've never had this before. I mean, in a Mexican restaurant."

"*Por favor,*" the man says, and offers more.

You set your food near his and push this to the woman. The woman opens the M&M's and shakes one out.

"*Gracias,*" she says and holds the piece in her mouth to let it melt.

The rain continues to pour around you.

"My work," you say pointing to the company building which is barely visible now with the rain falling. The lights make it look like a prison.

"*Si, trabajo,*" he says. He reaches into his satchel and pulls out some pecans.

"Not for long though." You hold up two fingers. "Two more weeks, then I have to go somewhere else. "

"*Mi trabajo,*" he says.

"Your work?" you ask. "You sell nuts?"

He gestures that he picks them.

"*Pacanas.*"

"Yes," you say. "Never tried picking nuts. Don't think it would work out that well for me. I'd get too many calluses. How do you say *calluses*? Of course, didn't work out that well here either."

You shrug and absent-minded pick at the tortilla.

"Your girl?" you say. "How old?"

"Si," he says. "*Ella es nuestra vida.*"

"Yes, very cute."

The couple looks at each other and smiles a relaxed smile for a while. The woman wipes off her forehead and wraps a blanket around the girl, who continues to sleep through the rumbling thunder.

The three of you sit for a while and listen to the thunder and rain. The desert chaparral is calm, with a faint purplish glow. Water drips down from the freeway above.

"When the storm stops," you say. "Go this way." You point out the opposite end of the underpass. "There."

"*Si,*" he says.

"Go around the parking lot and you find some streets. I can give you some more instructions."

He nods.

"Where are you going?"

He doesn't understand.

"*Su casa?*" you ask. "*Donde esta su casa?*" you ask hesitantly, stringing together the few Spanish words that you remember.

He smiles. "Guatemala," he says.

"Yes, but no home here. In the United States?"

He shakes his head.

"So, where do you go now? *Donde* now?"

He looks out the opposite end of the underpass, and smiles. He motions to his wife and little girl.

"Yes," you say. "They are very beautiful. I'm on my way home, now." You say. "I have an apartment. Although I'm not really sure what I'm going to do when I get back there. You'll be OK here under the freeway if you wanted to stay out of the rain. There's a Taco Bell not too far from here."

"Taco Bell," he says with a big smile.

"Yes, they have Mexican food."

"*No es tan bueno en Taco Bell.*"

"In a jam, they've got a great quesadilla."

He laughs at this.

"Si, their quesadilla is *muy bein,*" you say.

"*Mucho queso.*"

"Yes, cheese. I can never get enough cheese. It should be a food group of its own."

"*Si, queso. Pero, mi amigo, usted debe intentar un poco de alimento verdadero. Mi esposa prepara un pozole delicioso. Pozole.*"

"Posole? Never heard of it. Good?"

"*Si, muy delicioso.*"

"Someday, I'll have to try it," you say. "I suppose I should get going."

"*Mucho gusto,*" he says.

"Remember, just through there," you say pointing to the end of the underpass. "When you're ready."

"*Mucho gusto,*" he repeats and stands.

"Yes, thank you."

"Here," you say and you pull out the money in your wallet. It is not much but you figure that they will need it.

"*No, no,*" the man says. "*Encontraré el trabajo pronto.*"

"Please," you say, holding out the bills.

"*Gracias,*" the wife says and bows slightly.

You give a wave and step onto the dark sidewalk that leads to the parking annex.

Suddenly, the rain grows harder and you run quickly to your car parked near the end. You set your backpack on your feet, and rummage around for your keys. Although you normally put them in the small pocket, they are nowhere to be found. In the darkness, you fumble around in the large pocket, over the pens, the Rolaids, books, magazines, until you find them tucked into a corner and fish them out. Quickly you open the door, jump in and catch your breath.

Yeah, just scrap it, man" Burgie says, legs thrust in front with his high tops splayed under a bundle of shoelaces. It's already after midnight, but early for Burgie.

He's multi-tasking in his living room, a tub of ice cream in his lap, a soldering iron resting at his elbow and a rerun of *Beat the Geeks* on his muted set. His head has surrendered to the backrest of his thinking chair and you have just finished relating Alex's advice. "That's what Seymour would do too." *Seymour* would be Seymour Cray, father of the supercomputer, ultimate Odd Man Out, and local hero within the confines of Burgie's apartment.

Sitting across from him on an overstuffed couch, you feel like you are just another computer part in his presence, wedged as you are between a disemboweled tape drive and a vintage wall-mount enclosure, taking an audience with Burgie. It is a comfortable spot albeit a bit dusty. Burgie has settled in across from you, all ears, setting a circuit board and soldering iron down on the table next to him. Granted, it is a bit late (or early) for a visit, but you were desperate and in need of a Vulcan mind-meld. And Burgie, the ultimate night-owl, was the first person within a suitable driving radius that you felt would not turn you away.

We all will be scrapped one day, you think, replaced by the younger, smarter, faster models.

Burgie pushes his glasses up and looks at you closely. On the wall, Seymour Cray, shown with his team, circa 1960, with his ground-breaking CDC 1604 monolith, the first-ever high-performance supercomputer, the first of a new species of niche computers endowed with focused power and speed. The picture says it all. Cray's benevolence permeates the room. His smile is one of pure joy, the quiet contentment of a genius who broke all the rules. The monolith shares the spotlight like a proud son. Beneath its matte exterior, the real masterpiece created entirely from transistors by grad students who, at the time, did not know it was supposed to be impossible.

A single piece of furniture sites uncluttered at the center of the living room: the Love Seat. It is a round bench encircling a cylinder, upholstered in soft blue velvet. Not for anything remotely romantic, it's fashioned after the Cray-1, Cray's next giant leap in technology. At 1:2 scale, it's a reminder of great things, the successor machine configured in this way to shorten the path from the main computer processor to its memory. It's an accommodation to the speed of light, which was becoming an irritant to Cray, limiting the speed he could crank out. To circumvent it, Cray devised the love seat, encircling his single processor with reams of memory and pushing the enclosure skyward. The Cray-1 also marked a departure from the multi-processor model Seymour had dedicated the previous decade to perfecting. He scrapped it to pursue the ultimate single-fastest behemoth, jumping ship from CDC to form a whole new company, Cray Computers.

The love seat is remarkable, a piece of art really, an exact replica of the second generation, a reminder of breakthroughs that can be achieved outside the confines of conventions and rules.

With a toe, Burgie pushes his Baskin-Robbins tub of Cookie Dough toward you. You wave it off. You've still not recovered from something you ate in the van.

"Just move on," is his advice, although you really were not asking for it so directly.

"Gordon wasn't too happy today," you say. "He thinks my code stinks. I'm letting the entire office down. He even says that I've got to finish my current assignments before I go. Or he's going to blackball me."

"I mean with your life," he says. "Move on with your life."

Which is easy for Burgie to say, you think to yourself. After all he has his eBay business to fall back on. But you, what do you have? That's the problem. Nothing. Your job is the foundation of everything that you have. Your apartment, your car, your gadgets, magazines, food—everything is conditioned on that steady stream of money flowing into your checking account each month. Worse, you feel part of yourself is tied up with the job. Just driving into work each morning gives you a sense of satisfaction. Now, it seems, you are floundering.

"Well, I'm trying to. Move on that is."

With a toe, Burgie hooks his frosted tub and reels it in like a docile marlin. From a red plastic Ketchup bottle, he squirts some goo over the top, then some syrup from another, some nuts, some whipped cream from a commercial dispenser. A quick whipped squirt to the mouth is the appetizer, before he lifts the tub to his lap and begins the excavation of his top layer. It's the Endless Sundae Dip, and you are tempted.

"You sure?" he says through stuffed cheeks, lifting the squirt bottle.

"Yes," you say, but realize he is referring to the dip. "I mean, yes."

He hefts another large glob on a broken cone, then shapes it lovingly with his tongue. It's art in motion. He briefly closes his eyes to absorb the assortment of flavors.

"I guess I'm still processing it," you say. "Nothing makes any sense."

"Probably that processor of yours. Old technology," he says indicating your head. "You're probably bottle-necked up there, in your processor. That's my guess."

"Probably my stack," you say, glancing down at the line of bolts on the floor. "It just keeps filling up; things keep falling off."

"That's heap space. Your stack's usually handling short-term memory. Mid-term memory goes on the heap, the hippocampus actually, where it can be retrieved for a couple of days. We are basically heaps.

"Most things are just push and pop. Push it on your stack, then pop it off. That works as long as you don't need to do too much about it. You know, like think or make any decisions. But the more you need to think about things, the more you shuttle it out to your brain's heap. But if you are taking any amount of time with it, that information is going to be shuffled out to your heap and into your cortex. That stuff just gets plunked down anywhere inside that brain of yours."

"Well, I guess. Trouble is I can't find it. One minute I think I have a handle on things, that I see my way clear to what I want to do with my life. And the next moment, well, I can't figure it out. I forget what I decided to do."

He considers this with a thoughtful chew.

"So, you can't retrieve stuff?"

"I forget a lot," you explain. "It's almost as if I reset, lose track."

"Hmm," he says thoughtfully. He digs in for another large scoop of ice cream, followed by a squirt from his bottle. He munches, studying you.

"Well, most scientists are a bit sketchy on how retrieval works in the brain. It's not as if you have a disk full of memories in your cortex that you just go out and grab. Your gray matter has to burn new synapses to get to information. You have to recreate these each time you want to get to them. Almost like you relearn things each time, re-burn the synapses to get to the stuff you want to remember."

"Like a DVD," you say.

"But, of course, a lot faster. So, your processor has this natural cycling, which refreshes important things to remember. We take in everything around us and it gets processed, the synapses burned inside our heads, and the information stored away. And it's not just stored in one spot in the brain. You distribute the information in a holographic fashion, with bits being shuttled around different areas. It's a very efficient way to store information, a lot better than our DVD's these days. Instead of storing information on the surface like a DVD, the brain's volume is used. It's like a 3-D storage, where information is multiplexed inside each chunk. You can retrieve the information just by the angle you choose to access it."

Burgie glances up at the monitor overhead, catching a snippet of a rerun, then his eyes close.

"And of course, any memory that is infused with any strong feeling gets the amygdala involved. That's a walnut-sized nodule tucked in your midbrain. It can activate instantaneous responses, get you running when something awful is about to happen, or get you pumped up to fight."

"In fact, our brain works best when we can use our emotions to activate old memories. The amygdala just kicks in and circumvents the normal routes inside our heads to get a fast track on these memories."

"Some I'd rather not go back to, if you don't mind."

"Your brain naturally reacts to things around you. A good smell, a pretty smile, a loaded gun…"

"Or all three. That's how I feel."

"It can get confusing. But these are the triggers. They not only trigger memories, but they will trigger things to do. That's what you can use to get moving."

"I don't seem to move forward. That's my problem. I keep replaying the part about Gordon at the podium, the part I missed. I keep trying to hear his exact words. I hate getting it second hand."

"Yeah," Burgie says. "So much of everything is second hand these days."

"But I think it might have helped to hear the words," you say.

"I don't know," he says. "Gordon more or less avoided the exact words. So, I think it's just that gray sponge of yours. Tries to reiterate the problem to death. Probably the hypothalamus at play. Sounds like you're looping."

"What?"

"Looping," he says. "Your old sponge keeps mulling over things again and again. Can't seem to break out of the loop. This is a natural refreshing of the brain."

He motions with his spoon, indicating your head, then returns it to the tub.

"Of course, we all need loops, I'm not saying we don't. Even priority-driven interrupts are just big loops somewhere. Some process just checking to make sure that there is nothing more important happening."

"Well, I do keep thinking about things..."

"The same old things, again and again?" he asks. "Without any resolution?"

You shrug.

"Looping, all right."

"But I think of other things too," you say.

"But always come back to the same thoughts, right?"

"Usually."

"Can't seem to get beyond them."

"I try."

He reaches in for another large dollop.

"You're looping all right," he says. "There's only one way to break a loop, you know: from the outside. It's the most reliable."

"I've been outside. Nothing different."

"I mean outside of your loops. At the meta-level. Obviously, you are stuck in a process, and it keeps looping around and around. But you can't just order yourself to break out, can you? So, you've got to have a trigger—something that forces you to interrupt your endless loops. External events. Triggers, my friend, are always the trick. Our whole mental apparatus is set up to process triggers. That's how new synapses are created. That's how we get at things up here. Triggers."

"Where do you find these things?" you ask.

He laughs. "Triggers are all round us. It's just that we isolate ourselves—and hence our code—from their reach. They are external events that trigger our internal routines."

"I'm not sure I totally follow."

"Well, think back when you were learning to walk. You'd run into a wall and it would hurt. Your brain would connect the external

---

event of banging into a wall with unpleasant pain, and go in and modify its internal code not to do it again. Hitting the wall was the trigger. So, every time you began to walk and saw a big blank surface, your amygdala would interrupt whatever you were doing and trigger your balance response. You would recall the banging part and maneuver away from the wall. In your case, you are hitting a different kind of a wall."

He smiles, picking a piece of cone from his beard.

"You've got a process in there," he continues, "that is hacking away at the code, burning new synapses, rerouting your reactions. Your sponge is pretty damn malleable."

You nod, but are frankly bewildered anyway. Talking about it just makes you feel worse.

"Essentially you've got to detect your loops. Every time you find yourself looping, you have to change channels. Like having an internal remote, a clicker."

"I don't know…," you say.

"Hold that thought." He scoops up his circuit board and iron and walks off. His feet pad softly over the carpet, and he disappears into the bedroom next door

Overhead you notice a row of three 18-inch monitors playing reruns of *Heckyl and Jeckyl*, *Dr. Who*, and *Boy and His Dog*. You look around for a volume control and find a universal at the end of a long tether.

There is a loud flush. Then another. And Burgie slinks back in with his soldering gun smoldering.

"Core dump," he says, and you nod. "But to un-pause, my advice?"

You nod.

"Scrap it. Do a restart. Interrupt every loop that you begin. Force yourself to scrap your current routines, the ones you rely on each day to, you know, drive to work, get dressed, take a shower. Just stop doing these things. Then each new event will trigger fresh memories and fresh routines. It is the ultimate make-over. But from the inside out."

"You know people who have done this?"

"Rebooted?"

"Yes, I mean who have completely changed."

"Well, yes. A few. Look at Bruce Willis, he made those schlocky movies until *Pulp Fiction*, then he came back. Or John Travolta. Now he was old news until…"

"*Pulp Fiction?*"

"Well, you've got to admit, it was a great movie."

"But besides actors, I mean. Can I speak with someone who's been through it. Someone I can call."

"Can't say I have any numbers for Bruce or John."

"People you know of."

"Well," he thinks. "There's Señor Jim. He's definitely rebooted. But he's pretty stealthy."

You heard the name before.

"I just have questions is all," you say.

"I'm not sure how to get hold of him, although Kristo would know," he says. "But Kristo is a hard one to get any face time with. His emails go routinely unanswered, especially during game weeks. He's usually locked in on a couple of MMORPG's at a time. So, he doesn't come up for air."

He scratches himself, repositions the tub of ice cream and takes the remote. He becomes engrossed in the reruns, and soon you have your feet up on the couch.

"*Progress isn't made by early risers,*" Burgie says out of the blue. "*It's made by lazy men trying to find easier ways to do something.*"

"I guess."

"Robert Heinlein said that," he answers. "Can you *grok* it?"

"I better go," you say. Burgie reaches for another scoop of ice cream and nods. You find your way to the door as Burgie un-mutes the TV.

> *"The only time a woman really succeeds in changing a man is when he's a baby."*
> —*Natalie Wood*

You stop outside Burgie's apartment and stand in the dark, trying to think through your next steps. You're not ready to go back to your apartment, back to the same old thing. The same stairwell. The familiar walls, wood floors, chipped window sills, recognizable sounds. The same sun coming up on queue, bringing the same suffocating heat. Same you, same problems. You cannot shake it. It feels like a trap.

You drive north for a while, not knowing where you want to go. The roads rise up out of the valley, the city an uneven swell of lights below. A cool breeze streams through your window and up the sleeve of your shirt. It feels good.

You see movement in your mirror. The samurai returns your gaze with a look of impatience. He is waiting for you, saying little, his eyes staring you down with an intense push. You keep driving, although you have nowhere to go, not really.

"Stupid," the samurai says at last. You cannot face him. You pull over to the side of the road. There are only a few buildings around; it's mostly desert, with a few mesquites rustling by the side of the road. You pull the phone off your belt and dial a number.

"Yes?" Her voice surfaces over the line, puzzled and upset.

"Katie?" you say, surprised that she answered.

"Who is this?"

"It's me."

"Me?"

"Jenz. From the office," you say. "The one who's being laid off."

"Oh," she says with some recognition.

"I found your number," you say.

"What?"

The line is silent for a while.

"It's late, you know." she says.

"Sorry," you say.

"OK, let's talk tomorrow," she says.

"I just wanted to call and thank you for those forms. The ones that you got for me."

She is silent.

"I mean staying after and all."

"You're welcome."

"Bad time, huh?"

"Yes."

"I forgot my watch, so I'm a bit off."

"No clock?"

"The one in my car is broken."

"Where are you, anyway?"

"West side, I think."

"You need some sleep."

"You're right."

"A little less caffeine, OK?" she says.

"OK."

You switch ears and look at a car whizzing by. You are hanging on, racking your brain, trying to think what to actually say next, but you draw a solid blank, a deep empty well of thought. A big null.

"OK. I'm going to hang up now."

"Did I mention that I do read some books that aren't about computers. I mean, on occasion."

There is no reply.

"You had asked me, and I said that I liked movies. Remember."

More silence on the line.

"I didn't want you to get the wrong impression."

"No chance of that." She giggles.

"Yeah, thought I'd mention it."

"Listen, you're sweet. But I'm going to hang up now."

"It's just that I don't always think that well on my feet."

"Are you standing right now?"

"No, sitting."

"OK, you're not making any progress in that position either." She laughs again. "Bye."

The line goes dead and you look at your cell to check the connection. You continue to look at it, thinking of just what to do next. Nothing really comes to mind. You press Redial and hold your breath.

"Go to sleep," she says.

There is silence.

"Listen," you say, "you want to grab a cup of coffee? I mean, now that you're up and all."

"Not really."

"I guess I shouldn't have called again."

There is silence on the line.

"OK. Little chance that I'm going to get back to sleep," she says.

"Sorry..."

"So where *are* you exactly?"

"Well, maybe a little lost. I can't see any street signs. I'm having kind of a bad day. Not the worst, but ..."

"Can you find your way to River and Sixth."

"Yeah, I could."

"You can stop at a gas station and ask, you know."

"I suppose."

"All right, give me 15 minutes. There's an all-night place there. It's the only one that's open. But you are going to owe me a real dinner one of these days."

"Great," you say. "Sorry it's so late. I mean I lost track."

"OK," she says. "I suppose I can sleep later."

"Yeah," you say.

"And Jenz?"

"Yeah?"

"You'll be OK."

You nod as the line goes dead.

You find the intersection, but it's almost a full thirty minutes since the phone call. It is a strip mall with a 24-hour pancake house. A few cars are parked outside and you pull around the back to find a spot where you can regroup out of view.

In the rearview mirror, your eyebrows are furled and when you look at yourself, you have an odd, desperate look. Your hair has dried straight up. You try to smooth is down, but it springs back. You find a jacket crumpled in the back seat, and pull it over your shirt.

Inside, you spot her at a table in a gray sweatshirt, a cup of tea steaming in front of her, head resting on a hand. You wave to catch her attention, and she nods. She motions you with a limp wrist.

"Sorry," you say. "Sorry I'm late. I overshot it a skosh."

"That's OK," she says. She looks tired.

Your jacket is wrinkled and has two large grease spots in front, so you strip if off like a magician's trick and throw it on the seat next to you. Carefully, you slide in across from her. The booth has a cluster of condiments and bottles near the wall, above them a picture of a stack of pancakes, framed like a portrait over the table. It is a still life of sorts, syrup dripping off the top one with exaggerated highlights.

"I ordered some tea," she says lifting a tea bag out, then wrapping it around a spoon hastily.

"I could use some coffee," you say. "Do they have cappuccino, do you know? I could use a good cappuccino."

"This is a pancake house. Try some decaf. You look worse than you did before.."

"I need to keep a little wired."

"Well, I think if you came down a couple of notches, you'd have a better handle on reality."

"Well," you say, thinking about her comment. "I'm not really after a handle, per se. This whole job thing has made me think, you know, that there's got to be a better way."

She takes a long gulp from her tea.

"I mean, bigger changes," you say, looking at the condiments. "I've been struggling at work, and nothing seems to gel on my module. No matter how I try to cram everything in, well, I always end up with some pretty bad code. And bugs. Not that our machines are much good at work. There're slow."

"OK," she says holding up her hands.

"In fact, I have a sneaking suspicion that these machines are at the root of our problems."

"OK," she says. "Wait a sec."

"Just my opinion, actually."

"OK," she says. "Let's start over. Let's start out on the right foot, OK?"

As you talked, you stacked packets of sweetener in front of you. They collapse and spread out on your napkin.

"I don't really do well, not in the middle of the night," she says. "And can't follow techie talk."

"OK, sorry."

"You woke me up, remember?"

"Yeah, I remember."

She smiles. "Let's have a conversation. Get to know each other. Like that."

"OK," you say. "You're right. I feel kind of stupid anyway. I didn't realize it was this late."

"It's after 1 a.m. On a weekday," she says rolling her eyes.

You hastily put the packets back into the sugar container and concede the point. Obviously, everything is already off on the wrong foot.

"Jump right in," she says.

"It's just that," you begin. "Well. Thank you for coming."

"You're welcome," she says with a smile.

You smile back and scan the menu and find mostly food. You need coffee.

"Anything else?" she asks.

The waitress comes by, and you are rescued.

"A cappuccino," you say. "I didn't see it on the menu."

"That's because we don't have it."

"A cup of coffee, then," you say.

"A carafe," the waitress says when you ask about coffee. "That's all we serve. One cup or twenty cups. The same price."

"No espresso?" you ask.

"The coffee's is pretty thick," she says. "It's been stewing back there since yesterday."

"OK," you say and hand the menu back. "A small carafe."

"There's only one size," she says and smiles at Katie, as if she pities her.

"I'm OK," Katie says.

The waitress leaves and you wrack your brain for something to say, but draw a blank. You give a weak smile.

"You're a worry wort," she says. "Tell me, you and Burgie sure talk a lot of tech talk."

"Yeah, I guess that's all I know. There's always something new. For us, that's the excitement. A new chip or a new hack. We'd take a pay cut to get in on some of the newer development. It's amazing what you discover when you're coding. Time flies and you don't even realize that you're whizzing along. At least, when you're in a groove."

She smiles.

"Yes, it's a wonderful feeling," she says.

"But I feel like I am in a real rut right now."

"You mean, work."

"I mean *everything*."

She nods.

"It seems that I never get on the right path. Either I get interrupted, which happens a lot, or I keep going around in circles."

"Hey," she says. "You're just worn down by the layoff. A little less coffee and more vegetables. A fresh salad now and then..."

"Maybe," you say. "Anyway, I've decided that I can't go back. Not to work. Not to my apartment. Not to the life that I have."

She looks up. "That's a little crazy," she says.

"I know that as soon I as go back, I will slide into my old habits. I want to change myself. That's the thing. Become someone else."

"You mean, you're not going back to your apartment?"

"Nah, it doesn't feel right."

"Well, that's a little more crazy than I thought. Not even to turn out the lights? Or pay bills?"

"Well, I haven't come to that juncture just yet."

"So, you're going to keep driving around."

"Yeah. I guess. Nothing else comes to mind."

"And sleep?"

"I'll crash somewhere, with Burgie or somewhere."

"Don't *crash* crash," she says, sounding a little worried. "You're not looking that good."

"I feel I have to make a stand. This is as close as I can get to changing right now. Not to be the same, if you know what I mean."

Sounds like there's no going back, even if you want to."

"But I don't want to."

"Yes," she admits. "Some of us want to, though."

"Go back?"

"I think it might be nice," she says. "Sometimes, when I'm tired, you know."

"But where would you go?"

"To my former self," she says. "I look back and really miss it sometimes. I wasn't always like this. You know, my bum leg."

"I didn't want to, you know, pry."

"It's OK. I'm over it. I was once really into freeriding."

"Freeriding?"

"It's snowboarding in its purist form. No grooming, or half-pipes, just open country, natural terrain. And I was wonderful. I think I could have turned pro, if I wanted to. I was thinking about it, at least."

"You decided not to?"

"I hit a bank of snow too hard and flipped into a tree. I was going way too fast. So, I can't blame it on anyone else."

"That's how you…"

"Broke my ankle. Shattered it."

"Wow."

"Yeah, wow. For me, it was the end of the world. I was on pain killers for months. And they couldn't do too much. I was way off the trail. By time they found me, I was already pretty bad." She shakes her head. "It was really painful. And the ski patrol wouldn't come either."

"They wouldn't? Why? You were hurt."

"I was off the trail. They can't go there. Their insurance wouldn't cover it. So, my buddies called a private ski rescue. It took a while."

"I didn't realize."

"Yeah. So, I know how you feel. I know how the world can come to a quick end. And how unfair it can seem." She looks around, sadly. "But you know, I looked at the kids that were in the hospital there. With serious problems. So young. I realized that snowboarding was fun. But in the larger scheme of things, it was also pretty frivolous. I set my mind on other things." She looks at you. "Just like you should do."

"Boy, I didn't realize."

"This world has a lot of unfair things happen to people. I just had to get over my problems, and help the people, the children, who were far worse off than I was. That's what the whole experience taught me. I'm grateful, actually."

"Wow," you say.

She taps your hand gently. "You're sweet. Come on, you can stay at my place if you want. But I mean, just to sleep. It's pretty small, my place, but I have a couch. You have to put up with a cat."

"Well…"

"I hope you're not allergic to cats."

"No, I'm fine."

"I can't send you out to drive around in your car in the state you're in. You are not looking too good. If you really crash, or they find you tomorrow in some awful shape, well, I would blame myself." She looks at you and repeats, "Just to sleep."

"OK. I *am* tired."

"Just for the night. Besides, maybe I can wean you off your cappuccinos."

You follow close behind her as she weaves up a small paved road to the west of the city. She pulls into an alley, then parks next to a dilapidated guesthouse, with a bright porch light. You find parking further down the alley, then walk back.

She opens the screen door.

"Excuse the mess," she says stepping into a small living room. You look around and are surprised to find a perfectly neat living room.

A couch has a colorful quilt thrown over it, with a cat sitting on it, licking its paws. Next to the TV is a set of rolling files, with a stack of articles and magazines neatly stacked on top.

"It's my work. I can roll it out of the way. I just love working from the couch."

"I hope it's not a hassle," you say.

"No. It's fine. Will the couch be comfortable for you?"

"Perfect," you say.

"Because that's really all I have."

"No, it's fine."

"And you can just push Oscar off if he bothers you."

You position yourself on the couch and click on the TV. Oscar tiptoes over your lap and rubs against your arm. You mute the set and look at an old movie, kicking off your shoes and settling back.

"I am always doing that which I cannot do, in order that I may learn how to do it."
—*Pablo Picasso*

The cat's tail swipes your nose, and you jolt awake. You immediately sit up and the cat scampers to the floor. The room is filled with morning light. Behind you, the sounds of a shower echo, and the smell of coffee lifts you off the couch to a waiting Mr. Coffee in the kitchen. You find a large mug and pour the coffee quickly, loading it with milk and sugar. Blowing carefully, you sip the brew, feeling your head return to a morning buzz.

"Save some for me," you hear from the bathroom. You are on your second cup without realizing it. You set it down and check the remains in the pot.

"Sorry," you shout as you hold the pot up. There is a little left.

Katie steps from the bathroom, a towel wrapped around her chest, carefully hobbling across the tiles in her bare feet, hair still wet. She glances at the pot and frowns.

"Hey," she says. "There were four cups in there!"

"Well, actually a *skosh* more than three. Mr. Coffee cups are actually short cups so they can advertise the 10-cup capacity."

She disappears in the bedroom.

"Can I make you some breakfast?" you yell, swirling the remains, surveying her small apartment.

"You?" she asks.

"It's my weekend job," you say. Clicking on the TV, you settle into the couch, sitting on the sheets and trying to avoid Oscar who wanders back to your legs.

"Nah. If you are hungry, you can make something for yourself," she says, standing in back of you toweling off her hair and looking at the morning news. The fragrance of her shampoo drifts over to you. There is a hint of the sweet spice of her skin. You are at first hesitant to suggest any food, since your stomach has not regained its composure.

"You slept in your clothes?" she observes.

"Well, I usually do. It's quicker, you know. In the morning."

She is in a white blouse and jean skirt, and finishes toweling off her hair. It is tangled and spiky.

"OK," she says. "That would explain your fashion statement."

"I guess," you say and look for awhile at her green eyes. She disappears into the bathroom, and emerges with her hair combed back, then pads over to the coffee pot and pours the remains into a cup.

"We could make more," you say.

"That's OK," she says. "How'd you sleep?"

"OK, I guess, although my mouth feels kind of used."

"There's an extra toothbrush in the bathroom for you. And you can use the towels."

"I think I'm OK. Coffee has that cleansing effect."

She rolls her eyes at this. "You could use a strong dousing."

"Besides, I'm feeling pretty good this morning."

"Well, you look chipper."

"What time is it?"

"A little after five."

"Five? Wow, that's early."

"I thought you could get an early start on things. Besides I have some prying eyes two houses down."

"Oh," you say.

She looks around at the couch and living room.

"Can you roll those up?" she says, indicating the sheets on the couch. "You can stow them in the hamper in the bathroom."

"Why do you go in so early?"

"Oh, I'm not going in," she says. "It's the only time I have to myself. Some letters, some writing," she says.

"You can function this early?"

She nods

"Boy, that's a skill," you say. "Early morning hours—like 1 or 2—work a lot better for me."

"Well, just different biological clocks," she says.

"That must be it," you say. "Mine kind of cranked up to 3 gigahertz sometimes. So, I guess it's hard to slow that down at night."

"I mean some of us are morning people, and others are night people."

"That too."

"I'm a morning person," she says.

"I guess it's pre-set in our firmware."

"Anyway, most of the time it's not worth it. I don't write much that I like."

"You should try evenings then. I code much better late at night. At least, I used to."

"I doubt that would help," she says, gathering up a canvas briefcase, and stuffing papers and writing pads into it. "I'm in a slump. How about some bread or something? Coffee on an empty stomach is not that good for you."

"I don't mind. But if you had some toast…"

"Well," she smiles, "I could broil it. I don't really have a toaster."

"Yeah, it's such a single-tasker."

"A what?"

"Sorry, I watch way too much Alton Brown on Food Network!" you say. "Anyway, you'll get out of your slump."

She sets a loaf of bread on the counter.

"This is all I have. It's not too fresh, since I don't eat a lot of bread."

Moving into the kitchen, you hold the loaf up and give it a squeeze. It seems fresh enough: The crust doesn't crack.

"Seems pretty good," you say. "I'll just make some Zen Buns with it."

"Zen Buns?"

"Oh, yeah. I usually do it with leftover hamburger buns, but this will work just fine. But I need some butter and a saucepan."

From the refrigerator, she slides a butter container on the counter and places a knife next to the cutting board.

"Pan's hanging up there."

She leans against the counter and watches as you place the pan on the burner and crank up the heat.

"OK," you say. "As long as I'm using a pan, how about a Refrigerator Frittata."

"What's that?"

"Well, you need some eggs."

"I have some…"

"And then an assortment of leftovers." You smile. "Let me take a look and see."

You open the refrigerator door and peruse the shelves. You spot a small carton of Chinese leftovers, some veggies and cheese, and half of a club sandwich.

"Perfect," you say. "This usually takes about 4 minutes. It's perfect for a breakfast on the run."

"Really?" she says. "OK, I'll help."

"You don't have to," you say.

"Here," she says taking the ingredients out of your hands. "What do I do?"

"OK," you say. "First, mince the innards of that sandwich up, nice and fine."

"Mince it?" she asks incredulously.

"You wanted to help, right?"

She smiles. "OK, OK. You're the boss."

She shrugs and places the leftover sandwich on a cutting board. Meanwhile, you slice a third piece of bread. Coating each slice with a series of pats of butter, you set them on the pan. Immediately, the pieces simmer, and you quickly throw another pat on the skillet, letting it melt, before flipping each piece over. The bread is a golden brown, with crispy edges. Your mouth waters and she looks pleasantly surprised. The butter is quickly absorbed.

"You're doing great," you say. Her work is methodical. She rocks the knife over the bacon and turkey.

"This is fun," she says.

"Now, rough cut the veggies." You place a stack of vegetables on the side of the cutting board.

You move the bread to the side of the pan, then ladle in the Chinese leftovers. When she is finished, you add her ingredients together into the pan, stirring them and flipping them over for a good warm. You crack four eggs into a bowl and beat them with a fork.

"You're pretty good at this," she says.

"I like cooking," you say.

"Yes, I guess like it too." She looks up at you and smiles.

You give the ingredients another flip, then pour the eggs over the top, drenching them in a thick yellow glaze. The kitchen steams up and you stir the frittata lightly.

She pulls two large plates from her cabinet and sets them on the counter. You shut down the heat and spatula the slices onto the cutting board. With a large knife, you slice them like pizza, in small wedges. You spoon the frittata down the middle, and sprinkle some cheese for garnish.

"Presto," you say.

"I'm impressed," she says. "That was quick."

"And you've got real talent."

"Nah, just fun is all."

"Of course, your burners don't crank as many BTU's as they could."

"BTU's?"

"British Thermal Units. A really super burner does 15,000, but I like the commercial ones at 30 and 40,000. Those can cook. You can crank these bad boys out in 30 seconds a flip."

"Impressive." She smiles, and takes her plate. "Smells good."

"I like garlic and onion powder on mine. If you had some Parmesan, I would douse them with that also. That's really kicked up."

"This is fine," she says. "But if you want…"

"No, that's fine," you say, piling the other slices on your plate. You grab the pan and move it to the sink. With a quick pull of the faucet, steam shoots up from the surface. "Let's me clean this up for you. Real quick." A quick mop with a sponge and dishwashing liquid, and a rinse, and the counter looks better.

"Nice," she says. She motions for you to follow, and she steps out her front door to a cool morning. Around the side, a small yard sits behind a hedge of oleanders. She places her coffee and plate on the picnic table. "I like this time of day. Let's eat here, OK?"

"I haven't been up this time of day. Not much," you concede.

"Well, you should. It's a great time to just sit, or for me, to work."

You nod and sit next to her. She hands you a napkin, and smiles.

"*Bon appétit*," she says.

"Skol!" you say in a mock toast. "And you work every morning?"

"Well, most days." She takes a delicate bite of the Zen Bun. "This is good. Nice crunch."

You are munching and agree with stuffed cheeks. She takes a forkful of the frittata and smiles.

"It's discouraging, though," she says. "The problems of Africa are practically unsolvable. Famine, disease, corruption. They're a daily fact of life. I keep asking myself: Why bother?" She turns and looks at the sky brightening to the east. "Then I think of the faces of the children. They're stuck with a world their parents left them."

"Makes my problems look pretty puny," you say.

"The children give me hope that things can change."

"Yeah," you say.

"In your case, all you need is a little push," she says. "You're like an artist."

"Well," you say, "programming is very creative."

"Artists have long reinvented themselves. So, it's not such a foreign concept." She takes a sip of her tea. "Ever hear of Carlos Casagemas?" she asks.

"Not really," you say.

"It's a good story," she says. "Imagine Paris, the late 1890's. There was a young man, a son of a wealthy and well-established Spanish family. Carlos Casagemas. He fancied himself to be an artist. But in fact, he was a better drunk. And when he wasn't drinking, he was getting high on morphine and whatever else could be obtained. This was 1800's after all, and he had the money to do as he pleased.

"He was also in love with the wrong girl. Germaine was her name, an artist's model. He called her his *fiancé*, but that was pretty far from her understanding of what they had.

"Carlos would not even be a *blip* on our radar, not today. He would have wasted in the streets of Paris or back in his native Barcelona. There was nothing remarkable with his life.

"There are paintings of Carlos, if you look around, hanging in galleries around the world. Nowadays they command millions of dollars!"

"Wow."

"His name is bandied about. Details of his life are known.

"What made Carlos famous was his friendship," she continues, "with Pablo Picasso. The one man who changed the world of art. Have you ever seen a Picasso, I mean up close. Seen the strokes?" she asks.

You don't remember any strokes.

"Well, I mean one of his great works. They are deceptively simple. But, they are very powerful. Picasso painted in symbols."

"Kind of like coding…" you say, understanding.

"And with such range. The two of them—Carlos and Picasso—may have literally bumped into each other in a bar in the Left Bank. Both of them were Spanish, frequented the same bars, hung out in the Spanish circles.

"This was not the Picasso we know from pictures. Not the barrel-chested old man drawing on a beach next to his French villa. You've seen those pictures, right? Not the shrewd artist. No, this was the young Picasso, thin, with delicate features. Still the intense eyes. A wannabe who butchered French with a heavy Castilian accent, who pedaled copies of the latest styles. A foreigner. He looked like a fish out of water, an immigrant. This was the Picasso that was struggling. He was just another nobody trying to make a name for himself in the slums of Paris. Penniless.

"So, in one door walked Picasso, and in the other Carlos Casagemas, with the means. The next moment the two are sharing a loft in Montmartre, the dregs of Paris. Picasso had a moneyed companion and Casagemas had his ballast, someone to tell him when to stop, to tell him that all was not lost when he needed to hear it.

"Unfortunately, Casagemas was obsessed with Germaine, and could not leave her side. And of course, when she posed for other artists, he became unraveled. Meanwhile, Picasso cranked out some pretty bad stuff. Whatever was selling, whatever was in vogue, he would rip off: Delacroix, Manet, Daumier and Courbet. He was a hack."

"That's good," you say.

"Not a hacker. A hack. He did knock-offs. Yeah, they were interesting, but there were actually better painters of schlock in Paris around that time than Picasso. Meanwhile, Casagemas drifted into a deeper and deeper depression. Picasso also was running out of steam. He felt that he had not gotten any further with his art career, an astute observation.

"So, Picasso convinced Casagemas to return to Spain with him, to Màlaga. It was October 1900. Picasso had other plans to restart in Madrid. Soon after their arrival, Picasso left his friend to go to Madrid. There he was going to start an art magazine with another acquaintance. Meanwhile Casagemas grew more isolated and depressed. He wanted to be with Germaine. When Picasso did not return, he felt abandoned and returned to Paris without him.

"A few months later, Casagemas arrived at a dinner that included Germaine and other friends. He reportedly rose at the table and pulled a gun from beneath his coat. He fired at Germaine and she fell. Seeing her sprawled on the floor, he gasped and turned the gun on himself. The patrons fled and the police swarmed the restaurant. Germaine was unharmed. Casagemas was mortally wounded. He died a few hours later.

"When news reached Picasso, he was devastated. What had he done? There was blood on his hands and his dreams were overrun with images of Casagemas himself. This friend had touched his life deeply, more deeply than he had thought.

"He gave up whatever had drawn him back to Madrid, and instead he returned to Paris, to the hovel that he and Casagemas had shared. It was a hard trip and a tortured time for Picasso. The images ran from his dreams to his canvasses. And something amazing happened. Emotions for which he had no language found their way onto his brush. The paintings came alive and he dropped whatever pretenses he had. He no longer thought about *art* or what was good or bad. He just let everything flow into his paintings."

She looks up.

"An amazing guy," you say.

"Yes," she says with a small smile, "Symbols emerged. A language developed. He was changed. His personality and much about him shifted.

"When things lifted, everything was different about him, his canvas, his colors. He mainlined coffee until his eyes turned yellow."

You nod in admiration at this.

"He became relentless. This is what we see in pictures. Not someone who wanted to succeed anyway he could. But someone who was passionate about his art.

"In the space of two months, he produced 20 canvasses. All of this energy and vitality was released. He even took up with Germaine. Instead of pulling away, Picasso allowed himself to be pulled into a very powerful torrent of emotion. His friend's death was all around him. His paintings were haunted. He painted Casagemas in his casket surrounded by powerful emotional symbols. Something had been unleashed. And the art circles in Paris took notice."

She smiles and looks mournful. "I think we each have a Carlos and a Picasso inside. I think we struggle with giving it all up. Or, changing ourselves completely."

You think about this as she finishes the last of her frittata.

"I'd better be going," you say.

"OK," she says. "And thanks for the breakfast."

"Thank you." You smile. "It was fun."

She smiles. "See you at work." She pats you on the hand, then stands and gathers the plates, motioning for you to do the same.

You get into your car and back out the alley.

In the early morning glow, the streets have a dusty film. Lights turn yellow as you approach, and you slow down to wait patiently, red to green. Your car instinctively drifts toward Second Avenue like a homing pigeon. Up Stone Avenue, then across the tracks and down a small alleyway. When you turn onto Second, you slow as you reach the row of storefronts. Cartons and papers blow up on the sidewalk. There you stare up at your apartment, lights on as if someone new has moved in already, its brown stucco shedding white patches. Curtains flip loosely in from the windows that overlook the street. Downstairs you see Vermette moving behind the counter, carrying a box down the galley. The lights inside his diner are still dim. You pull up to the next traffic light, then a quick left turn down the back street, and you park in the back lot behind the diner. Vermette is standing over a broken garbage bag in his diner whites, smoking.

"Fricking dogs," he says, wheezing, lifting a split garbage bag as you get out of the car. He doesn't look up as you approach. "Knocked over the cans and rifled through damn everything." Some toast, gravy and half-eaten meatloaf peek out of the bag.

Vermette drops the bag on the ground and heads into the storage closet for a new one. You follow him in. He takes a long drag on his cigarette and, pulling it from his lip, tosses the ashes into the metal sink close by. Dishes are stacked on the sideboard. Shelves overhead are full of cans, paper towel rolls, and stacks of industrial napkins. The small back room smells of ammonia and grease.

"It's not Sunday," he says. His face is not much more than wrinkled skin hung from the bone. "You're screwed around."

"Yes, I guess," you say, leaning against the door jam. "Thought you could use the help."

"Never refuse." There is an inkling of a smile forming, but it is wiped clean as he lugs out a box. His diner whites are stiffly starched and creased like a military uniform.

As he lowers the ripped bag into a brand new one, you tie it off with a quick knot. Parking the cigarette on the sill, he bangs the screen door and trudges out to the back lot. It is already hot and sticky, and you immediately regret coming.

The diner came with the four upstairs apartments when Vermette bought it. He'd scraped together the money from trucking and an SBA loan. It's his retirement business. For a while, Vermette lived in one of the apartments, but when the neighborhood became too dilapidated and noisy, he moved out, opting to drive the few miles each morning to get his griddles going. Most days he is behind the counter by 6 a.m. Twice a week, he closes early and goes for dialysis at the VA. Sunday is his day off, and the day you usually don your whites for reduced rent and tips. He throws in free coffee in the mornings if you sit at the counter and order more than toast.

"You open yet?" he barks when he returns, retrieving his cigarette and inhaling another long drag, his eyes registering the damage.

"Just firing them up now," you say and walk to the front of the diner to start up the grills. From the freezer, you pull two frozen bags of hash browns, cellophaned bacon, flats of eggs and a couple of large cans of ground generic coffee.

As the grills heat up, you take a long knife from a drawer and cut through the first bag of potatoes. You stand at your favorite spot in the diner, a large, three-foot chunk of iron, caked with burnt grease and grime. At the front is a grease trough, with two long spatulas slung inside, handles pointing in your direction. Splash guards surround three sides, and a large whirling exhaust spins noisily overhead like a helicopter. You scrape down the deck, poking at burnt meat, sesame seeds, rice, pits and who knows what else. With a squirt bottle, you lube down the left side and dump half the bag up to the splash guard. The potatoes sizzle and you tweak back the heat. You shape the mass into a flattened mountain, much like Richard Dreyfuss in *Close Encounters of the Third Kind*, squaring up the corners and scooping a couple of stray handfuls from near the trough. These go on top. You shake some salt and pepper on it, then check the clock. There is still plenty of time, and Vermette has disappeared.

You heft a large mound of coffee into a new filter, and although it is double the mandated amount, you are beginning to feel slow, and need a good boost. You empty yesterday's slosh from the carafe and scrub it clean.

There is a row of knives slotted along the wood cutting bowl, old dull ones with heavy tangs and bent points. You slide the cellophaned bacon across the cutting board, then try without much

Jenz Johnson

success to slice it down the middle. It finally opens to a neat array of fatty slices, which you scoop onto the griddle. From the refrigerator, you unfold a chunk of margarine and smear it into an old Marine steel mug. This is placed near the potatoes to melt.

"Your apron and hat, kid!" Vermette shouts from the kitchen.

You wander back to retrieve it and find him on a stool, hands on his knees, smoke floating up into his eyes, looking a little piqued.

"You're not AWOL, are you?" he asks.

"Nah, just thought I'd put in some hours."

"Need a little extra cash?" he asks.

"It wouldn't hurt. Just got laid off."

He takes a drag and studies your face.

"That was quick," he says. He lets the smoke trail up in front of his eyes. "Let's shake a leg, then."

You wipe the sweat from your forehead and a few beads sizzle on the grill as you pass by. You grab an old sponge and proceed to squeegee down the tables and chairs, and the long counter. You scrub it until the counters shine. Vermette pokes his head out and gives it a quick inspection. He juts his chin at a spot you missed. You swab this quickly, then swing the *CLOSED* sign to *OPEN* and unlock the door.

From the small fridge under the counter, you take out a half-gallon of milk and mix it with an industrial pancake mix. You shake a large viscous portion of mix into the pitcher from a carton, then stir in some milk by approximation, lifting the spoon up to show Vermette (who is now watching) the drip. He waves the smoke from the back room. This you interpret as OK, and put the lid on. The mix is looking pretty gray, so you shake in a little Yellow Number 3 that Vermette keeps under the counter for this purpose. The bread is in place, and you plug in the waffle iron, setting it to low. Then you fetch the juice pitchers and put them into the fridge.

Most of this you do automatically, although you are more careful with Vermette in back. Most Sundays, he is mostly napping. You notice new spackle in the cracks of some of the tables. The parking lot looks raked of the odd trash that blew in. He has been sprucing up the place, although the coolers still rattle and the air is wet more than cool.

Vermette's regulars continue to come back. They love the food more for the quantity than anything else. He always heaps on the sides. Giant mounds of potatoes, lots of refills, piles of pancakes and toast. They don't mind waiting when you get behind, but if the refills aren't forthcoming, they boil over.

You pop more bread into the toaster and quickly create a stack for later.

The cowbell on the door knob jingles and old Grady, a regular, waddles up to the counter in his overalls. He motions a crooked finger to indicate he wants his coffee even before he reaches his spot. Behind him, another older man edges in with a cane and precariously mounts another one of the stools at the counter.

"What are you smiling about?" Grady asks.

You pour him a cup.

"Vermette's in back," you say.

"Screw 'im" he replies and takes a loud sip from his cup and frowns. "Any fresh joe?" He rejects the cup and pushes it toward you.

"That's it," you say.

"Swill," he pronounces and pulls the mug toward himself. "Hey, it's Tuesday. What the hell you doing here?"

You shrug.

When you return to the grill, the hash brown have stuck. You pry them off, and find solid black bottoms with an undercooked middle, still cold to the touch. So, you chop them together, using two spatulas and the squirt bottle. The bacon, meanwhile, looks about the same pale color and is cold. You pour the melted margarine into a squirt bottle. The grill is turned up, but nothing seems to be happening, so you decide to reverse out the hash browns with the bacon, pushing the mountain of potatoes along the grease trough, while nudging the bacon to the hot portion. By the end of the maneuver, both sides are looking about the same, sort of a "bacon browns." The bacon has sticky pieces of hash browns and the hash browns have uncooked bits of bacon. These will look better after more grill time.

Grady continues to sip and inspect your work.

A couple dressed in turbans and white clothes come in with book bags, the man in a light beige sweater with white pants, the woman in a white turban and flowing sari. Both of them wear Birkies and shuffle slowly through the glass door.

"Damn hippies," Grady says, loud enough to be heard.

The wife looks at the man who smiles and motions to a table in back.

You bring them menus and water.

"Coffee?" you ask as they settle in, adjusting their clothes to keep them off the floor. The table rocks from side to side.

"Do you have herb tea?" the woman asks. "Nothing with peppermint or rosehips."

"I'm afraid not," you say. "I can get you some hot water and lemon."

She indicates that would do.

"Coffee'll put hair on your chest, sonny," Grady says from the front.

"Don't mind him," you say.

The man in the turban runs his fingers through his beard examining the menu.

"Fricking hippies," Grady continues to mumble.

"I'll come back," you say, hearing the pancakes stop bubbling from across the counter.

The bacon browns look better and you give them another stir to blend in the burnt chunks.

The pancakes are square when you slide them on the plate, and the hash has gotten into everything now, with little burnt pieces poking out of the pancakes. You dollop syrup over the top, and squirt some ketchup on the hash browns to hide the bacon. A leaf of lettuce down the middle for garnish and camouflage and it looks deliverable.

You plunk it in front of the old timer with a bottle of hot sauce and refill his cup, sliding a setting and the napkin dispenser closer to him.

He studies the plate, assessing the portions and placement.

"Normally don't look this way," he says.

"Toast?" you ask, and he shakes his head. You return to the turbaned couple.

"Let's see," the bearded man says. "No wheat toast, no eggbeaters, no fruit?"

"Nope, nope and fruit cocktail," you say.

He smiles and considers the options.

"How about some oatmeal?" the woman asks.

"Can't vouch for the eat-by date," you say.

She looks concerned and swallows.

"It should be OK," she says quietly. "With some honey, if you have some."

"I think I can scrounge some up."

The front door opens and a threesome walks in chuckling. Local businessmen in bolo ties. They are acting rowdy and have take-out coffee in hand.

"OK, then," the turbaned man says. "Let's make it one pancake, toast, juice and that fruit cocktail."

"I'm not sure about the cocktail either," you say. "The can is pretty rusty, and so is the can-opener."

"So, let's skip the fruit cocktail. Any other fruit?"

"Lemons. And I suppose, ketchup, technically speaking. Tomatoes are fruit. I could try to throw something together."

He declines quickly, and you hustle back to the grill, tucking the order into the metal bar above it.

The squat one of the threesome signals for menus and coffee, and you quickly grab menus and coffee after rummaging in a cabinet for the oatmeal. There is a faded box and you pry off the top. Inside, it looks like sawdust.

"Two regulars, one unleaded," he says when you appear at the table. "What's the specials?"

"No special," you say. They probably do this each time they come in, since Vermette puts a NO SPECIALS! sign on each table, along with the NO SUBSTITUTIONS. The words are underlined and in a bold marker. They smile.

"Never are," he says and cracks a big smile.

"But," you continue, seizing the moment. "I'll make you one of my favorites."

He looks up rather surprised.

"You're new here," he says.

"I'm mostly in on Sundays. But I'm not sure it will be one of your favorites."

They look at each other.

"It's a Breakfast Tourniquet."

They squint, as if in pain.

"Should we ask what is in it?"

"Well," you begin checking to see if Vermette is in earshot, "you start with a couple of burgers and dry pancake mix..."

"Has anyone actually survived?" another businessman says looking worried.

"I'd have to leave out the pork rinds and corn nuts though. We barely stock what we need."

They hold up their hands and you stop.

"OK. We get the picture. I'll have your Number 2."

"Make that two, mine with pancakes and whipped cream. That's not a substitution is it?"

"No, not technically. But we're out of whipped cream," you say. "I can whip something else up, like lard or mayo. But frankly, it might change the complexion…"

"Never mind. Let's just stick with nothing."

"No. 2 for me," the other one says.

"That's three," you say.

They dress like car dealers, in plaid shirts, jeans with snaps on them and cowboy boots. There is a church up the street, so they may be part of the staff. Usually the church members did not wander down this far though. They would go to Stone or Speedway.

You pour the coffee and top off Grady's cup. He grunts, his head still close to his plate. He is having a hard time swallowing, and you wonder if the mix was too thick on the pancakes. You pull a mixing bowl from a shelf and practice cracking eggs with one hand and get about two in without shells. You find most of the shells.

The woman gazes across the street as you deliver the juices and toast. She starts as if you've caught her doing something wrong. "Waiting for the co-op?" you ask.

"We couldn't hold out this morning," the woman says and stares down at the toast slices, which have shrunken into parallelograms. She has a wisp of curly red hair that peeks out from under her turban. When she realizes what she has said, she starts to explain. "I mean, it smelled good."

"Convenience is nine-tenths of a good meal," you say.

There is a strange sound, and you retrieve the oatmeal before it smokes too much. You scrape it into a soup bowl and press the lumps out with a fork. You find some bread crumbs and sprinkle them on top to cover up some of the burnt spots. You find a couple single-serving packets of honey in a box of plastic forks and place them alongside the bowl.

You deliver the oatmeal to the woman.

"Thanks," she says looking down. As she continues to inspect her meal, you quietly move back to the counter.

The cowbell rings, and two coeds and an old man wander in, as if lost. They look around, waiting for a hostess to seat them until you motion them to one of the more stable tables. The old man shuffles to the counter and grunts to his cohorts. The coeds look up from their gabbing, then shuffle in their flip-flops to a table near the window. You know they will have trouble with that table, since the stem of the table always seems to loosen up and rock.

"Damn tarts!" Grady mumbles and pushes his plate closer as if to protect it.

"You have some coffee here?" the old man asks.

"Yes sir," you say, coming around the counter.

"I'll take that. Some griddle cakes, too. Make them big. And biscuits, do you have biscuits?"

"No, just toast. Or English muffins."

"Nah, then just the griddle cakes, OK? Make them big, you hear. Don't chintz on me."

The girls lean over the table, then laugh as you come over. They are wearing short tops and low-rise jeans with belts, almost matching. They have deep brown tans and smell of flowery perfume. They look like sisters, one blond, the other with jet black hair.

You hand them a couple of menus and place a couple of glasses of water on their table.

"You have bagels?" one asks.

"No, just toast," you say.

"But there's bagels right across the street, at the co-op," she says.

"They're not open," you say. "We have English muffins though. I have to defrost them."

She shakes her head.

"What about yogurt?" the other one asks.

You say, "Sorry," and hear the old man call you.

"What is this place?" she says to her friend and rolls her eyes. "Blueberry Muffins?"

You shake your head, and they don't look up.

"Or smoothies? My god."

They turn the menus over and scrutinize them.

"Can you come back?" one says.

"Or we can wait for the co-op?" one says.

"What about granola?" the other says, rubbing her nails. You notice her nails have small pictures painted on them. There is an ocean on one, or maybe a barn, it is hard to tell.

She catches you looking down, then leans back as if you are looking down her top.

"I could put together some granola," you say hastily.

"Really?" she says. "OK. And some pineapple juice."

She hands back the menu.

"Just orange or apple," you say.

"What about cranberry?"

"Orange or apple," you repeat.

"Grapefruit?"

You shake your head.

"All right," she says. She reaches down for her purse, which is on the floor.

"Which one?"

"Apple."

"And I will have the orange juice," the other says. "And the country-fried steak and eggs."

"What?" the blonde says looking up wide-eyed. "Are you crazy?"

"What does that come with?"

"The Number 9 comes with hash browns, pancakes, and toast. Or you can have grits."

"You have to be kidding," the other says shocked.

"I'm famished," her friend explains. "Besides I'm going on a liquid fast this week. Just juice and Coke. Maybe beer with Luke if we want to get crazy."

"You are out of your mind, girl," the other says. She looks up at you in disbelief.

On your way to the grills, Vermette motions to you.

"So," he says. "You going to have next month's rent on time?"

"I should," you say.

"Layoff's not a problem, then?"

"Well, just unsettling. But I'll start looking for another job soon."

He lights another cigarette, and you look back in the diner.

"You can put in some more hours here. If you want. Earn a little more cash. Those hippies tip well."

"Well, I don't know."

"The place is getting too much for me to handle," he says. "I suppose I could come up with something steady. Ever thought about that?"

"I got to get back," you say.

"Hey, kid," he says. "You OK?"

You shrug but are more worried about making granola without Vermette finding out about it. He hates caving in to the customers and especially loathes special requests.

"Hey, you're young. Don't look so worried."

"I got to get back," you say.

"... Can't be worse than Nam or paying fricking alimony." He shakes his head sullenly.

"I'm just a little unsettled," you say. "Have to sort things out."

"Hey, you'll bounce back. Look at me. Down to one kidney, no lungs to speak of, and I'm still kicking." He lets out a big wheeze. Smoke spews out like an exhaust pipe, and he doubles over on his chair and continues to hack without breathing. As he gives you the go-on-back sign, his shoulders bouncing up and down, the old men at the counter lean forward to see what is happening.

You wipe off a drinking glass and fill it with water from the sink.

"I'm OK, kid," he says, still hunched over. He catches his breath and slowly raises up, retrieving his butt gingerly from the floor.

"I should be getting back," you say. "Got a Number 9 to do." No one orders the Number 9. You open up the back freezer and he begins coughing again from the blast of cold air that streams out. Inside you rummage around for the box of chicken-fried steaks. They're a couple of them left next to a half-carved turkey carcass.

"A Number 9?" he says, his spirits brightening.

"Are these any good?" you ask, showing the ice-covered steaks.

He waves you on. "Make sure you put enough on the plate."

You carry the chicken-fried steak out, still steaming from the cold, and Grady looks at it as though it was something Vermette had coughed up.

"I'll be damned," he says.

"Hey, what about my pancakes?" the other old man asks.

You make a round of refills. The coeds are exchanging digital cameras across the table, pictures of them dancing in a nightclub, a couple of pictures of them in bikinis with beers in their hands. They laugh.

"Oh my god," they say over and over.

You quickly scrape down the grill, making as much space as you can, then squirt it with margarine. Granola, you think. That's just oats and nuts. You place the chicken-fried steak near the bacon and retrieve the box of oatmeal, shaking a small mound onto the grill. You add some grits and chop up some peanuts. You look at it, and it doesn't seem to transform into granola very quickly. You give it a squirt, then look around. There is a bottle of fake Maple syrup and you pour some over the top, then toss it. A splash of soy sauce for color. A shake of salt and pepper. Some sugar.

The steak begins to smoke, and you pour two large pancakes on the grill. They bleed over to the bacon, and you stop the leak with your spatula. You toss things around.

"Hey," the old man says from the counter. "Can I change my griddle cakes?"

"What's that smell?" Grady says.

Vermette motions you back.

"When you have time kid," he says, recovered, "you can mop down the latrine? I couldn't get to it last week." You eye the door to the bathroom.

"OK," you say. "But I got to get back."

"Hey," he continues without listening to you, "The Marines are looking. Ever thought about enlisting?"

"Not really."

"Got a buddy who could get you into Camp Lejeune," he says.

"I thought everyone gets into Camp Lejeune."

"But the nicer barracks," he says nodding. "The ones away from the older latrines."

You find the "granola" has darkened considerably and scoop it into a bowl. You fill a creamer with milk, and decorate the side with a lemon slice. The breading on the chicken-fried steak has cracks in it, but otherwise it looks OK. You heap the potatoes and toast and retrieve the pancakes.

The coeds look at the plates in astonishment.

"What is this?" the blonde asks. "This granola looks fried!"

"Fresh granola," you explain.

"I didn't want *fresh* granola. And it smells like bacon. And there's bits of something in there. My god. I wanted the other kind, the French Vanilla like they have at the co-op. Don't you have that? "

The plates are starting to feel heavy on your arm.

"That chicken steak looks like fucking concrete," the other coed says. "And there's bacon scum all over it."

"That's how we make it. Country style."

"That's not country style," she objects.

"No way," she says. "We're not eating this shit."

"Veronica, let's just go."

"It's our Number 9," you say. "Our most popular item."

"Let's get out of here," she says.

Everyone is now looking around.

"Damn whores," Grady says.

"I want to change my order."

"Me too," the other one says, and your arms are about to give. They keep their elbows on the table, refusing to take the plates.

"Change mine to the yogurt," she says.

"Yeah, me too," the other chimes in.

You arms are shaking now.

"We don't have yogurt," you remind them.

"Then, get some bagels. What kind of place is this?" she says. "This is ridiculous."

They are suddenly quiet, looking over your shoulder. Your shoulder is tapped, and when you turn around, it is Vermette, white hat in place, cigarette on his lip. His eyes are resolute.

"You order a Number 9?" he asks, lifting the plate from your arm. Steam lifts off and filters in their direction.

The blonde straightens up.

"It looks gross," the other says, but he slides it in front of her, moving the ketchup closer.

"It goes good with ketchup," he says.

"And you?" he says. He stares at her through smoke trailing up from his cigarette.

She freezes.

"You ordered..." and he looks at the bowl of hot makeshift granola. For a minute, there is a flicker of doubt in his face. For a brief microsecond, your eyes meet. But you see that he will not retreat and will keep his ground under heavy fire. You see the swamps in Nam, his troops gathered in the jungle, waiting for his order. You are part of his platoon and he has steeled you and the other men for battle.

He blinks and is again looking at the steaming dish, which is not on the menu.

"You ordered...," he says as he slides the steaming bowl in front of her, "this."

She looks down.

He slaps down the bill on the table.

"Enjoy your meal," he says, about-faces and walks to his stool in back.

The room steals peeks at the two coeds who have gathered up their forks slowly.

"Fricking crack heads," Grady intones under his breath.

14. granola

"By the time we've made it, we've had it."
—*Malcolm Forbes*

What in the hell was that?" Vermette asks when you come back to retrieve more potatoes from the freezer. The back room is filled with smoke, and he sits near the metal sink, cigarette shaking in his fingers. He is breathing hard.

"What?" you ask.

"Grilled Oatmeal?"

"Granola, actually."

"Gran-what?"

"Granola, it's popular now."

"Looked liked grilled oatmeal." He takes a long drag and looks at you with an icy glare, letting out a short cough.

"Maybe so," you decide. You wipe your hands on your apron and try to stand still, but you are wobbling from foot to foot. "With some grits and nuts."

He shakes his head in disappointment. "My C rations looked better," he says. "What are you trying to do here?"

You shrug.

"You know there's no specials," he says. "And you burned half the chicken-fried steak." He leans forward with a glare that demands the truth. He looks tired and disappointed, but more than anything else, he looks at you as if you have betrayed a code of honor.

You have no defense and look about the room. "The other half looked OK though," you say.

He takes a long drag and puts a clipboard with papers up on the steel counter. "Half doesn't cut it," he says coldly. "You can do better."

"I know," you say.

"You should be moving the hash browns after 15 minutes, and wiping down the grill on the hour. Your eggs are all mixed with burnt bits. And when did you start making bacon on the same side as the eggs?"

"What side am I supposed to make them on?"

"Jeez, kid. It's got to work like clockwork. Bus those tables when you deliver the bills, and wipe them down when they leave."

"I just got a little behind, is all. Normally, I would."

"And I mean, you are out there making specials. I bet you did substitutions too."

"Technically, no," you say. "Not substitutions. *Per se.*"

"Shit," he says. "That's disappointing, really disappointing. It's a steam-roller, kid. Once it gets started, there's no stopping it. Next thing you know, you will have English muffins instead of toast, or cottage cheese instead of hash browns."

You avoid his stare.

"We'd be just another fricking Denny's," he says. He squashes a beetle that was waddling across the floor. "How would we be any different?" he asks.

"More customers?" you volunteer.

"Who gives a rat's ass?," he says. "We'd be whoring ourselves, kid. That's what we would be doing, letting the riffraff determine our menu. Sure these civilians would love to have sandwiches in the morning, or a slice of pie. Their lives are undisciplined, and they squander whatever pride they have in themselves when they start down this road. This isn't an amusement park. They eat the grub we serve them, and it will stick to their ribs."

You remain quiet.

"Next thing you know, we'd have daily specials and lord knows what else."

He's breathing hard.

"That's not what I want," he says. "That's not what I planned."

There is a long silence.

"I'm talking about discipline. You have to stand up to them, kid. Sure they're going to ask you all kinds of stuff. They're going to try to bend you to their ways. But you have to resist. You have to stick to what you know is right. You've got to draw the line."

He finishes off his cigarette, a long ash balancing on the end.

"The country is just falling apart," he continues. "No rules. No one cares. People live their lives as if it will go on forever, and that they don't need rules or discipline. No offense intended, kid."

"None taken," you say.

"It's not the substitutions that bug me, kid. It's everything that it represents, the looseness, the lack of backbone. Everything willy-nilly."

He is winded.

"I better get back. I think I smell the waffles," you say.

"The point is that you got to stick to your guns. You have to do one thing well. If it's making omelets, then make omelets. If it's buttering toast, then butter toast. You see my point?"

You hesitate.

"Not quite," you say honestly.

"You got to find what you're good at, that's what I'm saying. If it's making that grilled oatmeal, well..." He hesitates. "Never mind. Get the fricking hell back in there."

When you return, the grill is smoking and the last of the customers leave coughing. You prop the front door wide open, and wave the smoke out with your apron. When the diner is aired out, you clear the tables. Few have left tips.

"This I conceive to be the chemical function of humor: to change the character of our thought."
—*Lin Yutang*

Dogs are sniffing around the garbage as you head toward your car. Next to it, two pigeons are courting and flapping their wings on the rusty roof of Vermette's pickup.

"Hey, no hello?" a hoarse voice asks.

You see your neighbor. He is squatting over a mirror outside the utility shed. He has a plastic box of potatoes at his feet, most likely from Vermette. He is in his sixties, and his deeply tanned face is full of wrinkles. He is cleanly dressed in an old sports coat and khakis, with a shock of white hair combed straight back. He carefully shaves the gray stubble from his neck, dunking the razor into a paper cup of water.

"Can't really talk now, Dino. I'm late as it is."

"Hey, 201, you're always late," he says, calling you by your apartment number. He takes a couple more strokes, lifting his chin and turning his face sideways.

"Hey pull up a chair," he says.

He rents the utility shed from Vermette for a very small amount each month, although Vermette suspects he's sitting on a motherload of cash.

"Can't," you say.

He laughs. "No job's that important. I can tell you that first hand."

"Yeah, thanks. I'll remember that for my last two weeks."

"Last two weeks, eh? They got tired of you that soon? Hey, no *problemo*, guy. It eventually happens to all of us. So, join the club."

"No thanks. Not just yet." You look around. There is a small portable stove, some plastic containers with leftovers, a newspaper. He sits back on his lawn chair.

"OK, suit yourself." He finishes his shaving, inspecting his face in the mirror and nodding with approval. With his towel, he wipes the soap off his ears, and smoothes back his hair with a comb. If we weren't sitting in front of a disheveled shed, he would look distinguished.

"Stay out of the technology sector, if you want my advice."

"I'll do that," you say.

"The fundamentals just don't have a lot going for them. Plus the yield curve is inverted. That's not good news."

"OK," you say struggling.

He nods to the containers near his stove.

"What do you call this stuff?"

"It's granola," you say. You recognize some of your concoctions from earlier this morning. Dino is probably the only enthusiastic diner the entire day.

"Tasted more like Grilled Oatmeal," he says with a smile. "It was dynamite. Very creative. Hey, listen, you heading off now?"

"Yep."

"Would you mind dropping me at the park? We're doing a potluck around noon."

"Yeah, OK."

He dumps the basin of water and brushes himself off.

"This will take just a second," he says. He quickly gets up and cleans off his plate into a garbage bag with his paper cup. He sets his basin and small camping stove inside the hut. He rolls a bag tightly and fastens it to the bottom of his backpack. It looks like he is ready for a mountain expedition.

"There," he says. He stuffs the paper in his shed and grabs a box and another garbage bag. "The key is traveling light. Great morning, huh? Not too hot…"

He lopes behind you, looking about. His water bottle sloshes with each step.

"What a car! This one's a classic," he says when you arrive at your car. It's coated with dust and has a bent hood. "You know, I do car washes. I spruce up the old man's truck from time to time."

"I've got another month or two before it really needs it."

"It would really buff up nice."

You unlock the car and he throws his pack in the back seat, then climbs in the passenger side. His feet move a stack of old wrappers to the side.

"Nice interior," he says.

"You know," you say off-hand, "you could take a bus."

"I do. But let's keep our environment in mind. You know that our country leads in carbon emissions. We can all do our part to cut our carbon footprint. I'm doing mine." He smiles.

On the road, he offers you a stick of gum that you decline. The morning traffic is thick, and even though there is barely a breeze coming in, he leans toward the window, letting the wind ruffle his white hair, his cheap cologne filling the car. He closes his eyes to enjoy the moment.

"Sure beats Chicago," he says. "It would be hot right about now."

"Well, it's pretty hot about now *here*."

"Yeah, but I mean Chicago's hot and humid. This is dry heat."

"So I've heard."

"I love the winters though. That really makes it all worth it, don't you think?"

"I wouldn't know."

The park is up the street, a real hang out for transients. Although your work is in the opposite direction, you turn north and find yourself at a standstill.

"You don't smell that great, guy."

"It hasn't been the best of days," you repeat.

"Yeah, I'm just getting a whiff of it now. Whew!" He holds his nose with a smile.

"But it's going to change soon," you say.

"Well, hopefully soon, because you aren't going to get many dates with that aroma."

It would have little impact at this point, you think.

"Still doing the computer stuff, as I remember?"

"Yep."

"Well, you're cooking isn't half bad. Actually, it *is* half bad, but the other half is pretty good. When it's not burnt."

"Hey, do you mind?"

"Yeah, well, I'm just saying. You have other talents."

"Tell that to my boss. He's on my case."

"Well, no job's worth all the grief if you ask me."

"I'll make a mental note of that."

"I say, get out while the getting is good. No amount of promotions is worth it. Anyway, you can find something else."

"I guess," you say.

"Not like me. My field was tough." He looks out the window. "Not a big demand for paste-up. Not these days. Linotype, ever hear of it?"

You draw a blank.

"Well," he continues. "No one has."

"What's that? Like mimeograph?"

"That's old technology too." He laughs. "Nope, linotype was the latest and greatest in my day. Fresh out of the high school, I learned from the best. My father. They were just making the move from hot type to cold type."

"Cold type?"

"Yep. It was good money for a while. My father went kicking and screaming down the tubes when they tried to bring in cold-type. Printers loved hot type."

"It was hot?"

"Oh yeah. Remember, newspapers used to run off of these large presses with rack after rack of type that was set by hand. Hot type was set with molten lead. The presses banged down pretty hard on those plates, so the type had to be encased. My father could crank it out. He did the whole enchilada. He'd set the slug by hand, hyphenation, patterning, page formats, leading—the whole deal. And you had to work backwards too! Each letter was shoved into place from right to left. Then you had to count up the points and put spacers at the end of your line. And then before you went onto the next line, you put another spacer between the lines. That's how leading got its name, from the lead spacers between lines."

"Really? Sounds like a lot of work."

"He read backwards better than he could forwards. But when the big guys started moving in the cold-type machines, his days were numbered. They said they needed it for the ads. You know, quick turn-around, last-minute changes. He saw the writing on the wall. He grew up around the grime and smoke of the composing rooms. He wasn't about to sit around with a bunch of women, take a pay cut and make paper dolls. That's what he called them, *paper dolls*. I couldn't imagine him with a scissors and a bottle of rubber cement. His fingers looked like sausages, fat and always grimy. So, he took an early retirement when it was offered. He made out all right."

"And you?"

"I hung in there a while. I had the fingers for the paste up. Well, I was his protégé at the paper, but no one figured the phototypesetting was going to bite the dust in three years. But it did.

You could set twice as much as the hot type, plus you had the ability to correct mistakes without breaking the slug. Didn't have to read backwards either, like you did on hot type. It was a sweet future."

"Until...?"

"Computers, my friend. Phototypesetting was the rage, then computerized typesetting. No paste up required. The computer was doing it all. Hyphenation, all the fonts, symbols out the kazoo. Pretty soon, there was no place for me. From the editor's desk to the new offset presses. Eliminated a whole bunch of us. The rest is history."

He looks around.

"Anyway, my prior life. Ben Franklin apprenticed as a typesetter, you know. A number of great men started as typesetters."

"Aren't you in the wrong century?"

"Well, 201, you don't find out until it's too late."

"That's why they invented calendars, so you know what century you're in..."

"Touché!" He laughs. "Anyway, it was my family's trade. Of course, it would have been nice to have a pension. But, hey, you don't need much. The markets have been good to me. I watch what I spend, so you know, I'm doing fine. I always loved the outdoors, so for me, it's perfect. I love my retirement."

He stretches back and leans his head out the window. The morning traffic is slow, but Dino still enjoys the hint of the breeze.

"Hey we're here, guy," he says. "This is close enough."

He reaches his hand over.

"So, anyway, I got to go," he says. "Remember, you got a gift, my friend, I can tell you that. Your grub's better than those fancy-pants restaurants. Your stuff, though, it is pretty sly, 'cause it's got some real subtext to it."

He nods appreciatively.

"Don't find that stuff in most dumpsters, you know."

He waves out the window. In the distance, a couple of bearded vagrants are smoking and look up.

"Much obliged," he says. "Hey why not come over to the park. The guys would get a kick meeting you. You're known as Mr. Sunday. You cook our Sunday brunches, indirectly, at least the stuff that Vermette will let me haul away."

"Nah, I better not."

"OK, catch you later. I got to enjoy my golden years. Great day, huh?"

He holds your gaze, shaking your hand.

"Great," you say, reaching into a pocket for a couple of dollars.

"Nah, just let me know when you want this classic of yours washed. Besides, you've done enough with the ride and all."

He turns and walks toward the park bench, a couple of men hooting when they see he's bringing food.

"I have measured out my life with coffee spoons."
—T. S. Eliot

Y ou realize when Dino closes the door that he is right. You don't really care all that much about going in to work. Your car starts up sluggishly, as if voicing its reluctance. Suddenly, you are on auto-pilot. You let the car go where it wants, along the backstreets.

You pull into a parking space a few spaces down from a small storefront. The sign says *Dojo Espresso*. When you walk in, a small bell rings from the glass door. Mats are piled up along the wall. The air has a pleasant scent of incense mixed with coffee. Overhead is a small banner with Japanese characters.

"Shoes, please!" says a voice.

You look down to see a neat row of tennis shoes, sandals and huaraches. Next to them, there is a bamboo shoe horn. You use it to remove your muddy shoes and place them next to the others.

There is laughter, and you wander behind a divider to a small espresso bar where three young men dressed in their martial arts outfits are sipping coffee and joking with one another.

"Is Alex here?" you ask.

"Yeah, but he's on the can, dude," one of them says. "You aren't here for lessons, are you? Because the new ones don't start until tomorrow."

"Not really," you say. "Just dropped by to see Alex."

"OK, well, then grab a seat. I'll fix you a shot. You a friend?"

"Sort of."

"Well, that's close enough for me. Why don't you come around the counter here and plunk down. I'm Tony."

He reaches out a hand.

"Nice to meet you."

"Take a good look at these," he says, pointing to large canvas sacks of coffee beans. "Just arrived."

"Incredible," chimes in his buddy.

"From Kona."

"Well," you say. "A latte sounds pretty good."

"A latte?" he smiles.

"With a double shot," you say.

"Now, may I make a suggestion here?" he asks as the eyes around the bar settle on you. "Latte's are really not the way to go, dude."

"No?"

"No. I mean it's nice for breakfast and all. And with a double shot, it's got a nice buzz on it, I wouldn't argue with you," he says. "But with the primo roast that we have here, you need to try an espresso. Most Italians never put milk in any coffee after breakfast, because there's no need. The espresso says it all. It's such a big earthy flavor with a nice kick."

"An espresso?"

"Yes. You see, the aroma and the crema are everything and if you mask it with milk, it's like putting ice in your beer. You lose it all."

"OK," you say. "I'll have an espresso then."

"Great."

He grinds up a small batch and scoops it into his basket.

"This is called tamping a puck and it is really an art form in itself. Did you see how I pressed it gently? But you will notice that the grind sits perfectly even with the top here in a nice level tamp."

He shows his creation.

"This is so that there is an even brew when the scalding water is forced through. Now, I can tamp it harder to give you a stronger brew. But, I usually go with a medium tamp."

He runs a demitasse under a stream of hot water from the sink.

"And the portafilter—that's this basket that carries your puck— fits up into the grouphead here." He twists the coffee in. "Now we force down a blast of water at around 200 degrees Fahrenheit. Anything cooler is going to add too much bitterness. Unlike a normal brew, you only get about 70 percent of the caffeine, but the nice part is there are no soluble acids. That's what gives it its smooth taste, if it's done right. No sour taste from the acid."

"70 percent?" You are surprised. "That's because of the smaller cup, right?"

"Mostly, although they use more Robusta in espresso and that has less caffeine ounce for ounce."

He holds up the portafilter so that you can take a look inside. The grind sits even with the top like devil's food cake.

"See how the grind sort of sticks together. The oil is released in the grinding to form minute little passageways through the puck. Think of them as small little canals running through the coffee grounds. When the water is forced through, it weaves around the canals lifting off the oils and filling the brew with flavor and texture."

You nod at this.

"Of course, the roast is by far the most important element at play. You have to start with the right beans. Alex has his own stash of *Arabica*, that he gets straight from the island. The plants are cared for meticulously, trimmed regularly, the new flowers plucked before they can overload the plant. This is after about seven years because they don't produce berries until then."

You notice a large canvas bag of beans behind the counter.

"Primo stuff," one of his buddies chimes in.

"Alex had a grower that was stepping on product with some Robusta, but that didn't last long. A nose like Alex can discern the TCA from 50 feet away. Alex calls it the Rio punch, since Brazil floods the market with this crap. So you have to find the right supplier."

He surveys the different bags, each stamped in black with names and countries.

"The beans are everything. I'm not saying the roast is not important. But without the raw product, where are you?

"I guess nowhere," you answer.

"Now take a small batch of beans, hammer them with a blast from our Big Bertha roaster, and in a blink, your average bean with only 200 or so volatile molecules is transformed into one with over 800 distinct chemical structures.

"And the aroma is just incredible. The whole place just fills up with this earthy heaven."

He smiles at this.

"Then you have to cook it at high temperatures for no more than 30 seconds and ..."

He pulls down on the pump with an even stroke, and you hear the water hit the coils inside his machine, forcing a stream through the puck. The result trickles into the espresso cup.

"A perfect cup. Look at it. Amazing."

He cradles the cup close to him, taking a long slow smell of the liquid.

"And look at the crema. You can tell everything from the foam. Did you know that? Too light and it is underextracted. A wrong grind or too little time in the basket most likely. If it has a hole in the middle, then the grind is probably too fine."

He looks carefully at the crema.

"If you find white bubbles that are too big or a big white center, then the cup is going to be bitter. The brewing time went over. But you will notice, a perfect brown color, coating the entire surface. Like this…"

He slides the cup to the counter where you are.

"Perfecto!" he says. "Go ahead and try it."

You take a sip, and you are amazed. The espresso is smooth and delicious, with a slight chocolate and cinnamon taste.

"This is good," you say.

"The best," Tony smiles. "You won't find a better cup anywhere in the state."

You notice Alex at your side. He has snuck up on you.

"Hey," he says. "This is a surprise."

"Just thought I'd drop by," you say.

"You've met Tony, our barista in training. And this is Richie and Clive."

They all nod.

"Just hanging out after a morning workout," he says. "Hey, where'd you disappear to last night? You could have crashed, you know."

"Well, I did. But I had a really weird dream."

He gives you a light slap on the back.

"Come on, I'll show you around."

"Well, I just thought I'd stop by," you say.

Alex is dressed in a judo uniform, black pants with Japanese characters up the side and a crisp white jacket. He takes you to the front and explains that setting up the dojo had been a dream since he was young. Over time, he built up a following, mostly students from the university.

"I couldn't get a decent cup of java so I added the espresso bar. The beans are hand-picked by a good friend back in Hawaii. I learned to roast them when I was hanging out there years ago. So I put them together with my aikido. The students can hang out here after a lesson or walk over for a cup between classes. It works out."

"And you sweep at the office?"

"Yep, run into folks on Wednesday nights, and they come in. Like you did today."

"I see."

"Can't complain, really. I like it."

He takes careful strides around the room.

"Mostly beginners, but we have a group of us that do tournaments with a couple of clubs in the area. We've been beating their butts for a while, so this attracts more good fighters. But you didn't come here to learn aikido did you?"

"I really should be at work now. Even though I'm usually late, I usually don't skip out like this."

"Yeah, don't sweat it. It usually is for a reason. Sometimes you are being prepared for a bigger battle. Let me show you around."

He walks to the center of a large matted room.

"This is the world as I know it," he says, indicating the perimeter as he turns slowly around. "And most of us are at the center of our own world. That's the first wrong assumption. We are actually characters in other people's world, as well. Sometimes, very important fixtures. But most people do this…"

And he closes his eyes walking blindly around, stumbling occasionally on an invisible stone, or coming to a screeching halt at an imaginary wall. He opens one eye.

"See?"

You nod at this. He is funny to watch, because his actions are exaggerated.

"Now, most people are thinking 'how do I look?' or 'what's for dinner?' If you open your eyes, you see people around you walking, interacting, you watch their moves, see them more clearly. That is something few people are able to do. We are so centered on ourselves, nothing else comes into view. OK, now try this. Walk toward me, just straight at me."

You take your hands out of your pockets and walk slowly toward him. At the same time, he walks toward you from the center of the room. He is looking around, as if admiring the scenery. Suddenly, you are nose to nose, almost colliding. You stop, but Alex doesn't, and he moves right into you, gently pushing you back until you sidestep him.

He keeps on walking, talking to you as he proceeds. "And so, we keep going. It was pretty much a collision, am I right?"

He turns around.

"OK, now again. This time, you avoid me."

This is an easy exercise to do. As Alex approaches, you take a different tack early on, and the collision never happens.

"See," he says. "That part is easy. But now, what if our paths are simply destined to collide, you know? What if you and I are just on a collision course, through no intent of our own. Let's say."

Again he starts to walk toward you. "Like this," he says, and he is almost upon you. You turn slightly, but he also turns, until you are stumbling into his chest. He grabs your arms to stop you.

"Well, see that's a problem, right?" he says. "You're OK, right?"

"Sure, but I don't see your point really."

He laughs. "The fact is, kid, you are on a collision course right now. Like I said, I think you've got a bigger battle to fight. Now, this time, you try to walk into me. Don't worry, it won't happen."

"Just walk into you."

"Yeah, start at the back of the room. Over there."

You go to where he points. Then, he motions to you, and you move slowly toward him, as he walks slowly toward you.

As you approach, he keeps walking straight at you, casually as if he were out for a stroll. When you are almost on top of him, he makes a small move and is suddenly behind you. It happens so quickly you don't see what he did.

"Hey, kid." He laughs. "I'm over here. What happened?"

"I wasn't expecting that," you say.

"That's the point. OK, it wasn't that fast was it?"

"To me it was," you say.

"Oh," he smiles. "I did that in slow motion. OK, again."

And you go through the same routine, walking slowly toward him. As you reach the same spot, you watch carefully, trying to second guess which side he will move to, but the same thing happens. He ends up in back of you.

He adjusts his jacket. "So, OK. I'll stand still. Now that's got to be a slam dunk."

"That's more like it," you say.

He goes to the center of the room, and stands with one leg slightly in front of the other. He smiles and relaxes, giving you the signal to come toward him.

You now walk more cagily, since you suspect something different is going to happen. It can't be this easy. As you approach, he is smiling and nodding.

"Hey, kid, looking good," he says. "I like how you're walking this time. Much more aware."

"Thanks," you say, but don't take your eyes off of him.

When you're almost upon him, he turns slightly to one side and gives you a small push in the same direction as your walk, and suddenly you are on the mat face down.

Jenz Johnson

"And kid, it gets better. The faster you come at me, the more force I have to work with. Go ahead, come at me faster."

"That's OK," you say getting up. "I get it."

"Do you? In a real battle, only one guy prevails. So, it gets a little more intense. You have to know your moves and see your opponent's moves a lot clearer.

"OK. If you like, we can just do some exercises. It will loosen you up, put some energy into you. And, the first thing is your posture."

He places his hands on your shoulders and forces your shoulder blades together. You immediately straighten up, and he smiles.

"How does that feel?"

You nod. You are suddenly feeling better.

The whole evening was a waste," Dan says.

"Yes, well, you moved like an elephant," Burgie says. "You can't call that graceful. You were an easy target all night." He moves a large chocolate doughnut to his mouth.

"Who cares!" says Dan. "It really sucked."

"I thought he did well," Señor Jim says.

Burgie stops chewing and looks up at the stragglers in the kitchen finishing the last of the snacks before disappearing into the night with their monitors and CPUs. He turns to you quietly.

"Señor Jim," Burgie says by way of introduction.

He smiles with a nod.

"Jim. Jim will do." He extends a hand.

"Well, this is great."

"You probably know me as Zen Dog," he says. "On Red Team."

"Oh, sorry about that. You guys got creamed."

"Great attack," he says. "Looked a bit haphazard, but nice teamwork."

"Jim here *rebooted*," Burgie says, looking at you. You look again at Jim, who gives a comical expression as if he couldn't help it.

"Oh," you say.

"No biggie," he says. "We all reboot at some time or another."

"Jim won't tell me anymore what he does for a living," Burgie mentions. "All I can say is that Yahoo was good to him."

"In their own ways," Jim says. "I do embedded systems now."

"A hacker at heart," Burgie interjects.

"Not that exciting."

"More exciting than what I am doing," you say, "being stuck."

"Stuck?"

"On a treadmill. I keep falling on my face. I was laid off, just last Monday. And before I go, my boss wants me to do the impossible."

"Sounds like a boss."

"Yeah," you say.

"Although The Impossible is not always so…impossible. It's just a higher gear," Jim says.

"Higher than I go," you reply. "I don't think I go beyond first. And these days, it's mostly in reverse."

Jim laughs at this and grabs your arm to shake you.

"Well, you're moving, so you're at least in second. If it's any consolation: the worse it gets, the better it gets. You'll do fine." He smiles warmly.

"I'm famished," Burgie says. "Let's go get something to eat."

"Well, I could use a good bowl of *menudo*," Jim says. "And it might help cheer you up.

"That's Mexican, right?" Burgie brightens. "I could use a huge burrito!"

"Yeah, I know a place," Jim says. "They have the best *menudo*, and it is worth going a few miles to get there."

"It would actually be great, if you have the time," you say.

"I have a quick errand to run," he says. "But let's meet up at *Miguel's*. Ever hear of it?"

Both you and Burgie shake your heads.

"You'll like it. Take Broadway through downtown and take the first left after the freeway underpass. Keep going south, about seven miles. You can't miss it."

"That's way on the South Side," Burgie says disappointed. "What about Taco Bell? It's closer."

"I've never been that far south," you say.

"Say 30 minutes," Jim says. "But I can't stay too long. I'll meet you there."

"Yeah, OK," you say.

Burgie rolls his eyes. "Seems kind of far to drive for Mexican food," he says.

Jim laughs and gives Burgie a slap on the back.

"You, my friend," Jim says, "will never change."

Two steaming bowls of *menudo* slide onto the table, and Burgie's eyes widen as a large plate piled high with beans, rice and a gigantic burrito is lowered in front of him. He cannot wait and immediately scoops up a forkful before the plate touches the table. He quickly airs out his mouth with short breaths, fanning himself with his free hand.

"Hot, hot," he says.

"*Por favor,*" the waitress says. "*Es caliente.*"

Burgie nods with a pained expression.

You look at the bowl, and see cilantro floating in a rich broth. "What is this?" you ask, pointing to the floating cubes.

"Just eat," Jim says with a smile.

You lower your spoon in the broth and fetch a square. It's spicy, but the square tastes like a sponge. You sit chewing, deciding whether it needs to be swallowed. You set the spoon down.

"Interesting," you say.

"Life-changing," Jim responds. He eats quietly, taking a tortilla from a stack in the center. He tears off a corner and dips it into the saucer of salsa in the middle of the table.

"Gaming can really develop an appetite," Jim says.

"You know it," Burgie says, rolling a long string of cheese like spaghetti with his fork. He lets the cheese slide off into his open mouth. He moans with delight and chews happily.

"You've rebooted?" you say after a while.

"A couple of times. The first time was an accident. The second time I realized what was happening. It's just like a second systems effect. The first system you code is not bad, but you really get it down the second time around. That's what happened to me."

"I want to reboot, too," you say. "I really do."

He laughs. "You will," he says. He takes a slow sip of his soup. "It's very nonlinear."

You nod at this. "I can handle nonlinear," you say.

"Most people can't he says. They want to be in control." He looks at your bowl. "How do you like your *menudo?*"

"Well," you say, "it's interesting."

"Not your cup of tea?"

"I guess not."

"The burrito is awesome," Burgie says, his cheeks stuffed. "Definitely worth the drive."

"*Menudo* is real food," Jim says.

"I guess it's an acquired taste,..." you say.

"This guy..." Burgie interrupts, his mouth stuffed, "...used to be fatter than me. If you can imagine that! He weighed in a good twenty pounds more than me, was a diehard geek, and was always dateless. Now look at him. Practically, well, respectable. It's enough to make me want to puke."

"Well," Jim concedes. "I guess my tastes have changed. We all change. When you look back, you're not the same person you were when you were in elementary school."

"Actually," Burgie says, "I am. I've been like this for a while." He moves a pile of beans to the middle of the plate. He scoops a sticky mass with his fork and loads it into his mouth. "I think it's burned in my ROM."

"For me, it happened during a game, strangely enough," says Jim. "I felt suddenly disconnected. Everything around me seemed distant and artificial, like I was looking through the wrong end of a telescope."

"A game," Burgie says, "*is* artificial."

"My hands got rubbery. The screen started to flicker."

"Quit joking around, now," Burgie says. "This isn't even funny. You sound zombied out. First off, it's impossible to become a zombie while gaming. You just needed to upgrade your console."

He laughs. "Yes, at a certain level, you're right," Jim says, smiling. "That would have been a whole lot easier. But the question was which console?"

"Yeah, well, depends on what you like?"

He smiles.

"What I hear," says Burgie, "is there's a next-generation Xbox under deep cover that Microsoft won't even name. It's the nameless console. The project doesn't even have a name."

Burgie looks at you, nodding slowly.

"You mean *Jasmine*," Jim says.

"What?"

"*Jasmine.*"

"Is that what it's called?"

"Black case, no controllers. Motion sensors."

"Yeah, I think…" Burgie says, tentatively.

"You didn't hear it from me," Jim says.

"No, no. Of course not," Burgie says between chews.

"But the point is," Jim continues, "it felt foreign and clumsy. I felt awkward with the very technology that I loved over the years. Computers have always been central to anything I had done. And without computers, what was there?"

It was as if Jim was reading your own feelings. The computers at work were beginning to feel more like work, as if you were trying to make it all work in a way that didn't make sense.

Jenz Johnson

"It didn't creep up on me, Jim says. "It happened all of a sudden."

The café around you is suddenly muted and only Jim's voice has any volume.

"That was scary. Because I saw that most of what I did was a game, at some level. Nothing else had changed but me. The game was still as graphically accomplished as I remembered. But it ceased to deliver the wallop. That night, in the heat of battle, I was disconnected. It was as if I was a game *playing* a game. Like I was standing between two barbershop mirrors and I saw the image of myself rippling back to infinity."

"The Turing Test," you say.

"Well, I froze."

"You did?" you say.

"I took my hand off my mouse, left my character standing in the middle of the desert of rocks, on the screen, and just walked out of my apartment."

You feel your heart beating hard against your chest.

"Got on my bike and pedaled. Just got out of there. Didn't know where I wanted to go. I ended up here. Miguel's." He looks around with a smile.

Burgie slows his chewing to listen.

"And, I was struck at how strange this soup was. It was delicious. Not your cup of tea I know. But I also realized that I wasn't thinking any more. It woke me up."

"And that's what did it?"

"When you're eating and enjoying yourself, you're not really thinking. I.e., computing."

"*Menudo?*"

"Not exactly. I wandered out to the desert. Looked at the city lights. Walked and walked." He shrugs. "Sounds a little crazy."

Burgie nods.

"There was a rocky pass that led up over the mountains. It was a way to Mexico. In a full moon, you can actually see the trails. I wondered along the path for quite a while. They call it *El Pase*, the Pass. It was very quiet. Up near the top, I spotted an outcropping of rock. It looked inviting, carved out just for me. I climbed around the back, and found a path that opened up to the whole valley. I felt different."

"You rebooted."

He smiles.

"We all have different triggers. It wasn't the soup. I think it was the walking mostly. Just getting away from things."

"Wow," you say.

"Where did you go?" Burgie asks.

"Nowhere."

"And you never went back to your place."

"No I went back. I went back to everything, but it was different. I wasn't just indulging myself anymore. You know gaming, and bingeing out."

"What's the point?" Burgie says.

"Exactly. That was how I felt. It lost its meaning. And *meaning* is at the bottom of everything we do."

"Well, not for me, exactly," says Burgie. "I'm more of a Sartre fan, you know, existentialism. *Life has no meaning.*"

"Sartre?" you ask.

Burgie nods.

"*Life has no meaning the moment you lose the illusion of being eternal,*" Jim says. "That's the quote."

"Well, the full context," Burgie concedes. "*Grab for all the gusto you can.* That's another motto. Schlitz. Circa 1970."

"Anyway, the point is this: *Meaning* is at the root of everything we do. So, wanting to change is on some level wanting to find something that gives your life meaning. For me, I realized that I simply lost focus. I had all the skills. It was a matter of rearranging my components to produce a better me."

"Like remixing?" you ask.

"Major remixing."

"And what happened?"

"I saw that I was a gamer at heart," Jim says with a big smile.

Burgie immediately brightens. "Señor Jim. You never disappoint."

"But my game is the *game* of gaming," he says.

"Whatever," Burgie says, waving off the details. "You were just pulling my leg about being zombied out with gaming."

"I loved figuring out the game. The rules. The strategies. The tactics. I loved everything abstract: set theory, calculus, probability plots. It wasn't playing the game that was my fascination, but deciphering the game." He gives you a studied look. "There's a difference."

"Sort of the game behind the game," you say.

"So, this *Jasmine*…" Burgie points his fork at Jim. "What *can* you tell me…?"

Jim ignores him. "Everything became the game. The stock market. Fascinating. Getting fit. Finding true love. Did I mention this?"

"No," you say. "No, you didn't."

"That's another meal in itself. Each has its own parameters, its own settings and strategies. What I saw was people played one game well. Maybe it was their jobs. Maybe it was their love lives. Family lives. But few people multi-tasked several games at the same time. That was my challenge. That's how I saw it. Take it all on and perfect it all."

"And you, what?" you ask, a bit confused.

"I was exactly the same guy when I walked out as when I returned. The difference is that everything was a game, where the rules and strategy were largely unknown. There was a winning side and a losing side to every situation."

"Really?"

He laughs. "The point is this: I was a different person when I realized this. It all happens up here." He taps his head. "And of course, in here," he says tapping his chest. "You have to see your own heart." He smiles. "I sat back down at my computer and I did things differently. I thought about things differently."

You look at him for a long time and see the satisfaction in his expression. Jim tilts the bowl and with his spoon ladles the remaining broth, bringing it to his lips.

"A good walk in the desert will clear your mind."

Burgie swallows the last of his burrito with a muted burp.

"This is my treat," he says. He takes out his wallet and places a $20 bill on the table.

You reach into your jeans for some money, and Jim holds up his hand.

"OK," you say. "Thanks."

"Great, thanks!" Burgie says.

"I really enjoyed our talk," you say. You are breathing hard, trying to think of something more to ask.

"Good luck," Jim says to you.

"Listen, this place. *El Pase.*"

"Yes, the Pass."

"It's close to here?"

"Well, you're not thinking of going up there?"

"Maybe a good spot to clear my thoughts."

"It's nowhere special."

"But, to the south?"

"Keep heading down this road."

"Maybe I will."

"You'll do fine." He gives you a gentle slap on the back. "Just keep going. Surf the web also. There's a ton of stuff."

"I didn't think there was."

"Just Google it. Look at www.rebootique.com. Check out some movies."

"OK, I will," you say.

Then, he nods and quickly leaves out a side door.

You walk quietly out to the dirt parking lot with Burgie. He pops a couple of peppermints into his mouth and gives a muffled burp. The night is quiet.

"Burgie," you say, "You were right. I just have to do it."

"Do what?" he says.

"I have to scrap my life. I can't go back," you say.

"Jim's a pretty cool guy," he says.

"I'm not going back to my place, Burgie, I can't. I feel the same way. I know what will happen. I'll fall into the same loops that I've been doing for the last umpteen years."

"Hey, slow down. What happened in there?"

"I'm just tired of it all. It's like I never get better. I see everything I do is wrong, and I keep doing it."

"But..." he says.

"I can't change it, not there."

"So, where are you going then?"

"I don't know," you say.

Burgie shakes his head. "You just need some sleep."

The wind picks up and branches scrape the roof of the restaurant.

Y ou wait quietly in your car as Burgie's Prius disappears from view. You hear the jutebox from Miguel's play a ballad with guitars and trumpets and sounds of voices and clanking dishes. The screen door slams and a couple of cooks drag a large garbage bag out to the dumpster. They light up cigarettes and laugh, talking in quick Spanish.

With your hands on the steering wheel, you look at your cupholder and see leftover latte from yesterday. You pop the lid and give a quick whiff, seeing foam, then up-end it quickly. The leftovers slide down in a slow congealed mass, bitter and slimy. You feel revived.

You start up the engine with a sudden jolt and your cold latte splashes up in the cup, spilling over the dashboard. Your glasses are knocked to the end of your nose, and you reach to steady them.

You pull your iPhone from its holder and find that there is poor reception. Wiping your forehead on a sleeve, you quickly start up the car and pull onto the main road, heading toward the lights in the distance. After a minute, the screen flickers and you see the signal strength grow stronger. You pull over to the shoulder and find a connection to the net. Smearing the screen, you find it, the movie Jim recommended: *Persona*. You tap it. There is a pause as the stream buffers up. Then the movie comes to life, filling the small screen in your hand.

You push your earplugs in and watch the opening frames. Bergman, the director, is speaking in code, maybe a hacker before there were PC's. The movie has its own logic and flow. It starts with a tight loop presetting values for a more elegant main routine. The visuals are a cache of ideas, of instructions, of secret intents. Now the message on the screen is encrypted. A patient. A nurse. A doctor. These are placeholders.

And there she is, staggering in her beauty, Liv, on a stage, suddenly forgetting her lines, then falling into silence, refusing to tell her secrets. You have seen her before in other movies. You love her freckles and girlish looks. And now Bebe, the nurse, receiving instructions from the doctor. In the movie, she looks so professional. She is to care for the patient, who refuses to speak.

You are staggered by Liv and Bebe. Their gorgeous Swedish curves, wisps of blonde hair drooping, pouting intelligence. They are the before and after, you can see it coming. You can see the slow process of crossing over, of the silence in one yielding to the curiosity of the other. They sit across from each other in the Scandinavian sun, in front of sails of boats on a nearby lake.

Then Bergman's voice is talking directly to you. The voice-over. You push the plugs further into your ears and turn the volume up. This is what you came to hear: Bergman stating that everything possesses hopelessness, this basic quality. Yes, life is hopeless. Your daily routine masks this, but you know that this futility lurks underneath. And, now, he says there is a gap, an abyss, he calls it, between the roles you take on for yourself and those you play for others, your firewall of programs. Each brick: "the abyss between what you are for others and what your are for yourself. The feeling of dizziness." The doctor's words cut through the scene with clinical precision.

You feel dizzy and fast forward to Liv and Bebe side by side on the screen. Their faces overlap, half of Liv and the other half, Bebe. You see the nurse absorbing the identity, the mannerisms of the patient. She is transforming in front of your eyes. The changes are not all that subtle, first with the cigarettes, how she lights them, then the eyes. She is sharing code, piggy-backing on routines already running on another processor.

Brakes squeal behind you and you look up. A car swerves around and continues down the road. Probably a drunk. You barely pause before shifting back to the movie.

The doctor's voice is explaining how life plays tricks on a person, and that the roles you assume cut you off from everything around you, that no one cares whether you are genuine.

You rewind this portion and he repeats that no one really cares whether you are genuine. "True or false," he says. Acting in theater, he says, is performed to play true. But in your real life roles, there is no true or false.

True and false are important in the hacker world, the ones-and-zeroes view. Burgie is saying humans can only differentiate between things. We can't decipher what is true or false—only if something is different. The act of "distinguishing" is our primary skill.

You think of G. Spencer Brown, in his book *The Laws of Form*. He also thought that mathematics could not assume there is a true and false. Rather, he based his system of logic only the state of being distinguished. That is, we don't have any intrinsic ability to know when something is true or false. Only that it is different.

From this viewpoint, the world can only be mathematically explained by using imaginary numbers such as the i in formulae to predict electrical forces and the motion of circles. Using them, everything falls into place. But without imaginary numbers, there would be no engineering, no jets or rockets, no computers. All because of a system of logic that has true and false, but also, "as if true" and "as if false," states that represent the appearance of truth or falsity.

Bebe suddenly faces the camera and says, "Can you be quite different people, all next to each other, at the same time? And then what happens to everything you believe in?" You see that Bebe's face has already changed, that she is the same person with side-by-side people inside. She says, we all are.

Then the husband enters the bedroom. It would be hard to know which of the two naked women he should sleep with. Bebe says that she is not his wife, but this doesn't seem to make a big difference to him. You see that her transformation is complete. And surprisingly, the patient is cured. But not completely. She is assuming another role, another persona. The doctor explains that life is theater, that you take on roles, and must let them come and go.

You realize that your car is careening out of control. You quickly swerve out of the way of something big in front of you. Your car skids to your left toward a darkened median and you brake quickly and throw the wheel around until everything collapses into slow motion. You brace yourself but there is no loud crash, no impact. Instead, through the windshield, you see a large green streak from the traffic light. You gun the gas petal and roar through the intersection.

A bolt of lightning streaks through the night sky. The rain falls in fast sheets, coating your windshield in film. You hunch forward, peering through the smudged windshield, your eyes burning and tired. A large construction sign looms ahead, warning of detours and delays. You slow down and navigate a steep drop from pavement to dirt. It is pitch black. No street lights. No traffic. You are in an old neighborhood. There is a large warehouse with broken windows and a burned-out second floor. The street turns into a series of potholes, with large pieces of pavement missing. You pass a couple of stores that are boarded up and a car up on bricks. Some faces look out from an alley.

You see lights ahead and pass some houses with corrugated metal roofs. Suddenly your road ends next to a house with one light on. You stop and listen to rain striking your roof. You pull out your iPhone, but there is no signal.

You step out and your shoes sink into the mud as you try to shield your glasses from the rain. A dog comes up to you, shivering and whining, sniffing at your cuffs.

"*¿Qué desea usted, vato?*" a voice says behind you.

A squat silhouette with a large-brimmed hat stands under the carport. He wears a bandana, a rain poncho and heavy construction boots.

"I'm trying to get to *El Pase*."

He laughs at this.

"Can you give me some directions? I think I made a wrong turn," you say.

"You are nowhere," he says and turns back to his truck under the carport. "Know anything about carburetors, my friend?" he asks.

You wipe your glasses on your wet shirt. "Not much," you say.

He grunts and hands the greasy flashlight to you. He moves around and starts the car which starts the hubcap rattling. The engine coughs, gasps and dies. He gets out, pulls out a brake fluid container from behind the hub cap and puts it to his lips. He takes a long gulp and grunts.

"Here," he says and hands over the greasy container. It is filled with tequila.

"No thanks," you say, but he pushes the bottle into your hands. It burns all the way down, and you cough.

From the house behind you, a door opens, and a short woman appears with a plate. You smell the aroma of fresh tortillas, and your eyes follow the plate. *"Tenga algo de comer por favor."*

She moves around the side of the car, casting a gaze suspiciously in your direction. She sets the stack on the car. The man leans forward and grabs a lime to suck on. She wipes her hands on her sweatshirt. She has long, jet-black hair and an Aztec nose. Her face looks somewhat distorted, as if one half doesn't work.

"Por favor," she says, indicating the tortillas.

"Thank you," you say, as you take a tortilla and fold it over. It is slightly crisp on the bottom, and tastes burnt, but the flavor is sublime. You reach for a lime and the tequila. The lime has salt already on it, and you drink a much bigger amount this time.

"You are lost," says the man and laughs. "Everyone is lost who comes here. No one comes here to *come here*. For $20, I will tell you how to get back. I make a good price for you. Get you past the *locos*."

"I'm not lost."

He has a broad smile as he leans against the post of the carport. The dogs sniff at the plate of tortillas and whimper. As you chew, you pull out your wallet and find some wet bills. There is not much left. And if you have to stop for gas, you may not have enough.

The man rubs the stubble on his chin, watching you try to figure out what to do.

"How about $10?"

"No, $20, my friend. Tip is included."

You tug out the twenty, and he grabs the bill with two fingers, raising it over his head like a prize, then kissing it and stuffing it into his shirt pocket.

He gets up and follows you back to your car. Opening the door, the man points directly behind you.

"This way," he says. "Then this way, then this way. This, this, this." He motions by chopping his hand back and forth in front of you.

"Do I turn at the mini-mart I saw?"

"Onto the dirt road."

"Not pavement?"

"No, the dirt road. Take the dirt one."

With a laugh, he pats you on the shoulder and steps back. You start the car, and it shakes to life. With a glance over your shoulder, you reverse over a chunk of pavement and are back on the street on your way to El Pase. You make the first, then the second. You avoid an old pickup truck cruising down the center of the road with its lights out. There is no dirt road.

With the engine running, you get out and step onto the mud. You see what appear to be car tracks in the desert. This must be it. You climb back in and gun the gas. The car crashes into an arroyo, and through some bushes. You speed up a small rise and down a narrow alley until it dead ends. You back up and turn around and pull into the first small street. It ends at a house with a rickety fence. You stop the car and get out. Sludging through the mud, you follow a broken fence around, and under a canopy, you see a silhouette of a man.

He roars with laughter. It is the same mechanic again, and he is plastered and he slips off of his tires and rolls around on the ground laughing.

"See, my friend. Only lost people come here."

And he laughs even harder. He is holding his sides, and tears are streaming down his cheeks.

He has my money," you explain.

You are in the kitchen, and the woman sits across from you at a small table. Her black hair is pulled back. She looks at you, her forehead deeply furrowed.

"I want to go to *El Pase*, but I need directions."

She nods, leaves the room, then returns with an old blanket, which she throws over your shoulders. You are still shivering in your soaked clothes. She slides a bowl of soup and a stack of fresh tortillas in front of you.

"*Por favor,*" she says.

"Thank you," you say before letting out a whopper of a sneeze that moves the bowl forward an inch. You try to keep the spoon from shaking in your hand. "Sorry," you say, and your throat begins to feel scratchy.

From a bedroom, the head of a young girl pokes out. She is 9, maybe 10, years old. She moves shyly to the table, and she reaches immediately for the tortillas, tearing off a corner and stuffing it into her small mouth. She chews and stares at you.

"You sneeze loud." The girl smiles and giggles. "Like a dog."

The mother talks to her, and she pulls her chair up, and takes her elbows off to the table.

"I want to stay up," she says. Then looking at you, she smiles. "Another one?" she asks her mother.

"*Si,*" the woman replies and instructs her daughter in Spanish.

"My mother says that you cannot stay here."

You nod and slurp the soup, a spicy broth with a couple of whole pinto beans lining the bottom and tortilla strips half-submerged. You begin to warm up, and your nose begins to run. With a napkin, you catch a drip before it shows itself.

"She knows the way back. Don't you think she is pretty?"

"I need to find *El Pase*."

"Her name is Lupé. Mine is Florita. I don't have a father."

Her mother instructs her to be quiet, and she is silent.

"Nice to meet you," you say. Your head seems totally empty.

Lupé looks up from her scrubbing at the sink and says something.

"My mother asks you not to come back."

You nod. "I wasn't planning on coming back this time."

"You look like Chewie." The girl giggles. "Can you make that sound?"

The girl pulls her chair closer.

"Isn't it late for you?" you ask.

"My mother does not speak any English. Besides it is summer, and I don't have school."

"Maybe I could use a phone," you say.

"We do not have one."

You pull out your iPhone. The signal strength is very low, but you try to dial a number. The call fails. You try again to the same results. You put the phone back.

"My mother says that you should eat so that you can warm up."

You lean forward and spoon more soup. It is delicious.

"Grandfather would know *El Pase*. He knows how to go anywhere."

The mother speaks rapid Spanish.

"She says I am not supposed to say more. But maybe you should wait until he gets back. He will be coming home soon."

You look at the mother, but she has turned her back to you. You look around the small kitchen, then take another spoonful of soup.

Isn't there any other way?" you ask.

"My mother says that you are too much in a rush. She says that we should wait for Grandfather. And we could tell stories while we wait," the girl says, watching you carefully. "Do you have any stories?"

You say that you don't have any. Your head continues to ache, and you find it hard to focus on anything. Looking around the kitchen, you see pictures of Virgin Mary, some done in crayon, others cut out from books. At the center is the table with four chairs. You want to get back in your car, but your body feels heavy.

"My mother tells me stories of my ancestors," says the girl. "Do you have ancestors?"

"Yes," you say. "But I have forgotten most of their stories."

This saddens the girl. She translates this for her mother. "My mother says to forget your ancestors' stories is very bad."

"I know that my grandfather spoke Spanish also."

"You do not look Mexican," the girl says. "And you do not speak Spanish."

"Actually he was from Russia," you say. "My grandfather came from Russia."

The girl smiles. "Does he have a story? My ancestors are Indians and lived in pyramids. Did your family live in pyramids?"

"No," you say. "Not pyramids."

"So, what do Russians live in?" she asks.

"Well, houses like yours. Well, maybe not as nice."

"So, you came from Russia too?"

"No, no," you say. "My grandfather left Russia when he was 17." It has been years since you have thought about your grandfather. "He had to leave his home. He was going to be drafted and sent to war. Either that or he was going to jail."

"Is it a sad story?" she asks.

"Well, I guess it ends happily. I'm here, you see."

She motions to you to continue.

"No one was to know. He was to come to Mexico."

"He was to come to Mexico?" the girl asks incredulous. "Not America? Everyone comes to America."

You tell about the potato fields where your grandfather went at night. Quietly along a back road, he and his older brothers walked. He was the youngest and could not keep up. So, every few minutes he would run as fast as he could to catch up. They would wait for him, but he was frightened since any moment soldiers could ride by in old rickety cars. In the field, the brothers would gather up potatoes in canvas bags. Then they would make their way back in the cover of darkness and dump the potatoes in a small cellar. The family lived on the potatoes.

His mother fawned over him and would wash his face as he told a story of the wolf he thought watched over him.

"A friendly wolf?" his mother would ask.

"Yes, a friend. He keeps an eye out for me."

"He is a good wolf, indeed," his mother would say. She would hug him and smell his hair.

But the day came when your grandfather had to leave. His older brother was already in Mexico and had sent the money. It was not a lot of money but enough to bribe people for your grandfather's safety. He would be taken to a safe house on the outskirts of town, then to the border in the back of a milk truck.

Your grandfather was told of the arrangements, and refused. He argued that he did not need to leave. That he belonged with them. That he needed to look out for his mother. That they needed him. His brothers quieted him. He would be taken away otherwise, to the front, or worse. He would die if he did not leave, they said. There was no coming back from the front. Bullets were everywhere. The army would not use him as a soldier, but as fodder.

But your grandfather would not be quieted. Not until his mother took him aside. "You must do this, Hershel," she said. "You must do this for me. I would not do anything to harm you. And you must be safe. Otherwise, what have I lived for?"

"His name was Hershel?" the girl asks.

"Yes."

"His mother sounds very nice, like mine."

Your grandfather sadly went about his chores the next day and the next. When he was within arm's reach, his mother would pull him to her and kiss his neck.

On the day he left, he wore just normal clothes. No suitcases. There was to be nothing unusual. He was not to tell his friends, nor were his brothers to speak of it to anyone.

Before daybreak, the small wagon pulled in front of the door. Your grandfather sat on the bed. His brothers were up, but no lights were on. His mother brought him a simple breakfast of bread.

When it was time, his brother helped him with his coat. He turned to his mother, but she was gone, to her room.

Her door was bolted. "Be strong, my son," she said quietly through the door. "Remember me." He knew he couldn't walk from her door to the wagon. But his brothers pushed him out into the darkness, tears running down their faces.

A boat carried him to Mexico.

"Did he like Mexico?" the girl asks.

"Yes, he liked Mexico," you say. He was taken in by an important tailor in Mexico City. My grandfather swept the floors. He would practice on scraps of material first. All types of cuts. Many years later, he would become a tailor himself, make clothes for people."

"My mother asks where in Mexico City your grandfather lived."

"I don't know," you say.

"She says she probably knew of him. There was a Hershel there. It is not a common name."

You see your grandfather's eyes. What would he say now to you? You see him at the dinner table behind his newspaper, weary from long days in the sun, years of hard work as a peddler in America.

"He ended up in America," you say. "He found his brother after searching for many years. And his brother brought him to America."

"Oh," she said. "That is very nice of his brother."

"Yes," you say.

The mother leans back. She takes out a small pipe, and a pouch filled with tobacco. She stuffs the pipe and lights it. Her eyes blink in the smoke.

"My mother says that you need to sleep. Tomorrow, she says we will ask Grandfather to help you find your way. You'll see. You will be fine."

The girl pushes her chair out and takes the remains of the table scraps in her hands. A dog follows her to his bowl, and she dumps the scraps there. The mother shows you to the grandfather's room. "You can sleep here my mother says."

Lupé has laid out a makeshift mattress of bedspreads on the floor. You take your shoes off. The room is dark, and you can see pictures of saints and the Virgin Mary on the wall. The walls are adobe, with small chunks missing. Your eyes become very heavy, and you feel the walls close gently in on you. The room slips into darkness.

22. launching

"The important thing is this: To be able, at any moment, to sacrifice what we are for what we could become."
—Charles Dubois

Y ou awake to a breeze lifting a small curtain and the eyes of Jesus and the pope on you. Across the room in a corner, you see two old yellow feet, and you hear the labored snoring of the old man. He is in a jumble of blankets and has one hand hanging lifeless over the side.

From the next room, you hear the clanging of pots and humming. The smell of eggs and bacon sifts through the door, and you pull yourself up, still exhausted. You see a small folded pile of clothes a hand-written note, *"Ware This!"* it says.

When you emerge to the brightly-lit kitchen, the girl smiles and waves.

"Buenas días," the mother says from the stove.

"Good morning!" the girl says. She is barefoot, in pink pajamas.

The mother quickly chops onions and chilies on an old wooden board.

"My mother says that you should sit down before you fall. That she will have something for you to eat."

You grab hold of the back of a chair.

"And then Grandfather will help you to find *El Pase.*"

The onions and chilies go into the frying pan with eggs and beans. It smells good.

Lupé talks gently to the girl, and she leaves the table, taking her doll with her. When she returns, her hair is pinned back. She takes dishes from Lupé and arranges them on the table. From a drawer she takes some forks, then places glasses on the table. She fills these with water from the tap. From the refrigerator, she takes a carton of milk and pours it into her glass.

"My mother says that you need to be brave like your grandfather."

"Yes, my grandfather *was* brave," you say despondently.

"She says there are many ways to be brave without big muscles." She laughs. "Maybe you are hungry now? We are having eggs. They are my favorite. But first my mother thinks you should go check on

Jorge, on your car and things. My mother says not to get him angry, though. That would be bad."

The mother looks at you, and you resign yourself to going outside. You find your shoes, still caked with mud, near the door, and walk out through a patch of mud and puddles. The air is cold, but birds are calling from the branches of the old trees.

As you duck between the overhanging branches, you glance around. You see other house and, behind them, mountains, with cactus jutting out from rocks and scrub bush. The front yard is mostly junk—an old swing set, some car parts, old plastic chairs, a rusty beer keg, and tools.

You make your way to the carport where you hear some banging and cursing. Jorge has a bottle in his hand, and is peering into the engine cavity of a car. He sees you and points at you as if he wants to tell you something.

He looks at your clothes and laughs. You notice that you are wearing an old mechanic's shirt with the name *Jorge* on it.

"It was not the carburetor," he says. "I think it was the starter. That was it. So, my friend. Thank you for the starter."

"What?"

"You did not need it."

"You took the starter from my car?" you ask.

He holds up a wrench to show you how he did it. "Because you were not using it," he says. He smiles and shows a mouthful of crooked teeth.

"How am I going to get back?" you ask.

"How are you going to get back when you are lost, my friend? You are not making too much sense." He tinkers with the gas line. "You tried last night. See, here you are."

"It's daylight now."

"They are the same roads, my friend. This has not changed. And you are the same driver, so you will just come back. I saved you some time."

You stand for a while looking at Jorge bent over his engine. When he does not look up, you return to the house.

Inside, the dishes are set, and you smell coffee. The girl takes a cup from the cabinet and goes to a pot on the stove. She gingerly lifts the coffee pot and tries to pour the coffee. The mother comes over and tenderly helps her. The cup is large, and the girl shuffles to the table with it in a towel, setting it down on the edge.

"Do you like sugar in your coffee?" she asks.

"Yes," you say.

She fetches the sugar in a large pink bag and places it next to the coffee. Still standing, you heap a couple of spoonfuls, then raise the cup to your lips. It is very bitter and strong with a tinge of cinnamon in it.

"It's good," you say. You sit down, and the girl sits next to you.

"My grandfather will be getting up soon," she says. "We can eat breakfast then," she says. "He likes to talk."

You begin to feel stronger.

"My car is torn apart," you say. "Jorge took my starter."

"Yes, Jorge likes to take things."

"Without a car, I'm stuck," you say.

The girl smiles at this.

"My mother will not like this. Do you go to school?"

"No," you say. You shake your head.

The mother says something from the stove and the girl quiets down.

"*Buenos días*," a voice says from behind you.

"Grandfather!" the girl says, and rushes to give him a hug. He pats her head gently.

"*Buenos días*," you repeat.

He looks at you curiously. He is tall and fit. His face is lined, and he smiles gently, his eyes gray-green. He stretches his back like a cat and yawns, then says something to the mother. She smiles, and the girl pulls out the chair for him.

"I told him that your name is not really Jorge," she girl says.

She explains to the grandfather, who leans gently closer to her as she translates. He nods and pats her head again, letting his hand brush the side of her cheek. He enjoys listening, and when she is finished, he plants a small kiss on the top of her head.

"*Ella es la niña más hermosa del mundo*," he says.

She beams.

"Maybe you can tell him that Jorge has taken my starter."

The old man chuckles.

"It's not that funny," you say quietly.

The mother comes to the table with a large steaming skillet of eggs and tortillas. She places it in the center with a wooden spoon and returns to the stove where she gathers bacon and tortillas on a wooden board. She brings these to the table.

The grandfather takes your plate. He loads it with eggs, tortillas and bacon, then sets it in front of you with the girl's help. *"Por favor,"* he says and motions with his outstretched hand.

"It is my favorite," the girl says. "Breakfast Nachos."

Everyone is looking at you. The steam has fogged your glasses so that you can barely see anyone. The girl stands next to you, napkin in hands, and draws small circles on your glasses until they clear up.

"There," she says. "Can you see now?"

"Come," the grandfather says. "Lupé has made you a very special breakfast. *Por favor.* You will feel better."

"Can you help me find *El Pase?"* you ask.

"First, my friend, you need to eat something."

You look down at the eggs, and you are suddenly famished.

"Thank you," you say to the mother. *"Gracias."*

She nods.

"You are very welcome," he says and lifts a large forkful to his mouth, smiling and chewing vigorously. The mother pours a mug of coffee for him, then sits at the table. Everyone is quiet. The girl picks out the chilies and onions, but eats the eggs and bacon with a smile.

"Do you know *El Pase?"* you ask.

"Ah, *El Pase.* Yes. But why do you want to go to Mexico?"

"I don't want to go to Mexico. Just to this pass."

"Yes, it is in the mountains. It is on the way to Mexico."

"Is it far from here?" you ask.

"Why do you want to go, my friend? Are the police after you? Did you steal this car?"

"No, no," you say. "I have a friend. Well, an acquaintance actually. He went there. He said it was beautiful. And I need a place to clear my thoughts."

"Ah," he says. "I see. I am not sure you will find what you are looking for there. Most people are very disappointed when they arrive."

"I just have to go there."

"It can be dangerous."

"Dangerous?"

"You want to go to this place badly."

You nod.

"Come, my friend," he says. "Eat. You will need your strength."

"Not until we are lost do we begin to understand ourselves."
—*Henry David Thoreau*

From the porch in back, the grandfather points a finger to a small mountain in the distance.

"It looks high. I didn't think it would be that high."

The backyard is partially surrounded by the same chain link fence as the front. There is a large mesquite tree, with a lopsided branch that hangs over a small shed. A small bike leans against it, with an assortment of buckets, cans and pipes scattered about.

"You will need a hat," the grandfather says, standing up.

"I have a hat for him," the little girl says and runs inside, returning with a pink bonnet.

"I'm not wearing that," you say, eyeing what seems to be an Easter bonnet with a large red bow on it.

"Go fetch one of Jorge's hats," he says to the girl.

Florita disappears inside.

"Are there any shortcuts?"

"I know all the shortcuts, don't worry," he says, placing his hands on your shoulders and looking directly into your eyes.

Florita returns with a baseball hat.

"Your backpack is safe here," the old man says. He surveys the backyard, then opens the screen door and wanders back into the kitchen. He returns with a bandana tied around his head, and he places an old straw cowboy hat on top, then tucks in his work shirt. Lupé brings him a wrapped package and places it with a small stack of tortillas into a satchel. She folds a cloth over some dried beef and places this on top, handing him the satchel and canteen with a nod. He thanks her and moves in the direction of the back door.

"This way, my friend." He places the long strap of the satchel across one shoulder and nods toward the yard.

You duck through the doorway and follow the old man into the late morning sun.

The alley is filled with weeds and trash cans, and you pick your way through the debris, avoiding planks of wood, plastic soda bottles and puddles of rain water. For an old man, he walks fast, with a spring in his gait. He looks over his shoulders to see if you are following.

The alley turns into an arroyo behind the row of houses, with small clumps of creosote bushes and prickly pear cactus lining the sides and a small ravine carved down the middle.

"We will follow this for a while. This is the way to *El Pase*. It is not too far," he says, shielding his eyes. His face is deeply lined and bronzed, with a series of dark spots across his temples. "It is a nice spot. You made a good choice." He pats you on the back and scrambles up the small bank onto an empty lot between two abandoned houses. You pick your way through the dried weeds and discarded tires, and follow the old man down a narrow dirt path that snakes through a tangle of ocotillo.

"Be careful," he says, and walks down the path to a mound of dirt piled next to a wall. The wall juts out along the edge of the lot, and he steps from the mound to the top, walking carefully out to the middle of the wall. "Here. When you jump, look here," he yells down to you, then jumps out of sight.

You scramble on top, carefully picking your way over the loose bricks. There is a warm gust of wind and you feel wobbly as you step sideways along the top.

"Down here," he yells from below, motioning to you. He is standing on a rough slope at the bottom, with creosote on either side. It is a farther drop than you think. As you stand there, you suddenly tense up. Your feet wobble, and you quickly lower yourself to your knees.

"You are thinking about something, my friend?"

"Another way down."

He laughs at this. "This is a very small jump."

"It's just that, well, I don't do so well with heights."

"It has nothing to do with heights. It is with your *cabeza*." He taps his head and it wobbles from side to side, as if loose.

"My head feels OK," you say. "It's just that jumping from walls is not my *forte*."

"OK, turn back," he says, throwing away the branch in frustration.

"This is stupid."

"You do as you please. You do not need my help." He puts his hat on and picks up his satchel.

As he begins to walk, you nervously yell down. "Wait!"

Slowly, you edge along the middle, checking for loose bricks as your knees drag along the top of the wall. You are afraid to look back, and there is little room to turn. Suddenly, your face is drenched with sweat and your arms begin to shake.

"This is *stupid*," you say louder, and then, in a flash, angry, you jump off, and quickly land on your side, sand flying up in your face. You are panting and sweating, slightly nauseous—and very angry.

"OK," you say between breaths. "There."

"See," he says with a big smile. "You are a good jumper."

You fix your glasses, which have slid down on your nose.

The old man unscrews the top of the canteen and offers it to you. You take the canteen from him, drinking the cool water and looking at him. You hand it back and he nods for you to continue.

"Come," he says. "Let's not take too long. The sun is becoming hot."

"You came from Mexico?" you ask as you walk through the brush.

"Yes," he says. "Many times."

"More than once?"

"Yes, it is something that I know well."

"But why did you go back?"

"To help people like you."

"You smuggle people? You're a coyote."

He laughs. "No, no. That, my friend is a very sad story. No, I try to help them. Some are left behind. Some lose their way. Some have no water. It is a sad story. I find them though."

"You take people over the border."

"No, just to water. I know where to find water, my friend." He smiles at this. "It is a gift. Come."

He leads you over a small hill. You follow closely, bending over to carefully climb up the rocks with your hands. When you turn past a large tree, you are in front of a trickling spring. Below it is a small pool of water. Moss lines the rocks, and he has already hung his satchel from a low branch. His hat is off, and he is wiping his forehead. Although the air smells like dead leaves, it is cool.

"See!" he says proudly.

You climb down and jump up to the small flat rock where the old man is standing, surveying the water. You look down and see a rather murky pool, crowded with moss and dead branches. A small picture of the Madonna is perched against a rock. There are small piles of rocks and ashes close by.

He gives you a small tug on your shirt and you find yourself kneeling next to him, as he mumbles a short prayer, and places a small offering of a tortilla and dried beef before the Madonna.

"She likes you," he says.

"That's good," you say.

"This is a good place to rest," he says. He walks slowly over the rocks back to his satchel hanging on the tree. He removes his poncho and lays it out, then sits down cross-legged. He offers you a seat on the poncho.

The sound of the waterfall is relaxing, and you lean back on your elbows, listening.

When you awake, the old man has his finger to his lips and signals that you are to remain quiet.

"*Buenas tardes*," he says loudly, then turning to you, he lowers his voice. "There are animals sometimes," he says in a whisper.

You can't imagine what kind of animals would make such a large motion in the bushes.

"Animals?"

"Yes," he says. "I have seen big cats and bears."

"Bears!"

You suddenly jump up.

"OK, just big cats." He laughs. "But they are not very friendly," he says. "Anyway, you should stay down."

You crouch again and study the bushes where the branches shake. You hear a chirping sound and then human voices.

Suddenly a man steps out.

"*Buenas tardes, amigo*," the man says. He is dressed in a t-shirt and jeans, with a satchel over his shoulders. The bushes move and a woman with a small girl in tow step behind him.

"*Buenas tardes*," she says, looking your way.

"Ah," the old man says. "I know these people."

You exchange nods with the couple, and the girl stares at you.

"*Buenas tardes*," you say.

"*Buenas tardes*, Jorge," the woman says.

You look around for Jorge, then realize that you are in his work shirt.

"No, I'm not Jorge," you say, shaking your head and pointing to the nametag. "That's not me."

"*Señor Andele*," the man says with a sheepish smile.

You recognize the family from the one that were trying to cross the freeway. It seems like years ago when they were huddled by the freeway, trying to find a way over the pavement.

"I know these people too," you say to the old man. "It's the second time I have run into them," you say. Then to the man you say "Senor Pecanas," and his wife smiles, her daughter peeks out from behind her skirt playfully. She smiles then ducks back.

"*Si*," the man says. "Juan."

The old man motions to them and they move forward, quietly extending hands to be shaken.

"Juan," you say nodding. The old man pats Juan on the back and talks warmly with him.

"Come," the old man says. "They should rest before their journey."

He motions to the family to move out of the sun and under the shade of a large cottonwood near the small stream. He gathers his satchel and poncho, as Juan relates a long story. The old man looks back and forth to the woman, who also confirms the story silently.

"Where are they going?" you ask, but the old man does not interrupt his conversation.

When he finally turns in your direction, he says. "Home."

"To Mexico?"

He nods then resumes his conversation with Juan, speaking also to his wife who talks very gently.

"They are going back to Mexico?" you ask.

"Si, si. They say America is a nice place to visit, but,…" he nods in the direction that you came.

The old man clears off a spot on a flat rock and motions for the wife to sit. She nods and carefully shows the girl where to sit, then sits down herself. The old man sets his satchel down and brings out some left-over tortillas from the morning. He offers them to the family and the woman nods. The old man sets the wrapped tortillas next to the girl. He also unscrews the cap of the canteen and presents it to the mother. The husband looks at his family and chews the tortilla. He nods as if to explain the situation to you.

"Maybe they should just try a little longer," you suggest.

The old man shrugs. "Well, I am afraid America is not as advertised. The TV makes it look much better than it is, you know."

"But, there is nothing they are going back to…" you say.

He looks at you.

"I mean," you continue, "why go back?"

"Well, they will have less things, that is true. Their house will be very small, yes."

"But it is also dangerous also, to return, did you explain this?"

"*Si, si,*" he says. "They know this. They regret that it is," the old man continues, "but they say, the Virgin Mother has looked out for them so far. She will look out for them on their journey back."

"But," you continue. "if they give up now, they may never come back here. I mean, it has not been that long has it? Maybe they should stay a little longer."

The old man relates your comments.

"They say you should not to take their decision personally. They liked what they saw. The work was OK. But it is not a place they want to raise their daughter. They are very particular."

The woman smiles and relates a short story that Juan and the old man laugh at.

"I wish there was some way I could help," you say.

The old man nods. "Besides, she says," the old man relates, "the food here is very bad, and the food at Taco Bell is probably the worst of all. They did not recognize any of it."

The woman continues to talk with the old man.

"The burritos are very big, but they taste like the outside of a cactus. No wonder they are so cheap."

They all laugh at her joke.

"And the Cokes are just like water from this pond," he says motioning down. "They are much better in Mexico. And they say, no one sings here," he says. "This is very strange. People just watch TV and talk on their phones. People do not have guitars, or play for each other. Where is the *alegría*? There is no reason to stay."

The woman smiles and gently nods to her husband.

"On TV, everyone was laughing together over nice meals. But they did not see any of these people. They do not see these meals. They do not think they really exist." The old man listens to them. "They say that it was a nice visit for them. But it is too much…what does Florita say?…" the old man says scratching his chin, "…*poop?*"

She sets out a thin blanket and the girl lies on it with her doll. She encourages the old man to sit down, which he does. He unfolds the cloth with food and with a small knife cuts a piece of dried beef, carefully wrapping it in a torn piece of tortilla. He offers it to the woman, and she takes it. He offers you a piece and then one to Juan.

"Thank you," you say, and take a quick bite. The meat is very tough but spicy. You gnaw at it awhile, until with little progress, you place the whole portion in your mouth. It is flavorful and you relax.

"But," he continues, "they are worried about you."

"Me?" you ask.

"They say you are looking very tired."

"I'm OK," you say.

"And that you smell bad," the old man continues. "They told me not to tell you this part, but maybe you should have a shower sometime soon."

The wife brings out a small bag of M&M's. You recognize it as the bag you gave her. She smiles warmly and shakes out one for you with a smile. The girl instinctively reaches for it, but when the woman whispers something to the girl, she stops and looks at you.

"No thanks," you say. "I'm trying to cut back."

She smiles and gives it to the girl who pops it quickly into her mouth.

"She says that you look more worried, not like the last time they met you. She says that you have lost many things. Maybe you have nothing left. I told them that you have lost your car and your way. She is very worried."

"I haven't lost everything…"

"And your job, you have lost your job. Look even your clothes."

"But I'm borrowing these."

"I did not tell her about Jorge, who is probably waiting for you. She wanted to give you the M&M's because maybe it will give you some energy. But I said that she should keep them. You know why?"

"Why?"

"Because they melt in your mouth and not in your hands!" He laughs loudly at this and turns to see your reaction. You are feeling confused and cannot imagine why the woman would worry about you. The couple smile as the old man translates.

"They liked my joke," he beams.

"But they have nothing," you say. "No money."

"Juan has money from his work. He worked very hard. Maybe not that many dollars," he says. "But you should not be too quick to judge them, my friend. For a family, with such a beautiful daughter, you see, they have other riches. You, my friend are in very bad shape. You are the one that has nothing." He pats you on your back and looks sympathetic. "Look you do not even have your clothes." He glances down at your overalls. "But do not worry, I told her that I will help you. Besides, Florita told me I must."

He nods and pops a small piece of tortilla into his mouth. He chews quietly.

"She wants to know if you would like some coffee. She can make some coffee for us."

You brighten at the thought of a warm cup of cappuccino.

"Yes," you say. "I'd really like a cup."

"Well," he says. "As long as you are not in too big of a hurry to get back."

But the woman has already taken out a small blackened can with a plastic top. Removing the top, she sets a newspaper next to her and, empties coffee grounds in a pile, then fills the can with water from a plastic bottle. She looks up and smiles. Juan meanwhile gathers small dried branches and scraps from the palettes. He leans over and with his matches lights a small wad of newspaper. The twigs immediately crackle and the fire pokes out of the stack. The woman spoons coffee into the can, and stirs.

"*Siéntese*," the woman says and invites you to sit down under the tree. Juan encourages you to join them.

The old man smiles as you take your place.

"You look quite at home," he says. "Are you sure you do not want to go to Mexico? I am sure that her grandmother would like to meet you."

He explains this to the family, who laugh easily as the woman takes a branch and a hanger and suspends the can over the flame. As she moves it in a circle, the sides of the can steam, and you hear the simmering of the liquid. When it boils, she quickly removes it and positions it over a tin cup that Juan slides to her. The coffee foams quickly and the smell is invigorating. You smile as she looks at you.

"She wants to know if you would like sugar in your coffee."

"Yes, and cream."

The old man laughs. "The cream part will be difficult, so maybe this time you can take it without?"

"Yes, I'm sorry."

You accept the cup and smell the coffee. "It smells delicious," you say. "*Muy bueno.*"

Jenz Johnson

"*Gracias*," she says, and motions that you should take a sip.

"She says that this will make you feel better."

You blow on the coffee until it is cool enough to sip. The coffee is very strong and rich.

"Yes, very good," you say, nodding.

"Gracias," she says.

In fact, the coffee is much better than any cup you buy in the drive-throughs. It has a thick consistency, but not too bitter.

"She says that she wishes she had her kitchen. She makes many things in her kitchen. And the coffee here is very bad. Maxwell House."

"Maxwell House? This is Maxwell House?"

"Si," she says.

"Some day she will have her kitchen again. It is not much, but she cooks much better than McDonald's."

You notice that no one else is drinking coffee.

"Am I the only one?" you ask.

"There is only one cup, so my friend, maybe you wish to pass it around."

"Oh, sorry," you say sheepishly.

The old man smiles and passes the cup to Juan, who also compliments the woman on the flavor. The old man sips with a big smile and the cup makes its round back to you.

"I told them about your father. That he spoke Spanish."

"Yes," you say. "Unfortunately I never learned."

"They say it is a shame. Spanish is such a beautiful language. It is the language of poetry."

"Yes," you say. The old man continues to talk softly with the couple, and they smile and nod occasionally. He glances over to the daughter who now is sound asleep. The woman pulls a small blanket over her and pushes the hair from the girl's forehead.

"Well, my friend. We must go. It is already getting late. They should rest. Their tour group is arriving soon."

"Their what?"

"They have signed up for a tour," he says nonchalantly. "It is easier going back, of course. They could get a ride from the *migre*. It is free after all. But they like to be in a group."

She nods at this, as if understanding the conversation.

"Besides, the food is better. She says that she likes running into you this way. That someday she would like to make you her special Chicken Mole."

"I'd like that," you say, then to the woman, "*muchas gracias.*"

"De nada," she replies.

"Mucho gusto," Juan says, and shakes your hand.

The old man tips his hat and you follow him down to the arroyo.

The old man is running in small steps up a rugged trail. He motions for you to catch up, and you quickly pick up your pace.

"We are being followed," he says with short breaths. He nods to your right, the direction that you came. When you look over, all you can see is the afternoon wind rustling the scrub bushes.

"Who?"

"I am afraid we will need to take a detour through another part of the desert. This path is well known. Even the big cats know it."

"Cats?" you ask.

"Mountain lions. They can smell the path and wait for their dinner to arrive."

"There aren't any mountain lions in the desert," you say.

"They come down from the mountains over there. See. The ranches further south attract them."

He moves his satchel to the front so to prevent it from bouncing around, then moves to a ridge overlooking a stretch of desert. He nods in the direction and jumps quickly onto a rock. You follow closely behind, stumbling on a manzanilla branch. Grabbing your elbow, he moves you to the second rock, and you try to balance yourself with one hand. "The cats will usually not follow you up on rocks," he says.

Letting go of your elbow, he scampers along a row of rocks. The desert below begins looking farther away. "This way," he says.

The small trail rises out of the desert floor and winds around to the small mountain. The old man walks in front, shoulders steady, moving quickly to higher ground. The desert grows smaller below, and you see the city in the distance.

The path is really not a path at all. It seems to be little more than a space between the plants. But the old man keeps a brisk pace, no matter what rocks or shrubs appear in the way.

A slight breeze blows over you, cooling your soaked shirt. You reach a small summit on an outcropping of rocks.

"Ah," the old man says with a smile, and with a quick jump, he is up on one of the rocks looking down. "This way."

You climb up the rock as best you can, grabbing onto the small handholds, then throwing a leg over an edge. As you stand up, you see a large flat rock with a dead tree next to it. "There," he says, pointing, "we have reached the rock."

With small jumps, he moves from rock to rock, until he is on the largest one where he stops and looks around. With a slow movement, he stretches. You move carefully over to him, watching your feet and crouching occasionally when stepping across to a new boulder.

He sets his satchel down, and finds some shade under the tree, sitting down and leaning back. "Come," he says.

You sit down and settle back against a rock, breathing hard. He takes a quick sip from the canteen and offers it to you.

"Do not drink too much," he says. "Take a small sip."

You hold the water to your lips and take a large gulp before you give the canteen back. He unfolds the cloth with food and with a small knife cuts a piece of dried beef, carefully wrapping it in a torn piece of tortilla. He offers it to you. You thank him, and take a quick bite. The meat is tough like belt leather. Your jaws ache was you chew arduously, slowing breaking the lump apart. He nods and pops a small piece into his mouth. He chews quietly. The wind picks up and you put a hand on your hat to make sure it does not blow away. You eat in silence, looking over the valley. The sky, which is bleached, now picks up more blue, and the far edges fall into shadow.

After he has eaten a few pieces of meat, he says. "It is best that you rest. I myself am tired."

Soon, he is breathing deeply, and the first sounds of snoring come muffled from under his poncho. You look up at the sky and close your eyes.

You are propped up on one elbow on your beach towel as the little Czech mathematician walks onto the sand. You recognize the goggle-shaped glasses. It is Kurt Gödel. Despite his glasses, he is buff in his shirt that's unbuttoned to wherever, hair perfectly askew. He's talking to his Spanish maid, who has accidentally spilled a bottle of wart remover on her dress. Now she is wearing one of his shirts, also unbuttoned, while he walks with the ocean to his back and tries to explain the simplicity of his proof.

"You see," he says, as she tries to pull the shirt together across her breasts, "I was able to show something so beautiful today. That every logical system we find ourselves in has a critical flaw. Has a fatal flaw, if you will."

"A flaw?" she asks with her strong accent.

"Yes. Even in the simplest of mathematics, there are things that you cannot prove. You cannot just write out a simple little proof for everything. Some things are just beyond knowing, beyond proving."

She pouts. "And how did you prove this?" She asks.

He turns. "I wrote out a simple little proof," he says.

"You are toying with me, Mr. Gödel. Is this what you want?"

And his eyes gaze where his shirt is being unbuttoned.

"Call me Kurt," he says.

"Kurt," she repeats.

"But you don't understand," he continues. "I can prove that I cannot prove some things. This is a mathematical certainty. But I cannot prove it with the mathematics itself. You see. That's the difference."

She blushes.

"So, within the system…" she begins.

"Yes," he replies, seeing a budding mathematician as her bosom rises and she gulps for air. "You can only really prove something about a system when you are outside of the system. You understand, don't you?"

She smiles, but her quizzical expression shows she is not quite sure whether she understands what he is referring to. "I think you're saying that you… and I… we are a system. Like this. Together. We have our own mathematics. " She reaches out and touches his bare chest with her fingertips.

"Yes," he responds blinking rapidly.

"We have functions that we can do together."

Blink, blink.

"And operations that we can do together…"

Blink.

"And," she continues, "we cannot prove many things together. There are some things that we cannot do. We have our limitations—in this system of ours."

"Yes," he says slowly. Where is her syllogism heading?

"It is not our fault. Not your fault. Not my fault."

His eyes widen.

"Nonetheless," she continues. "Our little system, for all its beauty, its wonderfulness, for all its possibilities, it is incomplete."

You watch Gödel's face, a full blown shock of recognition.

"I never thought of it that way," he says. "Precisely."

He is excited, realizing the capping glory to his up-to-then incomplete Incompleteness theorem. He races down the beach to transcribe the missing piece. Madly, he rushes into his hut and the mathematics come pouring out of his fingers. Papers fly about. He sees that our system of logic has far-reaching implications to life itself. That the same logic we throw around every day is completely useless at times. Could it be useless at the most important times in one's life? He ponders this.

This could easily be your stuckness. It could explain how you can sink into a place where there is no way out.

Getting unstuck is not going to be like stopping at a different coffee shop on the way to work. Or foregoing the extra shot in your third afternoon latte.

No, you are in the quicksand of life's paradoxes.

But maybe if you stay calm and collected, you will sink at a much slower pace.

◊　　◊　　◊

You wake up suddenly with a chill. The old man is feeding a small fire from a pile of branches he has collected, snapping dry brushwood and laying it carefully on the stack. He has dragged a dead branch closer to the fire and is examining how to break it up. The flames flash, then die down in the wind.

"How long did I sleep?" you ask. "I didn't think that I was *that* tired."

You sit up. There is a faint pink glow around the horizon, the chaparral hidden below except for a few larger trees that look like solitary figures, moving in the wind. You look out over the desert. A gentle rustling of the brush below sounds peaceful and comforting. Gradually the desert falls into darkness and you nibble at the meat the old man has laid out. The wind picks up and you move closer to the fire.

Overhead, the sky is lit up with great pockets of stars. Beyond the desert, the city glows pink and white. You see streets form a grid of lights. Except for the wind, it is silent and empty, except for a distance howl.

"Coyotes?"

The coyote howls in short yips that echo in the distance. Calls from other coyotes quietly join in.

"How much further?" you ask.

"We are here, my friend," the old man says.

"This is *El Paso*?"

He nods.

You look around. It is a small clearing that looks out over the city. A cool breeze lifts off the desert. You feel relaxed and peaceful, enjoying the warmth of the fire and the muted crackling of dried branches.

"My friend," he says. "Tell me about your home. The one you want to return to."

"My home. Well, my apartment is just, well, nice. I don't want to return there necessarily."

He nods.

"I mean, I want to return. But I want to know what I want to do."

"But you have a nice place?"

"Yes."

"With plenty of water."

"Yes."

"Good food?"

You smile at this.

"It is not bad, my friend."

"I guess not. It's just that I have to make up my mind about things. I love my job, but I will no longer have it when I return. I was laid off."

The old man feeds another small branch into the fire and listens.

"I never know what to do," you say. "That's my problem."

The old man looks around, following the edge of the mountain close by. From a side, you hear a low flutter, as if someone is opening a door. When you turn in the direction, you only see pitch black, and the tops of rocks from the fire.

"Did you hear that?" he asks.

"Yes," you say. "The wind."

"Shh," he says. He lets his gaze rise up. Above the spot where you were sitting, there is another outcropping of rocks. The flames now paint the façade of rocks in a flickering, yellow glow. Along the top edge, you suddenly see something move to the right. "Maybe it is time that you come to the other side of the fire. Slowly."

You stand up, dusting off your hands against the side of your overalls. He motions for you to move slowly. You step around the small flames of the fire jumping up when the wind momentarily subsides. Faintly, you still hear the sound, but it resembles a low rocking sound, almost like a deck of cards being slowly shuffled.

"What was that?" you say.

"Shh," he says. The shadow moves slightly to the left, a brief flash of a rock face, almost like the arm of a chair. It looks like a piece of furniture moving. The ledge is about twenty feet from you and you stare at it.

"We should go," you say. "Let's go."

"There is nowhere to go," he says.

Slowly your eyes adjust and you see the outline of a large animal breathing. It is standing on the rocks directly in front of you, looking down at you.

"A mountain lion." you say. "Oh, my God." You glance at the old man and see that his face is suddenly very solemn.

"Stand up," he says.

But you can't stand up. You are hunched forward, your knees shaking, feet splayed in the dirt. Over the tips of the flames, you see the cat's ears and face light up as it edges closer. Its huge body is crouched close to the edge and its eyes are now glued to you.

"What should we do?" you whisper.

The grandfather does not answer, but his head nods slightly to the left and down. You look over and see some small rocks and a few larger ones.

The cat suddenly snarls, and raises up slightly. You see his paws move along the edge of the rock, pressing the surface rhythmically like a massage as the old man slowly pushes a small pile of kindling into the blaze. The fire surges up and the cat growls loudly, edging back slightly.

"He doesn't like fire," you say.

"Everyone knows this," the old man says. "That's not going to save us." He moves quickly to drag a larger branch over.

"Now!" he shouts.

You grab a rock and throw it. The animal moves to one side. You fumble around, scrambling for other rocks and branches. You find another rock and throw it, striking the rocks in front of the cat. You look around for anything that you can throw and find a large branch. You thrust the branch forward, over the fire. The leaves ignite immediately and you heave it. The mountain lion steps back

Jenz Johnson

further. Your arms are aching. You stoop down and find another stone, wait until the cat stops moving, then heave the rock with all of your force toward it.

Suddenly the cat is in the air, lunging at you, his paws outstretched and claws extended, its eyes are bright orange, and teeth bared. It lands hard on the edge of the bonfire, leaves scattering. Its large brown body twists around. You slide to the dirt as the cat skids, then hastily jump to your feet and start running toward the edge. There is a loud roar and then dead silence. You have leaped forward, over the edge, into the abyss.

You are engulfed by the darkness, air rushing around you, legs pumping, arms paddling in the night. You hear the dead surface of the mountain, as your heart pounds in your ears, cool air on your face.

You slam hard on your feet, tumbling into sharp branches, spinning to your knees. You struggle up, hands bloodied in thorns, and try to see. The path is ablaze in moonlight, like a freeway, white and glowing. Your arms push aside the manzanilla and find the trail which runs below an outcropping then zigzags around large slabs of rock. You leap from one bright spot on the ground to another. The trail breaks off onto a small plateau and you keep moving, spotting the glow on the other side. Your feet hit a large edge of rocks, and you jump to one side. The trail opens up into a large wash, flooded in the moonlight, and you keep running through it.

Suddenly, you see a giant standing with an arm up, beckoning you. You look indirectly into its body. It's a large tree, a dead one with only a couple of large branches like arms. The bark is scratchy as you scramble up the trunk, using your fingers in the small cracks. Your feet feel around and find a large knot and you stand on it, reaching up. Carefully you maneuver up and find a series of small footholds. Finally you reach a large limb and straddle it, holding onto the trunk, panting and trembling. Your head is pounding. Below, the arroyo is faintly visible with a winding path of dark vegetation on either side.

After a few minutes, there are hoots and you hear claws on top of the tree. You look up to see the bird against the sky, head jerking around, surveying the landscape. One eye catches the light and stares down at you coldly. You lean forward against the trunk, hands still shaking, and close your eyes.

The old man nudges you.

Ants are crawling on your face and into your nose, and you find your face plastered to the bark, arms still gripping the sides. You release the trunk, and hastily wipe off the ants. The desert is just becoming visible, the blackness giving way to an early morning pink. You quickly look down, expecting to see the cat.

The old man is beaming at you, patting you on the shoulder.

"You did good, my friend."

"Where are we?" you ask.

Instead of answering, he straightens his poncho, pulling his hat tight over his forehead.

"Come," the old man says. "I'm hungry."

"I could have been killed."

The old man considers this as he gathers his satchel, which hangs from a branch, and lowers himself down. Carefully you back down the trunk. The bark has more crannies for your hands, and small broken branches that you did not see last night. Slowly you follow him down.

He begins trotting along a path into the brush. "Let's hurry," he says, jumping a bit, then speeding ahead with a skip to his step. You follow and soon find portions of the desert that you remember.

A small gully leads to a dirt wall with crevasses cut into its side. He finds a foothold and nods to you. You follow him to a level path above. There is a rickety set of stairs that leads up near the end of the wall. You step quickly and find yourself at the top in a vacant lot. There are street lights in the distance, and you slow down and walk calmly through tumbleweeds and discarded tires.

You follow the old man to a street.

"Where are we," you ask.

The old man turns at an alley and you almost run into him.

"We are here," he says, indicating everything about you. He shakes his head sadly as he walks along the side of Casa De Ríos to the rear. He stops at the chain link fence at the back. A couple of dogs wander over and sniff your overalls.

"Do we have to climb this?" you ask, looking up.

"No. You wait by the gate."

"Here?"

He scoffs and quickly backtracks as you lean against the fence. The sky is a turning from pink to violet, clouds thinning out near the mountains. You look to your left and right, trying to see if anyone is coming. In front of you, scrub brush and clusters of cholla spread out.

Jenz Johnson

Suddenly, the fence rattles and you see the old man.

"Wake up," he says, and opens the gate from the inside with a key.

You quickly enter and follow him to the rear door, and into a large kitchen. The smells are overwhelming, and a teenager near the back glances up as he empties a large box of tortilla chips into a plastic bin. You walk past a row of giant pots, bubbling with beans, water, and soups.

"This is Jorge?" a large man asks. You practically bump into him as you turn the corner. He is standing in the middle of a hallway, holding an unlit cigar, a sports coat pulled over a black polo shirt. His eyebrows are bushy and he has salt and pepper hair combed straight back.

"This is Mauricio," the old man says in a whisper, then to Mauricio, he says. "Yes, another Jorge."

"And he too is lost, I presume," Mauricio says.

"Lost, yes."

"Well, you should throw him back. He's just a small fish, too small to worry about."

"I would," the old man agrees, "but Florita likes him."

"Ah," he says. "She likes odd things, doesn't she?"

"Many odd things," the old man says, hat in hand, indicating himself as well.

"Well, then. You look good, my friend. More relaxed. But I do not see you. What is happening?"

"I am retired," he says. "More or less."

"Yes?"

The old man nods.

"You look well," Mauricio smiles. "And Lupé?"

"She is well also," the old man replies.

"You look hungry, gringo," Mauricio says turning to you.

You nod.

"He is always hungry," the old man explains.

"And you speak?"

"Yes. Sorry."

"He is very well-behaved," Mauricio comments to the old man.

"Yes, I am sorry to say."

"Jose," he shouts over your head. "Bring a bowl of *pozole* and some tortillas." He looks at you again. "You will eat like a king. Have you ever had green *pozole*?"

"No, sir."

"It is a specialty here," he says. He eyes the kitchen looking at the workers. It is a big kitchen with large refrigerators and stainless steel shelves next to a row of ovens and stoves. "Once you have it, you will be a changed man."

"This is true," says the old man, nodding.

"Sit there," he says, then nods to the old man, who pushes you back into the kitchen, and to a small alcove. There is a table with a large bowl of green leaves. You sit down, and a large bowl of soup arrives. The teenager looks at you, places a napkin and a spoon, then a small bowl of brittle bread chunks.

"You are very lucky," the old man says. "Mauricio, I think, likes you. At least he does not hate you."

"But how will I get back home."

"You talk too much. Eat your soup."

The old man ducks away and follows Mauricio. You look up to see the eyes of the kitchen on you. Most of the people have black hairnets pulled low over their foreheads, a few with greased-stained hats. They move around, clanking pots and sliding plates on a small shelf at the opposite end.

The soup is steaming in front of you. You take a piece of the old bread, and crumble it into the soup. It is green with chunks of chicken and hominy floating in it. Cooling a spoonful, you bring it to your mouth. The flavors are incredible. The broth has a deep, smoky flavor, with a spicy kick. In a short time, the bowl is empty and you set the spoon down.

The old man reappears, and a bowl of *pozole* is brought to him.

"OK," he says. "It is arranged. He made a phone call."

"The soup was really good."

"Yes, *pozole* is my favorite. They make it well."

"What's in it?"

"Listen," the old man says. "I am not here to give you a cooking lesson." He quickly slurps the soup, lowering his head to the bowl and spooning the broth over the rim. He glances up between slurps. "We must leave quickly, though. The old man stirs his soup, picking out a few strips of chicken with his fingers. He places them into his mouth.

Outside, he turns into an alley and you notice the house. It is quiet, and the fence sways. The worn shingles, creaky gate and dilapidated yard welcome you. You look at the windows, trying to see if anyone is up and about, but only see curtains and flower pots.

The old man slows down and walks quietly through the gate. He steps carefully over the stones leading through the yard, then up the back porch to the door. He stops and turns with his fingers to his lips, opening the door. You nod and unsling your satchel. Inside, there are smells of food and perfume. The table in the kitchen is cleared, except for crayons and a drawing of you. You stare at it. Your head is big, and hair pointing up. Your name is written above with a big arrow that points down to the figure. The old man smiles and pats you on the back.

He motions you into the bedroom, jutting his jaw out to the bed.

"Sleep," he whispers, folding his poncho over a chair. He finds his bed and pulls the sheet over him, hanging his hat on the bedpost.

It is still early morning, as you climb into your makeshift bed across the room. You look up at the ceiling. The plaster is broken along the edges, and a large crack is open down the middle.

When you awake, no one is there. Sheets are piled on each bed, and the room smells of bacon. You get up and wipe your eyes. As you stand up, you hear voices from the kitchen stopping.

You feel rested and alert, as you move quietly to the door, but your legs ache from the previous day's activities. When you open the door, Florita looks up from the table, crayon in hand. She smiles at you and waves.

"Grandfather," she shouts, "he is up!"

"Yes," the old man says, his back to you. "Finally."

Lupé says something in Spanish, and the girl quickly gets up and guides you to a place. A cup of coffee slides next to you and a plate of eggs and tortillas appears, steaming hot. The tortillas look fresh, slightly burned, but thin and brown.

"You slept a long time," the old man says.

"I guess I was tired."

"My mother says that you should eat now," the girl says. "You do not look so good."

You look back to Lupé who is at the sink, turning to indicate your plate.

"*Gracias*," you say.

"*De nada*," she replies, bowing slightly with a hint of a smile.

The plate is full of eggs and green strips, with a crumble of white cheese on top.

"These are Cactus Eggs," Florita says. "They are my favorite."

"Is the green stuff really cactus?"

"Oh yes," she says. "Prickly pear. Don't worry, there are no thorns." She laughs and waits for you to begin.

You push a forkful into your mouth, and the flavor is very similar to green peppers. "They're good. Tell your mother that her eggs are good!"

The girl smiles and Lupé nods.

"You are looking much better, my friend," the grandfather says.

"I feel better," you say. "I slept like a rock."

You are ravenous and eat with large forkfuls, your cheeks filling up. You gulp the coffee and feel ready to face the day. When you finish, Lupé places a hand on your shoulder, taking your plate. The grandfather gets up from the table.

"It is time for you to get started," he says. "Do you think you can find your way back?"

You stop chewing. "I thought you were going to show me. I mean, I don't know much more than I did yesterday."

"Ah, but you do," the grandfather says.

"And I still don't have my car." You look around the table. Florita seems worried and looks to the grandfather.

"This is not a big problem. Not like a mountain lion, am I right?" He laughs. You realize that he is probably right. "Yes, I am certain. Florita. Bring this Jorge his clothes. I think it is time that he gets started."

"But started doing what?" you ask, suddenly feeling your chest tighten. "Jorge out there has stolen my starter."

"See," the grandfather says with pride. "He is already much better than yesterday." Florita smiles too.

"Yes, Grandfather," she says. "I like him. And he will find his way back now."

"Yes, little one." The grandfather leans back on his chair and watches. You are suddenly standing and begin to pace.

"But I still don't know what I can do?" you say.

"Yes, yes," the grandfather says. "You have said this before. But none of us really know what to do. As I said, you are looking much better this morning."

Lupé turns around to look at you.

"My mother says that you still look like Pedro, our dog."

The grandfather laughs at this. "You are all ready, my friend. Look at yourself."

You realize that you are standing at the window staring out. You see the sun streaking across the front yard, but there is no sign of Jorge. You study the carport where his car is parked, but you cannot see anything.

"See," the grandfather says calmly. "You know more than you think you do. You have a direction already. You are no longer lost."

You see the dog moping in the front yard, shaking himself from the morning dew.

"Jorge likes to eat," the girl suggests. "There are some left in the pan."

"Yes," the grandfather says. "Give him the frying pan. Jorge can be very dangerous. But he is hungry too."

"See, there are some left," she says, pointing to the pan.

The grandfather walks to the window.

"I will tell you something," he says. "I don't like that Jorge. He has stayed here too long now. He eats our food. Lupé does his wash. His is lost just like you. He has been working on this car of his ever since. But he does not know anything about cars."

The girl is struggling with the pan. It has a lump of eggs and a couple of strips of bacon. She drags it off the stove slowly, but it is too heavy.

"Help Florita," he says.

You take it from the girl. The pan is not that heavy and fits your hand easily. You feel suddenly at ease.

"Do not look so surprised. There are many roads to where you are going. You sometimes have to pick one."

"But, why would he do anything for me? For breakfast? This doesn't make any sense. I don't want to die over a car part."

"But you said that this is important. We all must die, my little puppy. Why not over a car part, as you say?" He pulls the curtain to one side and you see Jorge stirring on a small cot with an arm over his eyes. He appears to be sleeping, with one leg on the cot and one off.

"No, I can't do this," you say stepping back. "This is crazy."

"You cannot stay here," the grandfather says. "Although you are not bright, neither is Jorge. He is probably very hungry by now." He smiles at this and gives you a push. "I am afraid, that you must figure this part out. It is time for you to go."

"Grandfather is right. You should listen," the girl says. "My mother does not think you will go outside." She smiles. "But I told her that she's wrong. That you are not lost any more."

You are standing over Jorge who is snoring very loudly. He looks up from under his arm, disoriented, beer near his feet. He rubs his eyes.

"Did you bring me my breakfast, *amigo*?" he says looking at the frying pan.

You have forgotten what you're going to say. You realize that there's not much you can say.

"I need my starter back," you say.

He laughs and tries to sit up. He is breathless. Bracing an elbow, he lifts halfway up, squinting into the sun that streams over your shoulder and into his eyes. "I need your starter, also," he says. "It's a damn good one."

"I need it." The frying pan weighs heavily in your hand.

"But, my friend ..."

"You stole it, Jorge."

"Borrowed maybe." He snickers. "It's found a new home."

"Stole. I need it back," you say.

He laughs. "And what, this frying pan is your wrench?" he asks. He laughs louder and repositions his elbow to handle his weight. "You are a cook, *vato*, not a mechanic."

"You aren't a mechanic either," you say. "Your car will never run."

With this, his face gets serious.

"My friend, this is not a very nice thing to say." He tries again to sit up.

"I'm not your friend," you say. You see him now as a drunk. There is stubble on his chin, and below his cap, his eyes are bloodshot and watering. He moves to sit up, shaking his head.

"I want my starter back. Now." Your hand holding the pan begins to move, just slightly. He looks at the frying pan and up at you.

There is a loud popping sound and without realizing it, you have smashed a head light. Jorge is now up, struggling to his feet. Eggs and bacon have scattered about the carport, sticking to the grill of the car.

"I want it back," you shout. Your hands are shaking, and you are pacing back and forth, looking at what else can be broken. You kick at a fender, again and again, until it loosens, then take the pan in both hands.

Jorge's arms are outstretched.

"Wait," he says. You swing, banging the top of the car.

"I will kill you for that," he yells.

"I will kill you first," you yell back and move closer.

You take aim at a side window. The sun is bright and hot, and you see the small carport filled with odd tools, bottles of beer, magazines and junk. Jorge staggers to the car.

"Wait, wait," he says. He braces himself on the fender. "Don't!"

"Then, give me my starter." You are uncontrollable. You are moving toward him, not sure just what you will do, the pan in both hands.

"No! Hold it," he says raising his hands to protect himself, looking sideways. "I don't have your starter," he says. His palms are up. "A bad joke." He motions to your car, which is parked where you left it. "See."

The car looks untouched, but dusty.

"See," he says. He walks carefully to the headlight that you have turned into a crushed pile of glass.

You lower the pan.

You walk to the front. The keys are still in the ignition. You get in and the car starts. You shut the car off.

You are breathing heavily, sweating. The inside of the window is fogging up, and the car smells like coffee.

◊   ◊   ◊

"My grandfather chose a very good weapon for you," the girl says when you return to the kitchen. "Didn't he? He is very smart."

The grandfather is standing at the window, and nods approvingly. The girl takes you by the hand and guides you back to your seat at the breakfast table. There is a half cup of coffee left.

"I have a very bad temper," you say. "I've always had a very bad one. I've tried to control it, but…"

"It's a very good one," the grandfather says. "It came to your rescue with Jorge. Otherwise, you would still be lost."

He stands, and you get up.

"Now, you must leave."

"But, how will I find my way back."

"That will not be a problem now."

"But the roads?"

"Just turn to your left and go straight," he says.

"But there are no straight roads out here."

"It doesn't matter. Just follow the mailman. He has done this before. No one messes with the mailman." The grandfather goes to the window and looks out. The girl is standing behind you with your old clothes. She has them in a paper bag and places them in your hands.

"I'm glad you came though." She gives you a hug.

"I am too," you say. You suddenly are at ease and feel well-rested. You look around you and feel different. Everything feels very different.

The mother places the frying pan in your hands.

"My mother says you must take your weapon," the girl says. "You may need it."

"I don't know…" you say.

"OK, my friend," the grandfather says. "The mailman is leaving."

You quickly run to the car, past the puddles, the mud and Jorge standing, still stunned next to his headlight. A small mail truck pulls into the yard, and the grandfather points to you. Your car starts up, and you wait for the mail truck to move into the street.

> *" The mind must be left to itself, utterly free to move about according to its own nature"*
> —*Shunryu Suzuki,* Zen Mind, Beginner's Mind

The road is no more than two tire tracks, cut into the rocky desert floor. A yellow sign warns of hairpin curves. You look up and see a sharp rise, rocks and boulders jutting out. You shift down and slowly climb up, the desert basin spreading out below.

The center line disappears as you edge around the first turn. Small rocks are scattered along the road side. The next turn is somewhat tighter, and you brake almost to a stop. As you reach the top, the valley opens up in front of you. There is a turnout and you pull off.

You find the iPhone tucked into a pocket of your damp clothes. You open the door and carefully set your feet on the dirt. You feel wobbly, but lift yourself up. You walk to the edge, near a cluster of boulders. The wind whips around the rocks, but otherwise, there is no movement, no cars.

You open up the iPhone's lid and find a strong signal. Your voicemail has piled up. You skip through most of it: Sam, Agnes, Blockbuster movies, Burgie, an automated mortgage ad, Vermette and the rest. You don't have the energy to listen.

You dial Katie's extension and her voice message picks up after a few rings. You hear her voice as she calmly explains how to leave a message.

You hesitate, then press *# to rerecord.

"It's me," you say. "I thought maybe we could see each other, I mean, get dinner, or something."

You shake your head and re-record it again.

"It's me," you say. "See you soon." You leave it at that, although there are a number of things that you wish you could say to her. You look at your iPhone then gaze out across the valley. There is a purple hue along the horizon and the color changes as the sun gets brighter.

You ring Burgie.

"Where have you been, man?"

"I took the scenic route."

"Your phone was off."

"I've been out of range for a while."

"Well, I should have figured that one out. That's you all over. Out of range."

"I feel like I'm on the top of the world."

"Well, there sure is a lot of static all right."

"Yeah, I'm on a mountain."

"OK. I guess that explains it then. Any idea where you are?"

"Heading north, northeast."

"OK."

"It's peaceful up here."

"OK. Not to bring you down or anything, but you've been out for days and everyone seems to be looking for you. You're checked out to the technical library. What is that?"

"Checked out?"

"Well, it's on the board so it's official. But frankly, Gordon is going into management meltdown. You know, angry, out of control, snapping at everyone, except Agnes, indecisive. Well, he's indecisive a lot. Anyway, he's murder to be around. Even more than usual. Seems to have come out of his shell though."

"Well, can't be helped."

"What?"

"The situation."

"I don't know. Coming to work might have helped a wee bit."

"I mean, I can't help where I am."

"You mean on the mountain?"

"I can't explain it," you say looking out, everything suddenly so peaceful, waiting for you. "OK, I'll try. First, I can't go back. There is nothing that I want back there. My apartment, my job, myself. It's all a big rut."

"Well, one of those ruts pays the bills."

"I try to visualize what my apartment looks like and I can't. I mean there is nothing that tugs me back there, except maybe to see Vermette. Have you dropped by?"

"Yeah, I went to your place, and he's closed down the diner. At least for a few days."

"Closed it?"

"Yep, that's what the sign said. 'Until further notice' is what it said."

There was silence on the other end of the line.

"You sound a whole lot better today."

"Yes, definitely. I can't figure out where or how, but suddenly I'm a little skewed, you know?"

"Well, skew I can understand. Be careful."

"I might need a place to crash tonight, though."

"Yeah, OK."

"And is Katie there at work?"

"Agnes's typist? Yeah, why?"

"Listen, I'm coming to work."

"Just stay clear of Gordon."

"That's why I'm coming in. I've got a score to settle."

"This is not sounding too good."

"Ever feel like you have a fight on your hands and there is just no avoiding it."

"Not really."

"That's how I feel."

You take a deep breath and study the valley.

Dust follows your car as you pull into the parking annex, the late morning sun shining through the passenger side window. You navigate over a deep trough down the center of the lot, and pull into a open space near the far end. The car stops, and you collect yourself. In the rearview mirror, you look unsettled, your face unshaven and dark. Although you feel tired, your eyes seem alert. From the backseat, you pull the large paper bag over and stuff it into your backpack. You ease into the heat, sliding the backpack over a shoulder, and look around.

Shuffling down the rows of cars, you stare at the office building on the other side of the freeway. The heat momentarily subsides when you reach the opening to the underpass. The cool air under the freeway smells of smoke and burnt tortillas. You walk carefully along the side. At the top of the embankment just under the freeway, a sleeping bag is half-open on a wooden shipping palette. There are remnants of a small fire, and the ashes stir in the breeze that rushes through the passageway. A couple of empty bean cans have rolled onto the road and you step over them, hitching up your backpack, and keeping a brisk pace. Overhead, the rumbling of morning traffic shakes the concrete.

You emerge into the sunlight and walk along the sidewalk, past the main parking lot filled with cars, along the neat rows of cactus, to the entrance. You spot Alex's van. In the shade, Kaufman leans on a concrete planter, puffing at a cigarette. He nods.

"Decided to come back, have we?" Kaufman says.

"Long story," you say.

"I'm sure. Anyway, everyone's looking for you." He takes another drag. "And I like your getup. Very blue collar."

You glance down at your blue overalls and shrug. "I was in a hurry to get back. Who's looking for me?"

"Dolores for one. She's holding court in the coffee room, regaling the brewsters on how you are dragging the company down. This from someone who doesn't know the difference between the Alt and Control keys."

"Probably Mac-itis," you say. "Who else is looking for me?"

"Of course, Gordon has his tit in a wringer. But I think it's really Agnes. But what do I know? All I see is that things are getting worse. Machines are left off. No one complains about fixing their machines any more. That's not a good sign."

"The ship is sinking," you say. "Maybe that's it."

He leans his head back as he takes a long, luxurious drag from his cigarette, letting a curl of smoke seep skyward, admiring the side of the building.

"More time for me," he says. "I'm not complaining."

He leans forward and lifts his eyes to the third floor, to the corner where Gordon has his office. "He's pacing up there. I can hear him. I think we have visitors. I moved the big LCD projector into the conference room just this morning. I don't do that unless someone important is showing up. Maybe it's a surprise visit. From a customer."

"Customers, you think?," you say. "Out of the blue like this?"

"Can't be good. We always get more notice than this, so we can string together a working demonstration. You know. Why so secretive? Hey, what do I know?"

"Another layoff?" you ask.

"Won't surprise me."

"Think I'll head up," you say. "Anyway, my days are numbered."

"Yeah, that's another way to look at it," he says, looking at his cigarette butt. "How're those fluorescent lights?"

"Can't remember," you say. "It feels like an eternity since I was here."

"Yeah. And another thing," he says. "Sam was sitting at your machine yesterday."

"He was?"

Kaufman nods. "Funny, huh, since your station logs out automatically. Odd." Kaufman says.

"Odd," you agree and head toward the main doors.

◊　◊　◊

As you shuffle down the corridor, people stop mid-sentence to glance over at you, cups raised to their lips, their eyes following you as if your gait will somehow tell them something. You nod but they continue to stare. There is more buzzing in the office, from groups tucked behind cubicles, talking and hunched over memos. You head toward your cubicle.

"Hey. Prodigal son returns." It is Sam's voice from behind. He walks with a folder under his arm, blue shirt and tie, with Paul next to him carrying a stack of manuals. "Ever hear of something like a dress code." He laughs nodding to your overalls.

"We don't have a dress code" you say, pulling on the front of your overalls. You stop and face Sam. "It's just temporary."

"It suits you," he says. "Get it."

"I get it."

"And did we get lost, and couldn't come in since Monday?"

"That about sums it up," you say.

"Were we really at the tech library on campus?" he asks. "Because that is what the board said."

"The board?" you ask surprised. "You mean Agnes' board."

"What other board do we have?"

"Deep in the stacks," you reply, although you don't recall telling Burgie anything about checking you out.

"It doesn't matter," he says. "Today should be a very interesting day. For you especially."

"It already is," you say.

"Because Gordon is really on the prowl now. But, you know, newbie, for such a neophyte, I have to hand it to you. To screw things up so much takes a real concerted effort." He pulls close and lowers his voice. "I think you should avoid the embarrassment and just start packing up. It wouldn't surprise me if they kicked your ass out of here. I say, it was a long time coming. They should have yanked you off this project long ago. Any one of my guys can do your stuff."

"You said *they*."

"Gordon."

"They?"

"You know what I meant," he says. "Don't act so smart."

"I just wanted to be clear, Sam."

"Consider yourself all clear."

"OK," you say. Sam looks around at a few heads turned his way, looking at him nervously.

"You might as well get started." He smiles. "Gordon is steaming. Don't say I didn't warn you. He's looking for you. So, you can't hide for very much longer."

"He asked to see me?"

"Not in so many words. But Agnes was casing your cubicle. What do you think?"

You adjust the strap of your backpack and feel the weight of the frying pan and clothes in it.

"I never saw that much in you," he says. "I have to confess that I thought he should have skipped hiring you. It would have saved us all the trouble." Up close, Sam is sweating. You can almost smell the panic. But before you can respond, Sam has turned and looked behind you. "Hey, it's the Bobbsey Twins…"

Down the corridor, Burgie and Jack walk toward you, Burgie lurching forward with his hands at his sides. Jack gives a small wave.

"This must be nice for you," Sam says with a smirk. "Your welcoming committee. I think you'll all get fired soon, if you ask me."

"Hey," you say as Burgie reaches you.

"Hey," he says, then glances at Sam.

"You look really funny," Jack says, looking at your chest.

"Yes, it's the clothes…"

"You could have shaved. " Jack says. "You have that panhandle look."

"Very fashionable," Sam interjects. "It's *you*." He laughs, and Paul joins in. "I'll leave you lovebirds to catch up."

As Sam disappears around the corner, Burgie gives you a serious look. "This place is really getting weird," he says. "We've got a big meeting tomorrow. What's that all about?"

"Where have you been?" Jack asks. "Were you looking for another job? Myra says you found something and were already working there."

"Nah," you say. "I wish that were true."

"Well," Burgie says. "Sam was sitting at your desk for a while."

"Trying out your chair, most likely," Jack says.

"Yeah, I heard," you say.

"And Alex put in a new coffee perk and yanked all the leftovers in the fridge. What's with that?"

"Visitors," you say.

"Visitors?" Burgie looks confused. "Why?"

"Who knows? Maybe customers…"

"Which ones?"

"Does it matter?" Jack adds, looking worried. "They're all mad at us. Maybe these deadlines are important after all."

"Anyway," Burgie says. "Agnes is in a huff. She's looking all over for you, even came down to see us. First floor dungeon. She never does that."

"Yeah," you say. "Gordon is after me, I think."

"Yeah," Jack says. "In a big way. You finish anything? Did you make any progress on your code?"

"In my own mind, I did," you say. "I know what I want to do with it."

"But, I mean, actual coding?"

"No, not exactly," you say.

"Oh boy. " Jack adds, his eyebrows furled. "It's probably too late now, huh?"

"It was too late last Monday," you say.

"Even Sam was looking worried, don't you think?" Burgie adds.

"Yeah," you say. "Something's up."

Jack nods quickly at this.

"I'm getting hungry," Burgie says. "Isn't it lunch time already?"

"Well, some things stay the same."

"Yeah," Burgie says. "Comforting isn't it?"

You stand at the counter with Agnes reading you your rights.

"I will tell you something, mister," she says, arms folded across her chest. "You will be lucky to survive this day. Mr. Lyman is very angry with you."

Katie's eyes find you, glancing up from her typing. She rolls her eyes, as if to say that the show has begun. You dare not smile, not now.

"I don't know where you were," Agnes says. "I don't for a minute believe that you called in. I certainly didn't receive the calls. But as far as I was concerned, you were truant. That's the long and short of it."

"Agnes," you say. "Maybe I can talk with Gordon now."

"When I'm finished, you can talk with him, young man." She holds a folder in front of her that's stuffed with memos. "This"—she holds up the folder—"is proof of your misdeeds. Every infraction is in here. I've made sure of it."

Katie is shaking her head "no." You see her in your periphery. It is hard to keep your eyes away from her. Her hair falls across her shoulders as she dutifully continues her typing. You want to shut Agnes up, for once. But now is not the time to say anything.

"You have eschewed all convention around this office. You really broke the rules this time, young man." She wants to say more, but she gets flustered, and stomps awkwardly back to her desk. Over her intercom, she announces that you have arrived. Gordon barks back to send you in.

"Time for your just desserts, young man," she says, glaring, and nods to the office door.

Gordon's office is as you remember it, only it looks neater, as if Gordon has tidied up. Gone is his putting green. There seems to be a couple more badminton trophies behind him. He wears small, half-frame glasses and looks cool and professional in his striped shirt and tie.

"You wanted to see me?" you ask, standing in front of his desk.

"Sit," he says without looking up, motioning to a chair. He lays his hand over a small stack of memos as you pull out a chair and ease down.

"I don't know where you have been this week, but I ..."

He finally looks at you.

"What in the world?" He is staring at your clothes. "What is this? What are you wearing..." He looks closely. "A mechanic's uniform?"

"My other clothes were soaked," you say. "From the rain."

"You don't have more than one change of clothes?"

"I was in a hurry," you say. "I came in because you wanted to see me."

"This is ridiculous. You mean to tell me that you have been wearing this all day?"

"Longer actually. Is this what you wanted to talk to me about?"

"This is some kind of joke with you, isn't it?"

"No, Mr. Lyman, not really."

"You think that you can essentially skip work, go work on your car somewhere, or something. Then show up here, late, and act like nothing is wrong."

"I was checked out."

His face is red, and he leans forward with an accusing finger. You focus on the top of his head, where he combs his hair over his bald spot. His scalp remains a pasty white color, while his ears and face turn bright red. You wonder if this is because the capillaries in his

Jenz Johnson

scalp are failing to deliver the oxygen needed to keep his hair growing, or if that it is common for most people.

"Well?" He is still staring at you, but grows more irritated as he notices that you're not looking directly at him, but rather slightly above him. At his bald spot.

"It's not a joke, sir," you say. "I was redesigning my module."

"Redesigning?"

"Yes."

"And, let me guess, you haven't been able to code much more than what you had on Monday, because of this redesign."

"The design is more important than the actual code, sir."

"You're supposed to be done with *XLib* by today. You seem to realize how important it is, and not just for the company. You fail at this and what employer will want you? You can't just decide not to do something, willy-nilly. "

"Well…" you begin.

"Where is it?" he repeats impatiently. "Your module."

"To be honest…"

"…That would be refreshing…" He leans toward you, glaring and fidgeting.

"As I've said, I've laid out a new design."

"I don't want new designs!" He bolts back in his chair as if hit by an errant paintball.

"No, sir."

"I want code."

"I can't code the way it was. The design is just all wrong."

"All wrong? All wrong?" he repeats, unable to understand what you are saying. "Well, then just make it *right*!"

"I mean, it's beyond repair. It needs a full re-write. From the ground up."

"What?" He throws his pen on the desk. "I can see that laying you off was probably the best decision I ever made. In fact, I should have done this sooner." He slams his hand on the desk. "Do you have any idea how juvenile you sound?"

"No."

"Of all of the people who could've done this piece of code, how you ended up with it, is beyond me."

"No one would touch it."

"Because it was so bloody simple. Anyone could write it! In their sleep! But you, you obviously have to have some sort of desire.

What? Some squeaky clean design?" He spits this last word as if it were distasteful. You wince and try to edge back in your chair.

You look again at his bald spot. His eyes are blazing, and you feel yourself being sucked in like a deer in a tractor beam.

"Who do you think you are?" he asks. "And you consider yourself to be some sort of what? Programmer?"

You don't answer.

"I'm not sure how you ever got on our payroll. But it's obvious from this conversation that your days are numbered."

His voice has grown loud, and you are thankful that you escaped most of the spittle that has begun to spray from his mouth, especially on the word *payroll*.

"See if you can get a job after I finish telling the whole business community about your incompetence. That's what it is: incompetence." He looks over his glasses, breathing harder. "You think you can get a job after I'm finished with you?"

You look down at your hands. You remember Florita with her big smile, and her grandfather looking at you proudly. That felt good. You open up your hands. You honestly don't know whether the hands belong to a programmer. They don't even look like your hands any more. They are too clean to be a mechanic's. They lay in your lap. You feel quietly detached from Gordon's rant.

"Well, do you?"

You don't say anything, but look up.

"Now, I will give you a little advice here. I can see just maybe you're rattled. Just maybe you've lost your way. Is this your first layoff?"

You look again at the top of his head.

"OK, then. Think about it. The company depends on you and your code. You bring in this piece of code and you are the hero. You will have everyone's thanks. You sit on your hands and whine, how do you think your peers will regard you? How can you even hold your head up?"

He is right, of course. You do whine. Even Florita noticed this.

"So," Gordon continues, "when you walk out of this office, you go straight to your desk and get cranking. You've got the whole weekend. You get cracking on your work and you put the time that is necessary to produce your code. I don't care what you do to get your desire back. I want to see progress. I want to see *XLib* completed on my desk by tomorrow morning, 8 AM sharp. Maybe, just maybe, I will forget about this conversation. Maybe we will both get through this.

Jenz Johnson

Maybe you will find some work in some company that thinks you have something to offer. Lord knows what they will see in you."

He is calm and almost smiling.

"Well?" he says.

"Sir…" you say, but cannot think of just how to complete the thought. You're not sure what you can say that would resolve the issue. Reality is setting in, and you realize that you will need to figure something out. Given some time to sort it all out, it would be possible. But thinking on the spot is somewhat of a stretch. Your stomach grinds, and you wonder if there was any coffee left in the lunchroom.

He waits impatiently.

"Do you think I could get a cup of coffee?"

He slams his hand down again on the desk, and you hear Agnes murmuring outside and the sound of her high heels.

"Customers are complaining. They're threatening me. You and your cohorts have contaminated everything that has gone out this door. Now, if that isn't enough, your little *XLib*, which everyone seems to need, is weeks behind. And to top this off, you can't get it *up* to do it. Am I getting the picture?"

"Not exactly."

"Listen!" He is fuming. This was not the answer that he was expecting.

"Because…"

"Because why? Because you can't write up this little stinking piece of code. Is that why?"

"Sir. It's all wrong.

"You know," he says, sounding calmer. "This is very interesting. I'm very enlightened by your analysis. But, frankly, I don't give a rat's ass. OK? I just want this thing done. I want it clean. And I want it, here, on my desk by tomorrow morning. Is that clear?"

"I don't think I can," you say.

"Well, this may sound odd, but I think you can."

"Sir…" you say and you stop for a small burp, your stomach beginning to grind.

"Anything else?" he asks. He stands up and motions you to the door. You push the chair carefully to its original position. He waits as you turn, and you move hesitantly out the office door.

◊　◊　◊

"I think you got what was coming to you," Agnes says, looking over her glasses.

"I did," you say. The reception area is empty except for Katie.

"Good." She closes the drawer at her desk and locks it, then putting on her gloves, she loops her arm through her purse. "Let's break for lunch, Katie. You can put the memos in my basket when you're finished."

Katie looks up at you as Agnes leaves. She has a concerned look on her face and wants to say something as your eyes meet. Suddenly, the door to Gordon's office opens quickly, and he storms out in long angry strides, briefcase in hand, without even looking up.

"Have a good lunch, Mr. Lyman," Katie says, but he is already halfway to the elevator. The heels of his shoes echo down the hallway. The reception area is quiet, and you lean your elbow against the counter.

"You look terrible," she asks. She looks at you closely.

You nod and with a smile say, "I'm OK."

"It didn't sound so good in there."

"I've never seen Gordon so mad," you say. "He even began to stammer."

"Agnes has been racing around collecting gossip. Her folder is really overflowing with your accomplishments."

You laugh at this. "Yeah, well, my reputation is pretty much sunk around here."

She laughs also. "And these clothes?"

You look down.

"Jorge?" she asks.

You nod. She laughs at this.

"This is choice," she says. "Well, you said that you were changing, but I'm not sure that this is the right direction."

"It was an eye-opener," you say.

"I'm sure this went down well with Gordon."

"Well, I guess it didn't help."

She gets up from her desk and comes around to the front. As she moves closer, your heart pounds. You cannot take your eyes off of her. She seems to float with each step.

"Can't be that bad," she says. "He usually gets rattled when the deadlines are missed. Must be the stress of the layoff."

"*He's* stressed." you say. She has her hair pulled back and is wearing a light sweater over jeans. There is a light fragrance of flowers that is surprising. "You covered for me, right?"

"I figured you'd lost hold of reality," she says dismissing it with a small wave of her hand. "I figured right, it looks like. At least, by Agnes' board, you were playing by the book."

The hallways are quiet, except the sound of a rolling trash can, as Alex begins his rounds.

"I kind of like this uniform." She reaches over and flicks the collar. "Makes you look kind of, well, ..." she smiles, as if really enjoying all of the drama, "salt of the earth." You laugh nervously. Her eyes are sparkling, and she is enjoying your discomfort. "Very exciting," she says.

"It wasn't planned. I just ended up in the rain, with a Mexican family."

She stops and looks at you, then laughs.

"And you told that to Gordon?"

"No."

She shakes her head. "But it sounds like you pressed all his buttons," she says. "Perfect timing. He's been in a foul mood all week. I wish I could have been a fly on the wall. It would have been worth it to see his face."

"Well, maybe I should do as he says."

She shrugs. "I think you need to take it easy. It looks like you're going to collapse anytime."

"I'm OK," you say. "I just need to sort this out somehow."

"You're thinking too much again," she says. "Hey, you owe me dinner."

You smile, and see that she is looking at you. You don't know what to say.

"Sound like a deal?" she asks.

"Yeah."

She extends a hand and you are surprised by her strong grip. She draws close, and you can feel her breath. She shakes her head.

"You reek," she says stepping back with a big smile. She gives your hand a tap, then steps around the counter and back to her desk. You watch her rearrange her folders.

"OK," you say.

She covers her keyboard and then slings her purse over her shoulder.

"See you after lunch," she says. "How's that?"

"Better than OK."

You watch her as she moves carefully down the hall.

You set your coffee on a stack of manuals and peruse the screen another time. The corridors are darkened; the clicking of your keyboard is the only sign of life. You scroll down and read through the method of one of your subclasses. It seems to get tangled up midway through. You are sure you wrote it differently, but now it seems convoluted.

"You aren't thinking of quitting are you?"

It is Linus Torvald's voice. You glance over to see Linus sitting comfortably on your desk, Nordic sweater pulled around his large frame, sipping at a mug of coffee. He smiles and raises his coffee.

"Because you are almost there."

"It doesn't feel that way," you say.

"It never does. But you know, the only way to make it work is to be persistent."

"I suppose," you say. "But there's a limit to persistence."

"Not really. You have to write the code the way you see it."

"I'm not sure it's going to work that way."

He shrugs. "You'll figure it out." He looks around your cubicle. "This is nice."

You open a manual and read through a package description.

"Remember when you used to write spiders?"

You smile. "Yeah."

"Wasn't too long ago was it? You got it to work, didn't you?"

"For the most part."

He nods and if he has made his point.

"But this is different," you say. "I haven't been able to figure this out for months."

"Then you already know what *not* to do." He looks surprised. "Probably looking in the wrong spot…"

You are about to object, but he is not listening. Instead, he leans against the cubicle wall, sets his mug down and closes his eyes as if to brace himself for a long night.

"Last man standing." Alex nods from the cubicle entrance, his trash bin next to him. "That's a good sign," he says.

You look up from the screen.

"Hey, Alex," you say.

"You know it's nighttime, don't you?"

"No," you say, a bit dazed and wired. "Not really."

"They were about to send a search party out for you last week. I heard all the news second-hand."

Alex smiles in a bright tie-dyed orange T-shirt and sandals, dreadlocks flopping from his head. He pulls a set of plugs from his ears and wraps them around an iPod hanging from his belt.

He takes out a handkerchief and, with a flourish, mops his brow, shakes the dreadlocks, and wipes his neck. "And who are we today?" he asks, jutting his chin at your work clothes. "You're not after my job, are you? Because you are looking very qualified."

"Well, my other clothes were kind of wet," you explain.

"I'm sure that explains it," he says.

"I spent the night in the *barrio*. A family gave me these clothes. Mine were wet."

"I see. And Jorge?"

You look at the name tag.

"He's a strange one," you say.

"Before or after you jacked his clothes?"

"Before," you say defensively. "I mean, after. I mean, it had nothing to do with the clothes."

Alex gives you a quick elbow that shoves you off balance. "Just kidding, kid!"

"I can explain."

Alex waves it off. "Your expression tells it all."

"I got lost in that thunderstorm," you continue. "The one that rolled through. Well, I thought I didn't have a car. I mean I *had* a car, but the starter was taken."

You stop and see Alex tilting his head like a puppy trying to understand. He stuffs his handkerchief back in a pocket and leans on his bin, expecting a lengthy story.

"I thought it was taken," you continue, "the starter, but it turned out that it wasn't and I had to use a pan of Cactus Eggs..."

"I'm sorry, guy," he says after he can no longer hold himself back, laughing, shaking his head. "Maybe you should skip this part."

"Yeah," you say, embarrassed. "OK, I was mixed up."

Jenz Johnson

"That part is believable," he says with a grin. "Let's leave it at that."

"Everything became crystal clear," you explain.

Alex nods. "Well, it happens all of a sudden sometimes," he says. "That's the way things work. One minute you are in a fog, and the next, well, you are dishing out breakfast." He laughs at this.

"I was fighting, Alex," you say.

"Yes," he says. "I can tell. Felt good, huh?"

"It wasn't as frightening as I thought it would be. Not when things were actually flying."

Alex takes a long look at you, as if inspecting you for any changes. He nods. "Hey," he says. "Walk with me, here. I have to get to that conference room to clean before tomorrow morning. You're looking sort of shaky."

"Maybe."

"Yes, you're going to do just fine."

You walk behind Alex feeling the pan rock in your backpack. He rolls the garbage bin down the hallway.

"Feels like a good day, doesn't it?" Alex says quietly, and you glance over to see him, eyes set in front of him.

"What's with the visitors?" you ask.

"I don't know," he continues, "but I only know that all of this— this meeting, the visitors—has been very abrupt. So, I expect that Gordon is in the crosshairs. You will need to pull yourself together. A good shave might do you good."

You get up and stretch. The corridor is empty. Your stomach feels suddenly empty. You could use a good meal.

"You also need to get a good sense of the terrain," he says.

"The conference room?"

"Yes," he says.

"But I already know the room."

"No," he says. "You don't. You know it from the standpoint of napping." You cannot argue. When the lights dim, it is the perfect environment for a quick snooze. Alex gives you a nudge. "You have to pick the best spot."

"But all of the seats are the same. It's a conference room, Alex."

"To the average person, yes, they are the same," he says. "But, you can't use the same eyes. You must use the seating to your advantage. Today, you have to pick the right spot. Each seat has its advantages. Each bump, each ravine is critical to a warrior."

"But it's carpeted," you say.

"OK, OK. But follow me on this one," he says. He turns down the long hallway that leads to the conference room. As you pass the coffee room, you see a few stragglers scouring the refrigerator for leftovers.

"Maybe I'll take a look in the fridge. I'm getting hungry."

"Today, I suggest you skip it."

"I'm famished," you say, completely surprised. "You're asking a lot."

"I know, it's sacrilegious. But you need all of your energies in one direction. And your stomach is not the direction I'd recommend. Come on."

Reluctantly, you follow Alex as he maneuvers his bin into the conference room. You click on the lights. The chairs are scattered, some under the table, others facing away. There are crumpled pieces of paper on the table, and the whiteboard is filled with scribbles and boxes.

"Walk around," Alex says. "Take a good look. I have to clean up, but you should walk around from the perspective of fighting."

The projector is set up on the conference table, with the projection screen pulled down.

"Gordon has something up his sleeve," Alex says. "I don't know what it is. All great battles are like this. The more you can prepare now, the better you will be. He's got a lot to hide."

"Really?"

"Oh, yeah. More than I understand."

"What's he going to do?" you ask. "He's upset, I know. But, it's just going to be a repeat of Monday, you know, berating us. That's Gordon's style."

"The memos are just piling up. More than can fit in the trash!"

"I mean, he is pushing me on *XLib*. But..."

"*XLib*?"

"It's needed to get the product out the door."

"Hmm. Well, at least you're thinking less like a coder. That's a good sign. Either you are the scapegoat here, or *XLib* is truly the center of the storm. And to think that you just disappeared this week. This must have hit Gordon with both barrels. Can you imagine? The guy who can help get the product out the door—you—suddenly checks out?"

"Yeah."

Alex pulls the chairs from away from the wall. From the side of the trash bin, he takes a broom and begins sweeping. He takes slow easy steps, first down one wall, then after moving he chairs back, up along the other walls.

"So, get ready," he says. "You won't get off that easy tomorrow."

He looks around the room now, paying attention to the chairs. There are subtle differences in the angle and placement. He walks carefully around the perimeter.

"I like the back," you say.

"Yes, it's a great hiding place. It was your favorite spot. You have to find a new one. So look around. Once the projector is turned on and the lights go off, the room changes. People in the back are basically out of view. They can easily be discounted. It's a weak spot."

"Then the front," you say. "On the left. Across from the podium."

"There's no question about it," Alex says.

You imagine people filing in, Sam's group to the right, Documentation up front, QA with them. The sections would sit together, with project managers closer. You turn around and look at the white board and projector. Some one has left an old schematic on the board, now smeared.

"OK," you say. "It's all coming into view. I know where everyone is going to sit."

"Good," Alex says.

You take a chair at the front and look at the board for a while.

"And I think I know what they're going to talk about. At least one of the topics."

"Good," he says. "And one more thing. Change those clothes. The overalls are OK, but you need to look credible. Whatever you say, people have to believe you. The visitors are here for a reason. So, let's not disappoint them."

You nod, then get up and erase the board.

"OK," you say. "My clothes are here"—patting the backpack.

Alex smiles. "You'll have to tell me about your exploits. But later." He collects the remaining trash and pushes the chairs into place. With a marker you sketch out some boxes and arrows on the whiteboard. You hear the hall get noisier, and you look for the right chair. There is one on the other side of the table, and you set your pad there, and put a pen on top to hold your spot.

29. catapulting

"Break on through to the other side.
Break on through."
—The Doors

You edge along the side of the room, voices buzzing as Gordon moves to the podium. Dolores looks up at you, her eyes watery and lips moving as if to memorize last-minute instructions. Rex is next to her, his moustache twitching nervously. At the front, the two visitors sit behind Gordon, both in polo shirts with the company logo. The lights dim and you move to your seat.

"Anywhere," Gordon says. He peers over his glasses and his eyes follow you as you move down the aisle. The room quiets and all eyes are on you now. Burgie, Jack and Myra look on solemnly from the corner. You look around for Katie, but she is nowhere to be seen.

"OK, people, we have a lot to cover," Gordon says. The screen fills up with bullet points.

"First. We have some visitors today, I'd like to introduce. From corporate, Roger Henley and Phil Morales. They've dropped in to hear your comments and to answer any questions that you may have. About the layoff. Or upcoming plans." Each raises a hand. "Nice to have you here," he says turning back. "We will arrange for your questions later. In fact, you can come up to the front after the meeting."

The first slide beams onto the screen to the sound of chairs moving and pages turning.

"First, I would like to jump to our upcoming release. It's an important one, folks." He looks down at his notes, then a quick glance to the two managers behind him with a knowing smile. "You've all seen this before."

"Mr. Lyman," you say. You are standing, in the bright light of the projector. Both managers look up, squinting in your direction.

"Yes?" Gordon says, surprised, shielding his eyes with a hand. "There will be time for questions. Later." He smiles cordially then returns to his notes.

"I didn't want to wait," you say, "to express my thanks."

Gordon looks up, surprised.

"Well, this is unexpected." There is a buzz in the room.

"I want to thank you for the opportunity to work here. I realized actually that you took a chance on me. And I appreciate it. A whole lot."

"Good," he says, a bit flabbergasted.

"I've learned a lot," you say, realizing that everything feels very different. "More than I expected."

"Glad I could further your education." He smiles cordially.

"In my next job, I won't make the same mistakes."

"OK, good, good," he say impatiently. "Let's get back to the business at hand."

"In fact, starting this morning, I'm going to stop doing things that are of no use." Gordon looks confused. "Miyamoto Musashi taught me that."

You feel a light hand on your shoulder, and you turn to see the samurai next to you with a smile. It is the first time you've seen him smile.

"You can have a seat, now. Just focus on your work, Jenz."

You shake your head, and Gordon looks up.

"I'm afraid it's no use," you say.

Agnes immediately stands up in the back of the room. She senses trouble. He motions for her to be seated. You hear voices close by telling you to sit down.

Gordon studies you.

"Enough," he says. He waits for you to sit down then turns back to the room. The noise tapers off and people begin opening up their notebooks. "I'm sure with a little concentration, you'll see your way."

"Mr. Lyman, our code is on its last legs. So, to fiddle with it is a waste of time."

He ignores you.

"Folks," he continues, "it's time we put our backs into it. I was going to get into this later in our meeting. But now's as good of a time as any. We need to double up, make that extra effort."

You are still standing, waiting for him to finish.

"OK, this has gone about as far as it needs to go. Please be seated. It's really *not* a choice, Jenz. These are your assignments and you have to complete them."

"But it *is* my choice," you say. "I never thought I had one before."

"Here's your choice," he snaps. "You can do the work you have on your docket. In the time you have left. Or you can take your things and leave. Now. "

He glares at you.

The room suddenly quiets and you look around at the faces. Dolores has stopped blinking, and her eyes are bright and anxious. Burgie is nervously fidgeting with his beard, but he gives you a nod. As if to say, go ahead. Sam is mouthing *do it* with a smirk.

"*When you are given a choice between life and death...,*" the samurai says.

You know the answer.

You close your notebook, placing a stack of typed notes on top. You don't need them anymore.

"Now sit," snaps Gordon. "Enough of your theatrics. You have work that needs to get done. You deliver. Your code. On time. Is that clear?"

The managers behind Gordon are talking with one another.

"Sometimes," you say, still on your feet, "you have to stand up for what you really believe. Even if it's a piece of code."

"I can get that sucker done," Sam says, standing up.

"Sit down, damn it, Sam," Gordon says, wiping the sweat from his brow. Sam slowly lowers himself back in his seat, straightening his tie.

"I'm not delaying our release while someone tries to figure out your code!" Gordon says.

"The problem isn't my module. We just can't tweak things that are fundamentally flawed. And that's what we've got here. A bunch of code that has been patched together, on its last legs, with no real design."

"I resent that comment." Sam is standing, fuming.

"Sit down!" Gordon says, and Sam lowers into his chair.

You hold up a small stack of paper. "I'm not saying give up. That's another thing I learned. Sometimes if you just keep searching for the right thing, even if you don't know exactly where you're going, you get closer than you think."

"Enough!"

"Now this has gone far enough." Roger is on his feet. He is angry. "Gordon, bring this meeting to order!

"Sometimes you have to bend the rules just a tad..."

Agnes is suddenly on her feet.

"It's all *his* fault," Agnes blurts out from the back of the room. She is on her feet, shaking a finger at you.

"Agnes," Gordon snaps. "Sit down. Now."

"He's been nothing but trouble.," she yells. "From Day 1."

"Agnes!" Gordon shouts.

The room turns to see Agnes, still pointing her finger, shaking emphatically.

"Can you bring this meeting to order?" Roger snaps.

"Sit down. Now."

"If he would have followed orders, this would have never happened. Never."

"Agnes!" Gordon yells.

"What would have never happened?" Roger asks, still standing. He looks back at Gordon who is glaring at Agnes through the dimly lit room. "Agnes?" Roger repeats.

"I can explain what Agnes is referring to," Gordon continues, nodding with a smile to Roger. "She is understandably upset."

Agnes is now rushing toward you from the back, knocking over chairs, and pushing aside chairs in her way.

"It's all *your* fault!" she yells.

She pushes past chairs, stumbling forward over feet and purses, her eyes blazing as you hold the stack of paper over your head. She elbows her way through the aisle, people trying to avoid her fury.

"Agnes!" Gordon shouts, but she is already crossing through the lights of the projection screen, her face white as a ghost.

The samurai grunts, "*Step back.*"

As Agnes approaches, you gently guide her into your chair, a move Alex had taught you. It swivels around, making a full 360 degree turn, her legs kicking. When she comes around, she tries to reach your papers, thrashing about. You move the chair away.

"Honestly," Roger shouts. He glares at her then at you. "You either sit still or both of you are out in the hall. Is that clear?"

She cannot sit still but restrains herself.

"And you, Mr...?"

"Jenz is my name."

"Then, Jenz. This is absolutely no way to behave. You are completely out of order. And insubordinate."

"Mr. Henley."

"Please be seated."

"You asked us for our comments. That's why you are here. What other time do we have?"

He looks around the room to find heads nodding.

"Many of us in this room have been laid off, after working long and hard. Others may lose their jobs soon. We need to change our direction. Dramatically. We can't just fiddle with the code any more. We're beyond that. We are heading down a road of no return. We will lose our customers."

"I can't have our meetings turn into free-for-alls."

The room buzzes.

"The truth is," you say, "I've been heading down a road myself. Looking all over for something that was right in front of me." You catch Katie looking up from the back corner, her eyes glistening in the light of the overhead.

Agnes suddenly erupts unable to control herself.

"If he would have followed orders, we would have never been in this position. I told Gordon all along to fire him. He's irresponsible. He's a thief too! Give me those!" she hisses as she snatches the papers from your hands and scurries to her seat.

"Agnes!" Roger snaps.

She clutches them to her chest and glares at you.

"He stole these from me!" she says.

"These papers are mine," you say.

"These are company private. We would have been just fine if he would have minded his own business." She begins to say more, but thinks twice of it, slowly slouching back in her seat, your stack of paper ensconced in her grip.

"I will take those," Roger says as he extends his arm. She looks at the paper before handing them over, then at you. Her face is white.

"What is this?" Roger asks studying the first page. Then he looks at Agnes. "He took this from you?" She is speechless

"I'm not sure what Agnes thought I had," you say. "This was a memo to Gordon on a whole new way to approach our system. I have been working on this all week."

Agnes shakes her head.

"What's this all about?" Roger asks, scanning though the memo.

"Our customers are no longer calling us," you say. "We should be talking about how to save our product. Not how to make deadlines!"

Roger looks over to Gordon.

"Support calls are down?" Roger asks.

"Well, yes, it's a good sign, though," Gordon says. "We are making excellent progress. I will have Sam give a report..."

"Mr. Henley,..." you begin, but he quiets you and turns to Agnes.

"Agnes?" he asks. "What did you think Jenz had?"

"Nothing," she says. "My mistake."

Gordon glares at Agnes.

"Gordon's email," Agnes admits. "I print it out for him."

"And?"

"Well, it was confidential. I thought he stole the email."

"And this email said what?" Henley asks.

"Well,…" she says looking to Gordon for help. "It was Gordon's mail. The customers were not always the most polite."

"Complaints?" Roger asks, bristling.

She nods.

"Why aren't our customers making support calls?"

"They're threatening us," she says upset. "With legal action. It's unfair." Her voice trails off and she slumps in the chair, her hands clenched in front of her.

"What?" Roger says surprised.

"Listen," Gordon suddenly says. "Agnes really doesn't know the in's and out's. I mean… This falls squarely on my shoulders."

"Legal action?" Roger asks. "You didn't tell me about any legal action."

Suddenly Gordon steps forward and points at you. "You sabotaged us. You sabotaged our product," Gordon says to you. "That's what Agnes was trying to say."

"He has never made a single deadline." It is a new voice from the back of the room. It is Sam, and you turn to see him raise his hand, standing in his shirt and tie. Now there is a rumble of hisses. He looks around defensively and says, "My group can bring this whole thing in. He doesn't know what he is talking about. It's his fault all right."

Now there are moans. You look around and see the samurai nodding. *"You must move quickly now,"* he says, and nods toward Roger who is glaring at Gordon.

"Thank you, Sam," Gordon says over the microphone, but the conversations continue. "Everyone, quiet please. I think we can point to the real cause of our problems."

Burgie and Myra are now standing. Burgie has raised his hand and is speaking softly. Gordon is talking to the managers. Suddenly, a book slams down on the conference table with a loud pop. Sam cringes and sits down immediately. The room echoes with the sound and people turn to see Myra with the book in hand, ready to slam it down again.

"Burgie would like to say something," she says. "All of you, slackers, quiet down. Sam, you couldn't run a project if your life depended on it."

The room erupts in laughter.

"Sit down," Gordon stammers, now furious, his pate red.

"I want to say something," Burgie begins softly.

This is the first time that Burgie has ever said anything at a meeting. The room hushes as Burgie fidgets with his shirt, adjusting his glasses, sweating. You notice that it is the first time you've seen him tuck in his shirt. Even his hair looks combed. Surprisingly he looks respectable.

Gordon leans to the microphone and is immediately shushed, with a few angry looks from the front row. Myra whispers something and smiles.

"Jenz is right," he says. "The support lines are quiet. Our customers aren't complaining any more. There're bugs out there—critical bugs—and not a peep. It's freaky."

The room is absolutely still.

"Like they don't care any more," he says. "If they were actually using our product, our phones would be ringing off the hook. And technically, our code is a mess. And this latest revision will simply not fly. Not as it is."

Gordon is furious. Around the room, heads nod in agreement.

Roger moves to the podium as Gordon backs away.

"This is unacceptable!" he says. "In all my years, I have never seen anything like this. What kind of an office are you running here, Gordon? It's an absolute mess!"

Gordon edges back to his seat.

"The truth is that this department is in trouble. And we, Phil and I, are the ones responsible. Yes, we take the responsibility. We have resisted taking drastic measures, but the simple fact is that we're not meeting our numbers here; the revenues for your products are terrible!"

He looks around.

"And it's our name, our reputation that gets hurt. Our company name gets dragged through the mud. I didn't realize things were so out of hand. And legal action? To be honest, I hardly think it's worth it," he says with real disgust.

You are standing with your hand raised.

"Enough," Roger says. "I've heard enough."

You continue to stand, as the room quiets as you speak. "With all due respect. It can be fixed. All of this. If it were my name, my reputation, I wouldn't just fold up shop. There is only one right way to do it. Level with our customers. They probably feel like the rest of us, that we have been kept in the dark for too long."

There is suddenly a smattering of clapping from the back of the room. You sit down and continue to look at Roger for his decision. The applause continues to grow until the entire meeting room is filled with cheers. You look around and suddenly feel that you have arrived home after a very long time away.

"What we see depends mainly on what we look for."
—*John Lubbock*

T hat was pure genius," Burgie says, standing in your cubicle, barely able to contain himself. He is hugging his large frame, standing stiffly at your cubicle entry.

Outside, the lunchtime crowd noisily ambles by, occasionally someone pokes in and gives you a thumbs up.

"You turned the tide in there," you say.

"You were both great," Jack says. He is on his tiptoes rocking back and forth with excitement.

"Damn!" Myra says with a proud grin. She has taken a position on top of your side desk, legs crossed, leaning against your shelves. "A little rough along the edges, but for your first summit, really fucking *great.*"

"Yeah," Jack says. "I thought Gordon would erupt any moment. Talk about Mt. Vesuvius."

"And Agnes was about to go another eight rounds on the conference table," Burgie says. "She was unbelievable."

"That would have been fun to watch!" Jack says, beaming. "Like foosball."

"Foosball?" Myra says, baffled.

"Well," he says, still smiling, "like air hockey then."

You smile.

"I doubt if you will last the day," Myra says, suddenly serious. She looks around at the others, and their smiles slowly fade. "Sorry to be a bearer of bad news, but a performance like that—rubbing your boss' nose in his own crap in front of his bosses—does not get rewarded. I don't care how many corporate types are taking notes. *You* are one cooked goose. Gordon is probably talking their ears off right now."

Burgie nods sadly in agreement. "Yeah," Burgie mumbles. "but he was already cooked."

"What's another week anyway?" you say. "Besides, I realized that I wasn't right for the job anyway."

"Well, you can forget about any references from this company," Myra says sadly.

"I've been in worse situations ," you say. "Gordon is no mountain lion!"

Burgie and Myra look confused.

"Long story," you say waving it off.

"Hey, sorry to interrupt," a young temp says. He pokes his head in with a smile. Then looking at you, he says, "this is for you. It's important."

He hands you a note requesting your immediate presence at Gordon's office.

"OK," you say. The temp nods and disappears. "I got to go. It's been fun. Hope I see you guys around."

"Hey," Myra says, her arms open. "A hug is required." Before you can react, she pulls you into a bear hug and plants a kiss on your cheek. "You're OK." She is beaming. "You're fucking OK," Myra says.

"Ditto," Burgie says. He looks inclined to give you a hug also, but resists. He just stands awkward with his arms at his side.

"Anyway," Myra continues, "let's go and celebrate. How about a good pizza buffet? That will lift spirits."

"Now you're talking," Burgie says, perking up.

"$6.95," Jack says. "We can afford that!"

"$4.95." Burgie corrects him.

"You have coupons?" Myra asks.

"I always have coupons," Burgie says seriously.

"This sounds great," Jack says. "It will be just like a wake."

"A wake?" Myra says.

"Well, you know…" Jack continues.

"You guys go ahead," you say.

You walk hastily down the empty corridor. Your pack feels heavy, your hair falls across your forehead as you move quietly to the elevator. The office feels like an abandoned warehouse, the fluorescent flickering overhead. When you round the corner, Alex is steering his trash bin, whistling a muted blues tune.

"Hey kid!" He unplugs his CD and pushes his headphones into a pocket.

You smile and give him a wave.

"Nice moves!" Alex beams.

"You saw it," you ask.

"Hey, wouldn't miss it. You were rifting. I haven't seen a better performance since Miles Davis at the Amphitheater. Yes, indeed, it was a sight to behold."

"Gordon wants to see me," you say holding up the note.

He nods.

"Hey, come around the *dojo*."

"I will," you say.

"And listen: Never give an inch."

> Plus ça change, plus c'est la même chose.
> *(The more things change, the more they are the same.)*
> —*French proverb*

You hold the small note in hand as you arrive at the reception counter, Katie typing nervously at her machine. She gets up quietly when she sees you and moves to the counter, looking anxiously down the empty corridor. Her perfume feels light and cool around you like a summer rain.

"I got this note," you say.

"Roger wants to see you," she says. She leans closer, her hand closing the neck of her pastel blue sweater. "In there." She nods to Gordon's office. She waits for you to respond.

"Roger?" you reply and she senses your question, nodding. "Where's Gordon?" She mouths the word *gone* and looks around.

"He's gone?" you say.

Katie immediately hushes you. "Quiet," she whispers loudly. "Agnes, too."

She smiles then motions toward the closed office door, and looks around. She watches you as you nod and turn to the office door behind you. You knock and from inside you hear a voice, "Come in."

Roger is sitting behind Gordon's desk. The room is now a collection of boxes and stacks. The desk sits naked in the center of the room, cleared of everything except the phone, a pad of paper and a pencil. To your left, Phil greets you from the couch close by. Roger stands and comes around to the front.

"That was quite a performance in there," he says.

"Performance?" you ask.

"What you said."

He touches the back of a seat. You nod and sit.

"First," he says. "You were out of line. It was disrespectful." He glares at you. "We don't condone this kind of behavior, but you did get our attention." He hesitates. "You may be right. We weren't told how bad things were. The problem was with management. That's our responsibility. But sometimes you just don't see what is right in front of you.

"Now, I'm not fully convinced about turning it around. I'll be honest.

"As a company, we—meaning all of the management team—have to bite the bullet. I don't think we have much of a choice now, although I would have liked to see us keep our commitments to the customer base. I'm not willing to throw in the towel just yet."

He is building to some question for you, but it is difficult to guess where he's heading. Occasionally he glances over at Roger. He takes some time, hands folded and looking closely at you for clues.

"How do I say this…," he starts. "We are wondering if you would be willing to finish up your module, maybe help us with a new design. If your cohorts are correct, there's a lot that needs rewriting. What I'm saying is this: would you have any interest in staying on?"

You sit up.

"I'm not sure," you say. "Maybe Gordon was right. Maybe I'm not the right one for the job after all. I've lost that passion…"

"You seem to be very impassioned at the meeting."

"Well, Mr. Henley," you say. "Yes. What I said in there is how I feel. The code is spaghetti right now. And what with all of the other bells and whistles, you aren't going to get what you want by the current deadlines. The code is going to give you real problems if you rush this part."

"We won't debate the issue."

Your hands sit motionless on the leather arm rests. You take in the whole room, stripped of its personality turned into a large closet.

"We're focused on our customer base now," he continues. "We've checked. Many of our most loyal ones are leaving. We may lose more. Certainly our stockholders will become more restless. Now Sam thinks he can fix the problem in a few days. Am I right?"

"You'd have to ask Sam how he feels about the whole thing."

"Yes, I probably will." Roger nods and seems satisfied with your answer.

"But if you want my opinion," you continue, "good code takes time. You really have to be dedicated."

"Yes," he says, tapping his fingers together.

"Can I ask you a question?" you ask.

"Yes."

"What happened to Gordon?" you ask.

"We liked Gordon," Roger says. "He was a good man."

You notice that all of Gordon's trophies were cleared from table, leaving round and square shadows on the credenza.

"We didn't have much choice," Phil says from the couch. You turn and he is looking out the window. "It wasn't just the meeting. Or his failure to keep us informed. We came here to take some sort of action. It was one of our options. Still…"

"So, to be honest, we're in a bind," Roger continues from the couch. "We expected that at least the product was finally on track. We're not that patient. When we see what must be done, there's no use in beating around the bush."

"It's a big task."

"We want you to stay," Phil says. He gets up and walks to the side of the desk, sitting casually on a corner. "I'm not saying that we agree with everything that you're proposing. But, you have the guts to tell it like it is. We need to hear it, even if it's not always what we want to hear."

"Yes," Roger agrees. "You have potential with this company. Maybe as a manager."

Phil nods.

They wait for an answer.

"Well, I don't know what to say. I thought you two were going to fire me."

They both laugh.

"You've already been laid off and we're going to fire you?"

Phil is shaking his head in disbelief, still laughing.

"So, what do you say?"

"I don't know what to say," and you don't.

◊   ◊   ◊

You carefully close the door, and find Katie at the counter anxiously looking at you.

"What happened?" she asks. "What happened in there?"

"I don't know," you say. "They want me to stay."

"You mean, you're not being laid off."

"I guess not," you say. "I've never been in a reverse layoff. But, I didn't know what to say in there. I'm not sure, Katie, if I want to stay here. That feels odd."

You look down the hallway. A few people coming back from lunch. You look at her and feel suddenly calm, as if a weight has been lifted from your shoulders. "I just don't know what to think about it all."

She nods and moves in front of the counter until she is close.

"You really did great at the meeting," she says, and for the first time smiles. "I barely knew it was you. You can surprise a person."

"I surprised myself," you say.

You keep your eyes on her as she straightens the in-baskets and magazines that are lying on the counter.

She looks up with a smile.

"I better get back to work," she says. "They want me to help them out today, you know, talk to others. And type memos. It's going to be a long day." She pushes back a loop of hair that has fallen over her forehead.

"I was thinking," you say, watching her. "If you aren't busy, I'd like to take you to that dinner. Maybe tonight. If you don't have any other plans."

She smiles.

> *"There is nothing like returning to a place that remains*
> *unchanged to find the ways in which you yourself have*
> *altered."*
> —Nelson Mandela, *"A Long Walk to Freedom"*

You follow the chain-link fence along the back alley, then turn into a dirt driveway, dust whipping up behind your car. The morning is warm, and the air is already busy with morning traffic. The motor turns a couple more times, then sputters to a stop.

"You sure about this?" you ask looking over.

Next to you Katie looks out the window, hair tied back, wearing a T-shirt and jeans. The car is filled with the sweet smell of her fragrance. With a smile and a nod, she unhooks her seatbelt and rolls down the window. Her hair settles gently on her T-shirt, and you look at her as she surveys the wilting oleanders and garbage bins.

"I love it," she says. When she looks back at you, her eyes are dark and shining with anticipation.

"OK," you say and open the door, hefting your backpack on your shoulder. You move around the front to her door, and she is smiling at you, watching you.

"You're raring to go," she says.

"You can tell?"

"It's on the marquee," she says.

You are standing behind your apartment building, looking up, the smells of bacon drifting out from the diner. There is a clattering of dishes and a loud cough from the screen door. You stare up at the second floor, then your eye follows the crumbling adobe down the sides, to the bushes and trees. In the shade a neighborhood dog licks his paw, looking up at you lazily.

"Hey, 201," says a voice from the utility shed. You can't locate its owner, as you look in the direction. From the corner of your eye, you spot a tanned face leaning out the door. You see his teeth through the shade, then find him reading a paper.

"Hey," he says. You see a darkened face, a pair of pink eyes blinking from the shade. His teeth appear with a smile.

"Dino?" you say. You now recognize the voice of the typesetter.

"Hey," he says. "Where've you been, 201? Missed you. Missed that grub of yours. I thought you'd be back sooner than this."

He has a wide grin and folds his paper.

"Well, here I am," you say.

"Yes, sir," he says. He rubs his eyes and glances up at your car. "Who's the cute one?"

"A friend," you say.

"A friend?" he says with a big smile.

You hesitate.

"OK, I'll shut up. Hey, where've you been? I haven't seen you these past mornings. Thought you might have moved. Your lights haven't been on."

"I've been gone," you say.

"Yeah, that part I knew. Listen," he continues, "the old man is coughing up a storm. He closed the place for a couple of days, then opened up all of a sudden. You better get in there. Something's up."

"I'll check on him," you say and look to the open door. You can make out Vermette's silhouette in the back window and hear him clanking pots, coughing.

Dino gives Katie a big, toothless smile.

"Hi," she says as she takes your arm.

"Hey, there's a pretty one," he says. He puts his paper down and sits up.

She has some change already in hand and sets it down.

"Hey, no," he says. "I'm OK. Don't let my gruff exterior fool you."

She dismisses this.

"Really, I'm well invested," he says. "Hey, I'll let you into a little secret." He is beaming. "Kind of like show and tell." He digs into his sleeping bag and hauls out a ball of rags the size of a baseball. "Take a look," he says, squinting.

He unravels the bundle, and pushes out an iPod. It is scuffed with a makeshift pair of earplugs.

"Wow," Katie says. "I can't even afford one of those."

"Yep, the market has been good," he says. "I bought it used."

He nods and wipes it off.

"Yep, pretty nice, huh?"

"Very nice," you say.

"I hate the music that comes with these things, but hey, it's a big status symbol at the park."

"I can see why," smiles Katie.

He rotates it around so you can see front and back.

"I won't keep you two," he says. He has a big smile on his face and he winks at you. "Hey, it's my job. Reading people."

Katie steps back then looks around at the back lot.

"OK, I'll shut up," Dino says. "I've got a Sports section to read, so catch you two lovebirds later." He winks and turns back to his paper.

You shuffle to the backdoor of the diner, and Vermette looks up from his favorite spot in back. A cigarette in hand, he sits slightly slumped over near the sink. Dishes from the previous day are piled up in soapy water.

"Hey, kid," he says with a wheeze. "A bit early, aren't we? It's only Saturday." He glances at Katie, and smiles as if he is seeing the daughter he never had.

"Yeah, I was in the neighborhood," you say. "This is Katie."

He stands and, parking his cigarette, extends a hand.

"You're a sight for sore eyes," he says, a small smile breaking across his face. He offers her a seat, but she declines.

"You OK?" you ask.

"Not the best, to be honest, kid. Had to close the place down last week. For a couple of days. First time in fourteen years. But I'm OK."

He sits back down and looks out the back door, as you set your pack down at your feet. You look around the backroom, the shelves packed with bundles of napkins, large cans of vegetables and stacks of dish towels. A couple of boxes are parked at Vermette's feet. He seems to be gathering the energy to unpack them.

"We have something we'd like to propose," you say finally.

He sits up, looking back and forth at you and Katie.

"We?" he asks.

She smiles and his face softens.

"I realized something, Mr. Vermette. That I really love working here."

He smiles at this, maybe for the first time.

"She's one hell of a diner, isn't she?" he says with pride.

"I'd like to propose something."

He studies you.

"A partnership, if you are agreeable. I mean, I'd like to work into a partnership. You spend less time doing the grunt work and more time enjoying your retirement."

"I'm not ready for retirement, kid. I have too many things I need to do."

"Yes, I realize that. I said that wrong. I guess I'm asking for a promotion, sir."

He studies you carefully.

"I'd like to be more than part-time, sir."

"I see," he says. He takes a long, wheezy drag on this cigarette. You look at him calmly as he blinks through the smoke, listening.

"I'd like to suggest we could expand the menu. To bring in more students. It might mean some dips, some yogurt occasionally. Some Breakfast Nachos and maybe a green *pozole.*"

He momentarily frowns.

"I guess I picked up some recipes along the way," you say. "The point is this, sir: I think it's time to change. I mean, I'd like to suggest some changes, if it's OK with you. I'd like to take some of the burden off your shoulders."

He looks at you intently. You look around and see everything neatly stacked and waiting.

"There is one thing that won't change, sir," you say. "Not on my watch."

Vermette waits, letting his cigarette burn on its own.

"*No specials,*" you say. "That's just the way it has to be, sir."

He almost smiles, looking at you, then at Katie, then back to you. You wait, sun warming your back, the smell of bacon and fresh coffee drifting in.

"Hell," Vermette says, shaking his head. "I'm going to regret this."

J enz Johnson lives in California and runs his own software business when he is not cooking. He is the author of underground classic *Giga Bites: The Hacker Cookbook* . He may be found online at *www.reboot2.com*.

Jenz Johnson

34. acknowledgements

The love of my life, Mimi, gave me the inspiration to pursue this journey, and Noah, my best friend, was there to give me encouragement and advice.

It is miraculous that my editor, Al, stuck with me through thick and thin. His guidance was pivotal. I am indebted to Herb, Skip, Gerry, Siri Datta and Tom for their reading of my early manuscripts and their insights. And my special thanks to Mary for her comments and edits of my final drafts. My good pals Burgie and Jim changed my life, and I humbly apologize for any inaccuracies in their stories.

My father, who was remarkably 101 when I wrote this, has been a constant example of how a person can pull himself by his bootstraps. He did so with patience and humor.

35. rules of thumb

Term	Description
biocomputer	The human computer, that is the brain and mind that processes information within each person.
bokken	A wooden sword used for practicing martial arts, such as kendo.
bug	An incorrect statement or behavior of a program that causes it to crash or to spew unwanted results. Not a good thing.
bushido	Meaning "way of the warrior," the Japanese code of conduct and a way of life for samurai, handed down by word of mouth.
CAT4	Category 4 type cabling that consists of four unshielded twisted-pair (UTP) wires that supports a slower data rate of 16 megabits per second and was used in token ring networks.
CAT6	Category 6 type cabling that contains four twisted copper wire pairs with each pair is made up 23 gauge copper wire as opposed to Cat 5's 24 gauge wire. This type supports the faster gigabyte speeds of most local area networks.
catapult	A type of trigger that launches a person into an entirely different phase of their lives or into a different persona. Can also refer to the act of launching.
class	A programming structure that defines a category of objects within a program, for example, a Spider, which is a type of entity in the program.
code	The act of programming a computer program, or the actual portion of computer programming. Short for

Term	Description
	source code.
CS	Computer Science
dojo	A training hall for martial arts
FIFO	First-In, First-Out. See queue.
hack	To work on a computer program (or anything for that matter) in an effort to produce the best result, usually with extreme attention to detail and using time-consuming trial-and-error techniques.
hacker	A person who enthusiastically explores the minute details of computers and how to stretch their capabilities. Also, someone who savors the challenge of overcoming or circumventing limitations inherent in computer systems, and by implication, all things.
instantiate	In programming, to create an object from a class or subclass. For example, a programmer can create a kitten from the general class of Cat.
Internet	The computer network where information is shared using the Internet Protocol (IP).
iPhone	Mobile phone from Apple
isomorphism	In mathematics, an operation that returns a number to its original set, such as adding two integers.
LAN	Local area network which is a network of computers usually within the same building that are linked physically by cabling.
LIFO	Last-In, First-Out. See stack.
looping	The continual execution of the same piece of code. In a person, it is their habitual and unquestioning

Term	Description
	way they do things. In a computer, it is usually endless, and will result in a crash. Whether machine or man, it is not good.
Net	Short for the Internet.
newbie	Sometimes abbreviated to newb is someone new to a game, a neophyte.
object	A type of thing in Object Oriented Programming (OOP). Much like real-world things, it has behaviors and properties. It is an instance of a particular class, for example a black-widow spider is an object of the class of Spider. Specific objects vs their classes are important distinctions in programming.
operating system	Like Microsoft Windows® or UNIX® , the fundamental software of a computer that handles the interaction between the computer hardware, its programs and the user. Usually the operating system allocates memory, the different devices of the computer, and handling of files.
OS	See operating system.
persona	A person's concept and manifestations of "self" as seen both by the person and those around them.
ping	A basic command entered into a machine to determine if it can reach another machine over the network. The term is used both as a noun and a verb. The command is used to troubleshoot networks.
predictive text	On cell phones with standard numeric keypads, it allows the phone to guess the words you are typing by matching the numbers with known words in the phone's memory.

Term	Description
prototype	A trial version of a program or a persona that is used to test the waters.
QA	Quality Assurance. The department or process that insures that software runs correctly and without bugs.
queue	A line of things, usually people. As a computer term, it refers to a data structure where an object is place into a list but is retrieved in the order it was placed into the list. (Also referred to as FIFO).
reboot	The transformation of a person usually through the adoption of a new persona, although it can also be understood to be a minor change in lifestyle, job, attitude or clothes.
recast	In programming terms, a variable of one type can be recast into another type, usually changing its usage and value. In much the same way, a person can recast their persona to be a different model of the same person.
ronin	(Literally *wave man* in Japanese, that is a person who is tossed about, like a wave in the sea) A masterless samurai during the feudal period of Japan.
samurai	A member of the warrior nobility in feudal Japan, whose sole purpose was to serve their feudal lord. Samurai were well trained in the art of battle, and followed a strict set of guidelines that dictated their behavior on and off the battlefield (Bushido).
snafu	A problem, such as a bug, that illustrates the SNAFU principle, the Army acronym for "Situation Normal, All Fucked Up."
stack	A list of things that a person has to do or to remember. More formally, it is a data structure in

Term	Description
	programming where the last object is placed into a list and is the first item retrieved later on. (Also referred to as LIFO).
subclass	The technique of creating new classes in a program using the general properties and behaviors of more abstract class.
throw exceptions	A programming term when the program is able to detect an error or unusual value of a variable (the exception) while executing and immediately transfer control to a block of code that can better handle the exception.
trigger	An event usually in real life that causes a person to take a new direction, adopt a new perspective or take action.
WAN	Wide area network, which is a network of computers that stretches over a larger area, usually connected through the phone networks, dedicated links, etc.
WiFi	Short for wireless fidelity, used to connect to the Internet over established protocols such as 802.11.
web	Short for World Wide Web, the Internet as most people know it, filled with pages of information that can be browsed from a computer and other types of devices.

Notes:

Notes:

Notes: